WINTER

BOOK TWO: THE GUARDIANS OF MAGIC SERIES

MELISSA NASH

RIVERSONG
BOOKS

An Imprint of Sulis International Press
Los Angeles | London

ISBN (print): 978-1-946849-80-9
ISBN (eBook): 978-1-946849-81-6

Published by Riversong Books
An Imprint of Sulis International
Los Angeles | London

www.sulisinternational.com

CONTENTS

Prologue Captured, Bound and Taken 1

Chapter 1 Venture into the City.......................9

Chapter 2 Enter the Prison Keep 21

Chapter 3 The Lyrian Citadel.......................33

Chapter 4 Farewell 45

Chapter 5 Riding Lessons.......................61

Chapter 6 An Old Friend.......................81

Chapter 7 The Lifthayll Bridge.......................95

Chapter 8 The Spring Market.......................109

Chapter 9 Reunion 121

Chapter 10 Battle at the Bridge.......................129

Chapter 11 Travelling Through Water and Air..........145

Chapter 12 A Night Out.......................159

Chapter 13 Preparing for War.......................173

Chapter 14 Questions 187

Chapter 15 A Visit to the Forge.......................193

Chapter 16 Village Council.......................203

Chapter 17 Into the West.......................219

Chapter 18 Elias and Evaine 229

Chapter 19 The Sea Wind.......................235

Chapter 20 The Boar 247

Chapter 21 Alexia.......................255

Chapter 22 Departure.......................265

Chapter 23 Events are Set in Motion 277

Chapter 24 The Eve of Battle.......................283

Chapter 25 A Breach in the Winterburn 289

Chapter 26 Battle on the Hill.......................299

Chapter 27 Over the Ridge.......................311

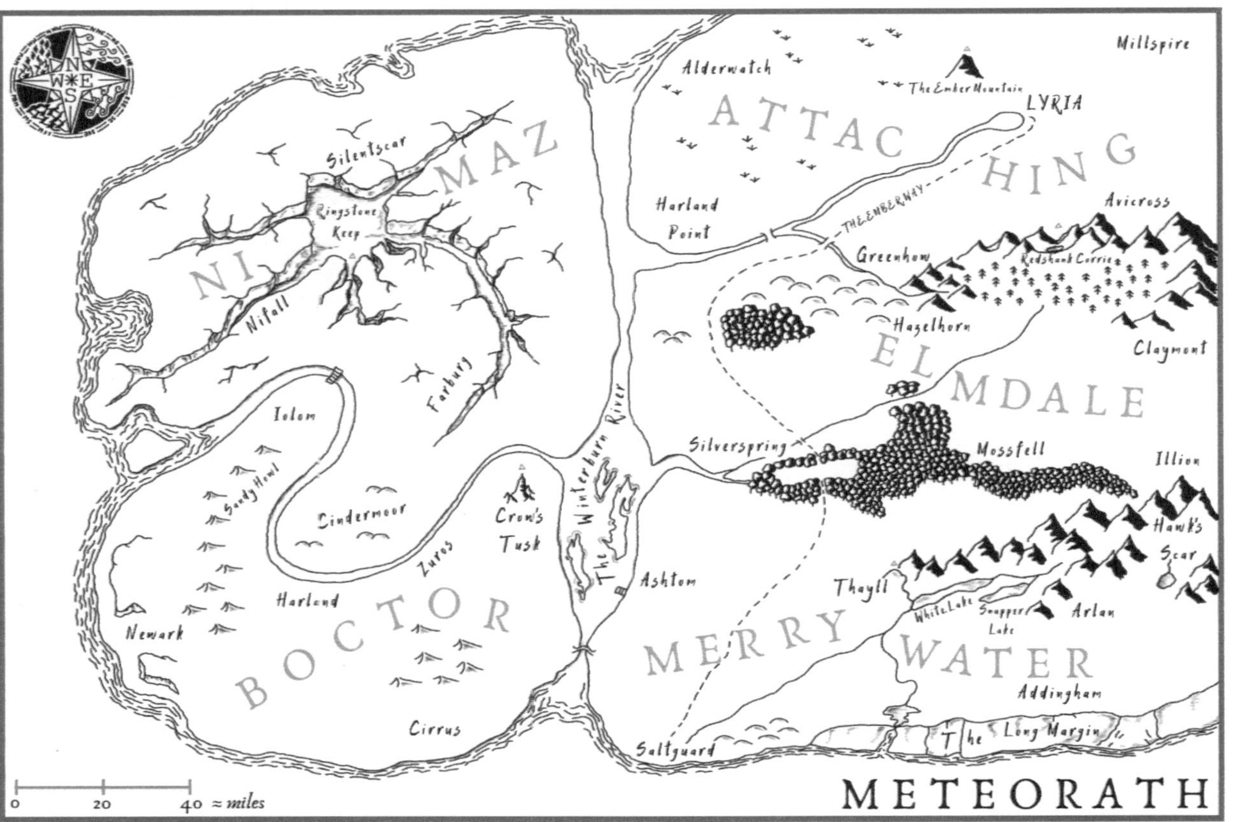

METEORATH
Millspire
Alderwatch
The Ember Mountain
LYRIA
ATTAC
HING
Harland Point
THE ENBERWAY
Greenhow
Avicross
Redshank Corrie
Hazelhorn
Claymont
ELMDALE
NI
MAZ
Silentscar
Ringstone Keep
Nifall
Farbury
Iolom
Sandy Howl
Cindermoor
Zuros
Crow's Tusk
Harland
Newark
BOCTOR
Cirrus
The Winterburn River
Silverspring
Mossfell
Illion
Hawk's Scar
Ashton
Thayll
White Lake
Snapper Lake
Arlan
MERRY
WATER
Addingham
Saltguard
The Long Margin
0   20   40 ≈ miles
N E W S

For Liam/Tom

Prologue
Captured, Bound and Taken

~Alejandro~

Night fell heavy on the glass chapel that evening. The city below was sleeping, but Alejandro could find no rest for himself. He knew that someone had been in the chapel, his home, just days previously. Nothing was out of place inside, except for two burnt-down candles discarded on the stone floor, but the intrusion was enough to make Alejandro no longer feel safe here.

He knew the time had come to leave the city. Guards were searching for him in connection to a peculiar incident at the Sickle Inn, and Alejandro could no longer risk showing his face in the streets to play music and earn money to survive. He did not wish to get caught, and his situation had become increasingly more desperate over the last few days.

Alejandro thought back to that day at the inn. He had stopped visiting these taverns because he knew the kind of reception he would receive from a select few shopkeepers also drinking inside, but on that day he had been drawn in by a strange, yet familiar sense of power, the same that resonated throughout the chapel and the same that he had ended up displaying at the inn. There had been three young women sitting near the bar that day and Alejandro was certain that at least one of them also had the talent to access this power.

He wondered if he had ruined his only chance to ever find them again, or whether, just maybe, it had been the same three who had tried to visit him here. Never before had Alejandro met anyone who might be like him and the thought excited him that just maybe he was not alone. He gave the candles a second unsettled examination, speculating whether it had been good or bad luck that the one day he had chosen to leave the safety of the chapel had been the same day other people had come by.

The more likely scenario though was that guards or shopkeepers from the city had been here, and Alejandro knew deep down that he had to leave before he risked landing himself in even more trouble, but he was reluctant to go because there was nowhere else in the region of Attaching that held such a large concentration of people and nowhere outside that he believed he would be able to make a living out of music, so he was scared to go.

By now, the chapel was so dark that he could barely see anything at all. Sunset was Alejandro's favourite time of day in the chapel. The walls were constructed from glass set into clay, so whenever the sun shone on the building, the entrance hall had a unique iridescence to it. The warm light of a vivid sunset created vibrant shades of purple, red and orange on the walls inside and cast rainbows over the beams in the rafters. As the candles slowly burnt down around him, a statuette of a finely dressed older man was illuminated briefly in one of the nooks of the walls, one of five that adorned the chapel. Sculpted onto a pedestal, the stone carving observed Alejandro with stony eyes as he paced around the chamber, deciding what to do.

Getting no closer to being able to get to sleep, Alejandro got up and put on a hooded, warm coat. At this time, he judged that he could safely go down to the city with little risk of being recognised. Perhaps a walk would clear his head and help him think through what to do next. He left the chapel and made his way carefully down the hillside into the city, not stopping until he reached the shadow of tall buildings, where he merged effortlessly into the shadows. Alejandro skirted around the street corners but quickly found his way to where all the roads in the city led.

The Lyrian Citadel glowed softly in the moonlight, but Alejandro did not dare approach it any closer. The building thronged with guards belonging to King Pala, and not to mention the King himself. But rising behind the Citadel was another significant mark on the landscape. Ember Mountain, the giant volcano of Attaching towered over the city wherever you stood, and whereas the castle glowed white, the conical mountain behind it was almost pitch black, with only its outer edges faintly visible against the darkness.

Alejandro shuffled his way around the houses, hugging the walls. He took up the hood of his robe to conceal his face and stole across to the opposite side of the square. Pausing there for a moment to check his surroundings, Alejandro took a moment to realise that once again, he could detect a strange, almost scent, in the air around the open courtyard. He froze, trying to locate where it was coming from.

Directly across from where he was standing, a figure stood on an open doorstep, illuminated by light from inside. As he watched, they took a final glance down the street and stepped back inside, clicking the door shut.

Alejandro slowly circled nearer the house, and as he got closer, he became more confident that this building was the origin of the sense of power he had picked up. The trail led away from the door, however, down the street and towards the direction where the figure had been looking, all the while fading fast.

Alejandro quickly turned away from the house and followed the invisible tracks down towards a well-lit alleyway that led to several of the inns where he was not welcome. Alejandro faltered; most of them would still be open. This route was not one he would typically take, and what if somebody recognised him? Far ahead, Alejandro spotted a cloaked and hooded company of four walking underneath the light of a street torch into the darkness of the evening and drawn in by reckless curiosity, Alejandro decided to follow.

He was forced to stop several times along the alleyway to avoid people he did not want to meet. The final cloaked figure glanced backwards one time, and Alejandro immediately recognised her face from the inn. He pushed further on but there were so many people and guards patrolling the main street that he was forced to cut through side alleys and back onto the main thoroughfare. The group of four disappeared from view several times ahead, but with a rare bit of luck, Alejandro managed not to lose them altogether.

Finally, the streets quietened, and he picked up his pace once more. Looking ahead, Alejandro realised he was now almost at the border-wall of the city. In a panic, he remembered there would be guards posted at the gate ahead and quickly hid from sight, realising how reckless he was being and considering whether it was now too late to flee back to the chapel.

Far over to the right, he detected movement by the wall in the distance and recognised four figures grouped by the outer city walls near the gate. It then occurred to Alejandro to wonder why they were trying to leave the city in the dead of night. Perhaps he was not the only one being searched for by the guards. Intrigued, Alejandro edged closer as quickly as he dared, aware of the watch's presence on the walls.

They whispered a conversation, but it was impossible for Alejandro to hear anything. Then suddenly, one raised her arm with a command, and the other three began to run for the city walls while the guard's back was turned. At that moment, Alejandro was torn. He was about to let them disappear once again. The fourth figure stayed where she was, concentrating on the guard. Desperation took him, and Alejandro ran forwards, grabbing the last girl by the arm before she ran too.

She screamed in surprise and lashed out at him as he physically took hold of her wrist.

"Wait!" Alejandro cried, "please!"

He immediately regretted his actions. The young woman eyed him in fear and wrestled free of his grip before she spun to flee back to the city. No, Alejandro thought wildly, he could not lose them all again. They were the only ones who could give him some answers. In his panic to stop her, he let his instincts take control. A fierce green tendril burst out from the ground at his feet. The vine wrapped itself around the girl's wrist and brought her to a halt. Alejandro caught up to her, planning to explain everything, as she tried to yank free of a chain she could not break. When he reached her, it was only then that he realised he did not detect the same power from this particular individual. He had made another mistake.

She looked at him with wide eyes.

"Who are you?"

It was the others that he had wanted to stop. He released his hold on the girl and turned back towards the city walls, but then turmoil broke loose. Guards materialised from every direction thinkable, as if they had crawled out of the very stone, and Alejandro cursed his stupidity. The King's soldiers surrounded the pair of them with nocked arrows ready to deal out death to them both, as a tall guard bearing a shield broke through the ranks.

"Bind them and take them up to the Citadel. The King will decide what is to be done. Don't let that one do anything unnatural, or we'll cause pain to the girl here. Do you understand me?"

"No, wait-"

A gag bound itself firmly over his mouth, and Alejandro fell silent. His hands too were bound by coarse rope, and beside him, Alejandro saw the same happen to the woman. They were shoved forward and commanded to walk.

Alejandro was marched through the streets on a similar course to earlier. He frantically considered using his abilities once again to free himself but then paused. There was a chance that he could escape maybe but not with the girl as well. Too many guards surrounded them. He was likely to hurt her if he tried anything, and he had done enough to her already. From her expression, Alejandro was not sure if she was more afraid of him or the guards.

They reached the Citadel doors and were hastily dragged inside, down long dark corridors that led to the prison. Through the fear and confusion, Alejandro dimly registered what an unexpected circumstance it was to be inside the household of the King. Then he was flung to a cold, stone floor, and all other thoughts were knocked from his mind.

"Is this the one?" a guard asked from above him.

"No. It seems the King was correct in thinking that there were more."

Dark eyes peered in through the bars from above him. A metal door boomed shut, and Alejandro lay uncertain, alone in the dark, filled with guilt and dreading what lay ahead for him from here.

Chapter 1
Venture into the City

~Aurielle~

Aurielle stood at the summit of the volcano and stared down the settlement of Lyria spread out below her. She had thought they might have finished with the city but it seemed not. Their friend, Gail, who had helped them reach the volcano, now needed rescuing herself. As it was their fault she had been captured and taken to the Lyrian Citadel in the first place, they had resolved to try and get her out.

In the small cave behind her, which had become their home these past few nights, she heard the sound of Shumuti and Sara's voices. The three of them had been sent here to find the individual in Lyria who could use Magic, the same as she and Shumuti could, but it turned out they had unearthed not one but two people who fit that description.

The first Magic user they had found sat with Shumuti and Sara now in the cave behind her. Gabriel had agreed to return home with them to train in how to control his Magic better. The second, however, they had failed to find before the King had, and they believed he might now be locked up with Gail, deep inside the prison of the Citadel.

Shumuti had been of the opinion that perhaps they could bargain with the King for Gail and the other prisoner's release, but from her past experience, Sara had raised her concerns over the intentions of the King and his guards, and Aurielle was inclined to side with her. If the King had already locked up one Magic user, they had no reason to believe he would treat them any differently. Having left the King's guard recently himself, Gabriel had also reluctantly agreed that King Pala had been acting differently lately. Therefore, they had tenuously decided to find a way to extract Gail and the second prisoner and leave hopefully before the King even knew they were there.

Seemingly, the King was searching for people with unusual talents like theirs, but his intentions remained unknown. Until now, they had always strived to keep Magic a secret, believing that was the best way to protect it. Aurielle winced at how they had assured Gail's aunt, Wyn, that they would free her niece. Gabriel believed he could get them inside the Lyrian Citadel and down into the prison cells. Honestly, she was not sure that they could pull it off, but it felt too late to back down now.

Aurielle concentrated her attention on the Citadel, recalling in her mind the sketched plan that Gabriel had drawn for them, which showed the locations of the King's chambers, the guard's quarters and more importantly, the small prison keep beneath the main foundations of the Citadel. Once she was satisfied that she could recall the layout without difficulty, Aurielle gave the city one last uneasy glance and turned back into the cave. Wyn sat beside Sara near the entrance, with the same anxious expression on her face that Aurielle had seen ever since the older woman had climbed to the summit of the volcano to relay the bad news to them. Aurielle had run out of comforting words to say, so instead she passed by the two of them and walked over to where Shumuti and Gabriel were sitting pouring over a map.

"I need you to tell us your plan on getting inside," Shumuti said.

"It won't be easy," Gabriel said, "the guards set a watch on the outer walls of the main Citadel gate, so there will be no entering unnoticed that way, and they have a view of the whole surrounding area. It will be difficult to sneak up right under their noses." He looked apologetically at Shumuti. "To be honest, I'm not sure-"

"I thought you had an idea," Aurielle said.

"I do have an idea. I found what I had been looking for earlier. I wasn't sure if I still had it. Wait here."

Gabriel disappeared back into one of the tunnels in the mountain. He returned a moment later, carrying a bundle of white and red cloth in his arms. He laid the fabric down in front of them, and Aurielle saw distinctly the insignia of the King, the head of a wolf, emblazoned on the front.

"This is my old guard uniform," Gabriel said.

"Do you think you can get inside wearing this?" Shumuti asked.

"It depends who is on duty," Gabriel answered.

"That dœsn't sound like a foolproof plan," Aurielle said.

"Far from it," Gabriel agreed, "which is why I suggest a modification to it. Instead of trying to steal our way into the prison keep, what if I claim to have found one of you in the wild and captured you? I tell any guards I meet that I want to return to the King's guard and bring one of you as proof that I intend to stick to my word. Then, once we get into the Citadel, I can escort one of you to the prison myself, where we can free your friend and maybe the man you are looking for, if he is there as well."

Aurielle glanced at Shumuti to see how convinced she looked. Her friend was silent, going over the plan in her head.

"It still seems risky," Shumuti said, "but it may be the best chance we have to get down there. As long as we can get to Gail, we can make our way back."

"I think we should keep in mind what your father said to us, Shumuti," Aurielle said, "and avoid seeing the King if we can, by getting in and out as quickly as possible."

"If we were taking Seaglen's advice, we would not be stepping foot anywhere near the Citadel in the first place," Shumuti said, "but that choice has been taken from us. Still, I am wary of the consequences of what we decide to do tomorrow."

"We are also putting a lot of faith in you not to hand us over to the King," Aurielle said to Gabriel.

"You still don't trust me, do you?"

"We still hardly know you," Aurielle said, thinking back to her encounter with him on the mountaintop a few mornings ago.

"I am no longer loyal to the King," Gabriel said, "maybe he did care for me when I was growing up because he hoped I would be a good Captain of his guard, but when I heard myself described by him as a secret weapon, I wondered how much I still meant to him."

"Well, I have confidence in you." Shumuti looked Gabriel in the eye. "I'm willing to enter the Lyrian Citadel with you."

"What if Gabriel loses control of his Magic again while you're inside the Citadel?" Aurielle asked.

"It shouldn't happen again so soon," he said, "but there is always a chance, I suppose."

"Then I should go with you," Aurielle said, "if any of us are going to be at risk, I'm the only one who might stand a chance at stopping you."

Gabriel and Shumuti looked at her in surprise, and eventually, Shumuti nodded in agreement.

"There is another way to bypass the walls and enter the city," Gabriel said, outlining a route on the map. "This one. But it's a long road, and it eventually leads to the docks where you said your boat is moored in Lyria. You and Sara should take this way in case something goes wrong with us. Hopefully, we'll already be there when you arrive."

"If not, we'll assume that you need rescuing," Shumuti said.

"If it gets to that stage, I don't know if you should come in after us," Gabriel said, "we can always fight the King's soldiers with Magic and escape as you say, but the damage we will have to create to do so may be enormous."

"That is the last resort," Shumuti said, "the King is not our enemy after all. We don't want to tear his city apart. But I think he will be reluctant to let you out from under his gaze if you return to him, Gabriel."

"All I need to do is convince the others of my loyalty," he said, "I've already escaped once from there."

Aurielle turned her head back in the direction of Wyn. "Then I guess we have little choice but to try."

It was not getting into the Lyrian Citadel that worried Aurielle, but more forcefully into her mind came her memories from her brief glimpse of King Pala and his sharp, piercing gaze. They were about to meddle in serious affairs, and she did not want to think about what would happen if he caught them.

"All right then," Shumuti said, "let's go back to Lyria."

Sara and Wyn walked over to join them.

"Are we set?" Sara asked.

"As good as we are going to be," Shumuti said.

"What about him?" Wyn asked, nodding towards Gabriel, "will he be joining you?"

"Of course," Gabriel replied.

"We need to get ready," Aurielle said, standing quickly and trying to distract herself from what they were about to do, "I'll clean up here."

Shumuti and Sara leapt into action after her as they set about clearing the cave and preparing what they would need. Gabriel disappeared down one of the many tunnels of the volcano and Aurielle nervously set about packing up her bag. Once she was ready, she glanced at all of Gabriel's things covering the floor and stepped back, refusing to clean up his stuff for him. In her eyes, they were still not companions yet, even if Shumuti had accepted him as one of them.

They had agreed it would be best to start at dawn, to make the trek back down the volcano less treacherous and to ensure that they got at least a few hours rest. That would mean that they would be able to make the journey back to Lyria in a single day. Gabriel still had not returned, so the four of them settled down to sleep. Aurielle was just about to close her eyes when she saw him enter. His mouth twitched as he noticed his belongings strewn across the floor and Aurielle gave a small smile of satisfaction before closing her eyes and settling off to sleep.

The heat of wet breath on her face and the pressure of something pushing down on her chest woke Aurielle with a start in the early hours of the morning. A pair of large, dark eyes stared down at her and a long snout hovered inches from her nose. The pressure on her chest was a leaden paw, and Aurielle froze, unable to breathe even if she wanted to as the towering wolf above her sniffed her face. The glint of several sharp teeth was just visible under the curl of its mouth. Out of the corner of her vision, she realised she was lying in one of the tunnels and not the central cave where they all usually slept. Something or someone had moved her during the night.

Suddenly, the animal backed away and removed its weight, causing her to start breathing hastily. She sat up, but the wolf had dematerialised back into the darkness. Taken aback slightly by what had just happened, she finally shook herself and scrambled to her feet, wondering why she was now in the tunnels. She had never walked in her sleep before.

Her thoughts sprang back to the others, wondering if they were now in danger. Aurielle set off at a run up the passage, towards the light that should lead back to the main cave. Everyone was there, still asleep on the floor and the wolf sat just beside Gabriel's sleeping form, as though protecting him. She faltered for a minute, and in the light, she realised that the black, tan and grey animal was not much taller than a dog, more like an oversized puppy in fact, with ears and legs that were still too large. She glanced between Gabriel and the small wolf, beginning to wonder if it had been no accident that she had found herself in the passage.

Aurielle marched over to Gabriel's bed and yanked his coat off of him. The wolf growled, and Gabriel awoke with a cry as Aurielle towered over him. He put everything together in an instant and grabbed the scruff of the wolf's neck to stop the animal from leaping up at Aurielle.

"You..." Aurielle said, glaring at Gabriel, "you..."

"A sentence please, Aurielle," Gabriel said, stroking the wolf to calm it down and trying not to laugh.

"You're not funny." Aurielle glowered down at him.

"Aurielle?" She heard Shumuti's voice. "What's the matter?"

"This animal is yours?" Aurielle ignored her and accused Gabriel.

"His name is Aztec." Gabriel stroked the creature's fur. "And yes, he is my friend."

"Why didn't you mention that you own a wolf?"

"He is important to me. I had to be sure I could trust you before telling you."

"Are you saying you trust me now?"

"Well, one of us has to start to, if this is going to work."

"You dragged me out of the cave last night and dumped me in one of the tunnels so you could scare me with your pet, as revenge for not clearing away your gear last night."

"Did you, Gabriel?" Shumuti asked, with a trace of amusement.

"Aztec has never met any other people before," Gabriel said, "I wasn't sure how he was going to react. I thought it best to introduce you one by one."

"Introduce me?" Aurielle asked.

"I think he likes you," Gabriel said.

"Where's he been all this time?" Aurielle asked.

"I said he's my friend," Gabriel said, "I don't control when Aztec comes back to me. He roams all over the volcano and moors, and sometimes I don't see him for weeks. Perhaps I should have mentioned him before, I'll admit. but I didn't want to ruin the surprise. He's gorgeous, isn't he?"

"He's beautiful," Shumuti said, coming tentatively over, "may I?"

Gabriel nodded, and Shumuti came over and scratched the wolf behind his ear. Aurielle watched on and sighed with a sinking feeling that she had lost this. Shumuti had always had a soft spot for the dogs in Thayll, and this animal was particularly striking with his patchy copper and grey coat, broad bushy tail and intent amber eyes.

"How did you end up befriending him?" Shumuti asked, "we saw wolves on the mountain on the way here."

"I found him alone as a cub when I first got here," Gabriel said, "I don't know how he lost the rest of the pack, but he was so small and weak, I couldn't just leave him. I didn't think he would survive alone out in the wild, so I brought him up here with me."

"We can't take him with us now, can we?" Aurielle asked.

"He is my final condition," Gabriel said to Shumuti, "if I come with you, Aztec comes as well."

Aurielle rolled her eyes in exasperation as she failed to fight back the smile on her face. "Well, of course, Shumuti is going to say yes."

"You're right," Shumuti said, "there's no way I can say no to a face like that."

"And no, Gabriel," Aurielle added, getting her word in before him, "she's not talking about your face."

Gabriel smirked and ruffled Aztec's ears.

Aurielle strode over to her bedding area in defeat as Sara rushed over as well to introduce herself to Aztec. Wyn looked slightly bemused by what had just taken place and when she spoke it was clear her mind had been focused elsewhere.

"How long before we leave?" she asked.

Shumuti tore her eyes away from the wolf, and her expression hardened once more. "Now. We leave now."

That focused everybody's attention. Aurielle forgot her quarrel with Gabriel and collected her pack. As the dawn birdsong chorus ended on the mountain, they were ready to set off.

Gabriel and Aztec found the unmarked trails that led the way down the side of the volcano quickly, the young wolf disappearing off ahead and marking the way forward. Gabriel was followed next by Sara, then Wyn, then Shumuti and finally, Aurielle. Going down the steep track was trickier than going up had been and so the journey was slow. Wyn had a staff with her to help, but even so, Aurielle found that she was continually on edge to any signs that the older woman might fall.

She glanced ahead at Gabriel, realising how strange it was to see him dressed in a colour that was not black. Strapped onto the underneath of his pack were two longswords, partially concealed under a black rag. Her sword was safely hanging at her side, and Wyn was the only one of the five of them not carrying a weapon. Instead, what Aurielle did notice was that on her belt was the pouch of runes that she had used with Shumuti, Sara and herself. The thought crossed Aurielle's mind to ask whether she would offer to read these stones for Gabriel now that he was one of them, but Wyn had not mentioned it as yet.

They trudged on back down the volcano slope as the sun continued to rise. Morning faded as the warmer midday replaced it and the glow warmed their backs. They did not stop until the foot of the volcano, where they had a proper meal and a quick rest, but Wyn was impatient and reminded them of the speed needed to return to Lyria. They passed along the winding track, and it was not before long that Shumuti, Sara and Aurielle felt some recognition of the terrain on which they were walking. Gabriel still led the way, but Wyn, who was still showing an extraordinary determination for speed, followed him closely. Sara had dropped back in the line and was now alongside Shumuti and Aurielle at the back together.

"Is this the place where we saw the wolves?" Sara whispered.

"I think you're right," Aurielle said.

"They wouldn't be here now though." Shumuti looked around uncertainly. "It's the middle of the day."

"Sara! Shumuti! Aurielle!" Their heads shot up. "Hurry up, will you?"

Wyn turned away, increasing her speed. The three of them ran to keep up, not realising how far they had fallen behind. They joined the other two by a small standing stone set beside the path. A trickle of remembrance entered Aurielle's mind as she recalled sprinting past this stone before in the dark, on their way up the mountain. Aztec sniffed the rock with interest.

"This stone marks the end of the territory belonging to the wolves," Gabriel said, "I didn't tell you that was where you were before because I didn't er...want to frighten you."

His eyes flickered in Aurielle's direction, and she opened her mouth indignantly.

"What are all those marks?" Sara asked, staring at the stone.

"Claw marks," Gabriel answered, "made by the wolves to mark their territory or sharpen their claws, I suppose. But sometimes I can't help thinking that they mean something else. But it's beyond me, and Aztec isn't a very good translator."

The young wolf howled in reply. Shumuti knelt by the marks and had a closer look. She beckoned to Aurielle, and she went to join her. Markings made from wolf claws covered the stone. Some were long and thin while others were shorter and thicker. Most of them were overlapping into scratchy triangles and crosshatches. They examined it, fascinated.

"Things to do," Wyn said, "no time to waste here."

"Right," Sara said.

Reluctantly, they stood up and followed Gabriel's lead as he set out once more. Aurielle looked back as they walked off at the waystone set against the horizon. For a second Aurielle thought she glimpsed a shadow sniffing the stone, but then it was gone.

The rest of the day passed without event and as dusk fell, they at last reached sight of the city walls. The group halted behind the crest of a small hillock and rested, trying to decide how best to tackle the next challenge ahead of them.

"This is where we split up," Gabriel said.

"Are you certain you want to go?" Shumuti asked Aurielle quietly.

Aurielle nodded her head. "Don't worry about me."

"Wait," Sara said. "What if I was to go with one of you instead? I can't use Magic like you. I'm nowhere near as valuable if one of us gets caught."

"No, I'll go," Aurielle said, "if something bad happens, Gabriel and I can fight our way out if we have to."

"Now," Shumuti said, "give us all of your bags, and we'll store them in the boat."

"Get Stannair ready to sail," Aurielle said, handing her pack over, "we might need a quick escape from the city."

With everything finalised and decided, they parted ways and split up. Shumuti, Sara, Wyn and Aztec scuttled away over the plains, keeping low to the ground. They soon vanished from sight, but Aurielle and Gabriel remained illuminated by the spotlight of the moon and walked forward to meet their audience at the gate.

Chapter 2
Enter the Prison Keep

~Gabriel~

A thick length of rope bound Aurielle's arms together. Gabriel carried her sword as well as his own, and on the surface, he dressed the part of a guard belonging to King Pala and the Lyrian Citadel. He took a deep breath as they slowly walked under the shadow of the high walls, wondering if he was fully prepared to be back. They approached the city wall gate and Gabriel knocked as he had been taught to do. Then they waited.

"Who seeks passage into Lyria at this hour?" a voice cried from the walls.

"A guard of the King," Gabriel answered back.

"And what was your business outside of the city walls?"

"I bring a prisoner...with unique talents."

There was silence for a few seconds.

"Quickly!" shouted another voice with higher authority, "open the gate!"

"Open the gate!"

Gabriel stepped back as a soft groan symbolised the creak of the thick, wooden door to the city swinging open before them. A burning torch was thrust into his face by a guard. To his relief, he did not recognise the bearer. Aurielle was briefly examined as well before more binds were added to those that Gabriel had tied.

"I wish to escort her to the Citadel," Gabriel said quickly.

"Of course you do." The guard grinned. "Two of my men will escort you both up there."

Gabriel noticed the badge on his shoulder that indicated this man was the Captain of the Guard. It was strange that Gabriel did not know him.

"Can I pass?"

"Go ahead," the Captain replied, "I wouldn't want to delay the delight of the King. I shall send a runner ahead of you to deliver the news. You, boy!"

"Captain?"

"Send a message to the Citadel."

"Aye, sir!"

The messenger ran off into the gloom. The Guard Captain surveyed them expectantly under his mask, and Gabriel took the opportunity to study him back, picking out a notable scar on the man's face, connecting his right eyebrow all the way to the ear. Gabriel took hold of Aurielle and marched her off along the street. The two extra guards of their escort walked ahead of them. Aurielle glanced at Gabriel as they walked, but thankfully, she did not dare speak. He tried to give her a reassuring smile back, but the sight of the Lyrian Citadel up ahead turned his expression to stone.

The Citadel rose out of the darkness as they got closer, sitting atop its mount at the centre of the city. Eventually, they reached the summit of the small hill and the gates of the fortress. They passed through with no trouble, due to the message sent ahead of them, and so they entered the grounds themselves, passing under the gate and into the home of the King of Attaching.

Even Aurielle, in her bound state, looked up in wonder as they crossed the gardens and entered inside a pearly white and red building, which opened up into the vast hallway beyond. Gabriel had tried to describe the inside of the Citadel to them but looking up at it now, he knew he had not done it justice. The walls and ceilings were teeming with paintings and carvings of ancient history and intricate patterns depicting landmarks and events all across the country of Meteorath. Veins of metallic silver ran over the glass of the windows and under the pale glow of the moon, the twisting design on the windows reflected back onto the floor. The whole place was beautiful, but still, Gabriel was not glad to be back.

A slight movement at the end of the hallway caught his attention. A door at the opposite end opened and out strode two more armoured guards of proud stature; one carrying a horn and the other a standard bearing the emblem of Attaching, the same that Gabriel now wore on himself. He knew these two as the personal guard of the King and so immediately made to turn right, to lead Aurielle towards the direction of the prison but their escort stood in his way.

"You will present her to the King," the guard said.

"Now?" Gabriel asked, "he dœsn't want to wait until morning to see her?"

"Now."

Gabriel faltered and felt Aurielle panic slightly beside him. He had not been prepared for this encounter so soon.

Their escort forced a change in direction and began to walk Gabriel and Aurielle forward, directly down the middle of the hall. As they progressed further and further inside, Gabriel noticed more guards placed at regular intervals along the walls of the room, holding spears, more than he remembered usually being stationed in this chamber. Then the armoured guard blew two clear notes on his horn, followed by a longer, deeper one. Their escort halted halfway across the floor and the room was silent, charged with expectation.

The doors at the end of the hall swung open a second time, for a split second revealing a crackling fire in the room behind them. Then a shimmer appeared in the doorway and out stepped a man more regal than any other who walked this hallway.

King Pala wore a midnight blue robe, with a black velvet cloak draped across one shoulder, embroidered with silver thread. Always elegantly dressed, his moustache and small, triangular beard were also neatly trimmed and his hair was cut just to touch his shoulders. He paced evenly forward, striding across the chamber with the two guards in tow. The King caught Gabriel's gaze immediately, and Gabriel tried his best not to look away, trying to gauge what the King's feelings towards him now were.

All the guards around them dropped to their knees in a bow. Gabriel looked around with a small frown. The King had not normally expected such formality with his guards in private. For a second, Gabriel considered following suit but held his ground. By the time he focused his attention back towards the King, Gabriel had discovered that he had reached them, flanked on either side by the standard-bearer and the second armoured guard.

"Your time away has not changed you, Gabriel." The King looked down at him with a steely glint in his eye.

"No, but things here seem to have while I've been gone," Gabriel said, glancing at the men who still had not risen.

He thought he saw a flicker of anger in the King's eyes.

"I didn't mean to disturb you this late," Gabriel said, "I had thought that my prisoner could be dealt with in the morning."

"You underestimate your own importance, Gabriel," the King said, "who is this?"

He indicated Aurielle.

"I found her outside the city," Gabriel replied, "I believe...she is the sort of person you have been looking for."

"Well this is unexpected," the King said, "maybe you have changed a little. I thought I had to finally come to terms with the fact that you would refuse to turn in one of your own."

"My own?"

The King waved his remark aside. "You know what I mean. Girl, what is your name?"

"Aurielle."

"Well, Aurielle," the King said, "I wish to speak to you in private. I will call for you after, Gabriel. Do I take it that your return here means you wish to regain your place in my guard?"

"Yes." Gabriel tried not to make his answer hollow. "If there is a place for me, my King."

"We shall speak about it later."

"What will you do with her?" Gabriel asked quickly, his heartbeat quickening. Their plan was beginning to fall apart already.

"Gabriel," the King said, "your return to the Citadel is currently in a very fragile position. Do you wish to question me again?"

"No."

One of the King's guards yanked Gabriel free of his grip on Aurielle's ropes and pulled her one step away from him. She looked back, and for the first time since knowing Aurielle, Gabriel saw fear in her eyes. Under the gaze of the King, he did not dare show any emotion or reassurance back.

"Your room is still empty," the King said, "you may have it back, for the time being."

King Pala turned away and his guards followed, pulling Aurielle behind them. As they began to walk back to the end of the hall, Gabriel's hand found its way to his sword. For a second, he considered giving up on the plan there and then. Then a second thought struck him that if they fought their way out now, the prisoners would remain in the keep. Perhaps there was still a way he could get them all out.

Aurielle disappeared behind the door to the King's private quarters, and Gabriel knew he had little time. He turned in the direction of the door that led to where he used to live in the Citadel. As he walked, he tried to keep his pace unhurried, feeling the eyes of almost every other guard in the hall on his back.

When he got into the corridor, he realised that one of them was actually following him. He passed through onto a spiral stairway that led up and down. Up was the way to the guard's living area but, struck by a sudden idea, Gabriel turned down instead, towards the kitchens.

As he had hoped, the kitchens were bustling with soldiers who had just come off duty. He found a large crowd and pushed between them, ducking down and circled back the way he had come, passing through another door that led to the back of the kitchens. Peering back through a crack in the door, he saw the guard that had been tailing him stop and look around, searching for where he had gone. Suppressing a smile, Gabriel shut the door and turned to find he was staring into the face of one of the Citadel's cooks.

"None of you lot are allowed back here," he told Gabriel in a gruff tone.

"I'm to bring food to the prisoners," Gabriel lied.

"Well in that case," the cook said, "about time. Here."

Grateful for this fragile piece of luck, Gabriel accepted the basket of stale leftovers.

"May I take the back route through here to the keep?" he asked, "it's much quicker."

The cook grunted, and Gabriel wasted no time taking that as a yes, hurrying on past. He passed through another set of doors and crossed out onto the outer walls of the Citadel. At the end of the wall was a tower, inside which was a set of steps leading down to the prison below. Gabriel descended the spiral quickly, returning the nod of a guard he passed on the way.

Down the stairway, Gabriel immediately turned left and came face-to-face with a second guard. Wondering how long his luck would hold, he opened his mouth.

"I've come with food for the prisoners."

The guard stood down without question and Gabriel passed through. The tunnel down to the prison keep was dark and gloomy, so Gabriel was glad when a line of lit torches appeared on the walls. The way he had just entered the keep was the only possible route to get in or out, so down here there was no guard set.

Gabriel passed the first few cells without luck. The smell down here was incredible, and Gabriel found it hard to concentrate on using his other senses to search. From what Wyn had said of Gail, Gabriel was reasonably sure that he had seen her working around the Citadel before and would recognise her. The man, Gabriel would not, but he would know the presence of Magic instantly.

He moved further into the prison, but there was still no sign of either of them. Fear started pricking at him as he proceeded on to the next row of cells. Finally, he paused at a face he thought he recognised.

"Gail?" He knelt next to the bars of the cell.

The cell's inhabitant had been sleeping, but at the sound of his voice, she instantly awoke and brushed her hair away from her face, looking up at him nervously.

"I know you," she whispered, "why have you come?"

"My name is Gabriel," he answered quietly, "I am going to get you out of here."

"What are you talking about? You're here to free me? Am I still dreaming?"

"No," Gabriel answered, "this is more of a nightmare, I think. Listen to me, were you brought here alone?"

"No," she answered slowly, "there was a man. He's the reason I'm in here. Unless it's because I helped them leave, but I shouldn't be telling you that."

Her eyes widened fearfully.

"Helped who? Are you talking about Shumuti, Aurielle and Sara?"

Gail retreated to the back wall of her cell. "I'm not telling you anything else!"

He pushed some food through the bars.

"Don't worry. I'm here to help you. Tell me where the man you came here with is, and I promise I'll get you both out of here."

She looked at him distrustfully but pointed to the row of cells opposite.

"At the end," she whispered.

Gabriel studied the lock that kept her cell shut for a couple of seconds. Concentrating for a moment, he felt for his connection to Magic and collected the energy around him. He saw Gail's eyes widen again as the padlock holding her captive began to glow and shimmer from the heat that Gabriel was creating. As he was concentrating, Gabriel felt a sudden rush of energy that he could not control and with an unexpected bang, the lock exploded clean off the door, ricocheting against a nearby wall and melting from the excessive heat in front of their eyes on the floor. Trying to pretend that he had meant that to happen, Gabriel breathed a small sigh of relief that nothing more serious had gone wrong.

"Be careful not to touch it." Gabriel slid back the bolt and swung open the door to the cell.

"You're like them." Gail crept forward with interest once again. "Are you honestly not with the other guards?"

"If I were, don't you think I would have had the key?"

He left Gail to decide whether to follow him or not and headed towards the location of the second prisoner. As he moved closer, Gabriel immediately knew where to find him. He was already standing by the bars of his cell when Gabriel arrived, staring out equally as curiously. Curls of brown hair partially covered his dark eyes that were flecked with green and Gabriel guessed from the length of the beard beginning to show on his face that he had been held captive for a good number of days now.

"What's your name?"

"Alejandro," he said, "who are you?"

"Gabriel. I've come to try to get you out of here. Though honestly, I don't know why you haven't tried to escape already."

"Listen, Gabriel. I cannot break myself out of here. If I use my power, they will kill the girl I was brought here with. Every time I use it something goes horribly wrong. I can't, I have done enough damage already."

He shrank back into the cell, guiltily.

"You mean her?" Gabriel indicated Gail, who had crept up to his side.

"You're all right?" he asked her in shock, returning to the bars of the cell.

"For now," she said.

"I'm so, so sorry," Alejandro said, "for all of this."

Gabriel heard the sound of footsteps above them.

"You can apologise to her later," he said, "we have little time to get out of here, and it's not going to go smoothly."

"Right," Alejandro said.

"Here. For some strength." Gabriel tossed him some food, which Alejandro wolfed down. "I'll get you out."

"Don't worry. I can manage it myself."

Gabriel watched in fascination as Alejandro placed his hand against the bottom of the bars where they dug into the floor. There was a loud crack and a small rumble from the earth. Gabriel drew back as a fissure appeared in the stone directly in-line with the row of bars and ran up either side of his cell. The support now weakened, the bars fell out of place and Alejandro pushed the whole front to the ground. The metal fell to the floor with a clatter.

"Are you all right?" Gabriel asked, watching Alejandro stumble slightly from the effort.

"I'll be fine."

"Your Magic is different than mine."

"Magic? Is that what you call it?"

"Do you have a plan?" Gail interjected.

"No," Gabriel said, "we did. But that's long past. We have one more person to save before we can get out of here. I think we have little choice left now other than to fight our way out. Do you feel up to it, Alejandro?"

"Just about. But why are you helping us?"

"I'm not working alone," Gabriel said, "my friends have been trying to find you for a while now. Come on, we need to get back upstairs, if we're not already too late."

Gabriel led the way back up the spiral staircase to the entrance of the keep. Pausing, he saw that the guard had changed over. He faltered as the new sentry turned and Gabriel recognised him as the soldier who had followed him initially from the main hall.

"I knew there was something off about you," the guard said, "you might have been the King's favourite once, but you're nothing more than a traitor now. King Pala will have you killed for this, you know. It's my job to make sure you don't leave the keep until he comes for you."

"You think you can stop me?" Gabriel asked.

The guard made a move forward and Gabriel sensed the Magic but still only had a second's warning before he felt the ground rumble and shift once more. He caught his balance, but the guard did not, tumbling down the stairs into the darkness of the prison below them. Gabriel turned back to Alejandro, who was looking like he was ready to collapse.

"That took more effort than I expected."

Gabriel rushed to support him so he could stand.

"You're in no fit state to fight," he said, "Gail, here, take Aurielle's sword."

She quickly obliged, looking unsure what to do with the weapon and came under Alejandro's other arm, so they could support him down the corridor. Gabriel was becoming less and less confident by the minute.

"Where now?" Gail asked.

"I have to save one more person, but you two need to get out of here. At the side of the wall are stairs to the training courtyard. From there, you can sneak out the side entrance to the back of the kitchens. There's a back exit out to the grounds that way. Get down to the docks if you can, Shumuti and Sara are waiting for you there."

"I know the way you mean," Gail said.

A noise at the end of the corridor alerted them. Gabriel pressed himself flat against the wall. Four figures were coming through the door. He turned to Gail, knowing that if she met any soldiers on the way out, she had no hope.

"I'll try and lead them away from the passage. Once you see an opening, take Alejandro and run for the kitchens."

"This is a terrible plan," Alejandro said, leaning up against the wall.

"Shut up," Gabriel said, knowing he was right, "Gail, do as I say."

Gail gulped and nodded.

The guards emerged into the light. Gabriel selected his target and prepared to attack.

Chapter 3
The Lyrian Citadel

Sara, Shumuti, Wyn and Aztec stole down to the river that wound its way into the marina. They scurried along the bank, running lightly and silently. Wyn was beginning to fall behind a little and Sara had started to hear her breath become ragged. She was about to suggest they took a short break, but in the next minute, water sprung up into view, and she knew that their destination was not far. The four of them were like shadows as they bypassed the single guard at the bank. He glanced back for a second as though he thought he detected something flying by, but they had already moved on.

Wyn left them at a small side alleyway into Lyria's streets. She would go back to her sister, Isa, and wished them luck before departing. The alley shadows engulfed her and alone with Shumuti, Sara suddenly felt wary. Around the corner, guards lined the bank on the left. Sara clutched Shumuti's shoulder along with Aztec's fur, as they flung themselves into a crouch, concealed in the bushes.

"Wouldn't it be simpler to turn back and follow Wyn?" Sara asked, not feeling too hopeful about their chances.

"We can't," Shumuti answered, "we need to get to Stannair. We're supposed to meet the others there."

"I don't think the boat will be any use to us if a quick exit is what we need," Sara said, peering ahead into the dimly lit marina.

"If I need to, I can work the wind," Shumuti said, "don't worry, it's just this once. We need the boat to get back to Merrywater. Otherwise, we're travelling on foot."

She turned away as if that settled the matter. The group of guards ahead of them moved off down the street and back towards the main body of the city.

"Come on, now's our chance," Shumuti said, skulking forward towards the docks.

Sara sighed and moved after her as Shumuti edged forwards towards the first row of boats. Off in the distance were silhouettes of guards on the far bank, but nothing barred their immediate path to Stannair. Sara and Shumuti drew their hoods up to shadow their faces as they wound their way around the marina to find their boat. They had just made it around to the opposite side when a blaring horn resonated three long blasts around the circular basin. Sara and Shumuti jumped and hid behind a stacked pile of crates as several soldiers ran by.

Sara poked her head around the corner. "What was that?"

"I do not think it means good news."

"Did it come from the Citadel?"

"We should hurry."

With the soldiers gone, they ran out in the open and quickly ducked under the shadow of a long boat with the name, Stannair, etched into a plaque on the side. Back to their old home at last, Shumuti led the way up onto the deck, unlocked the hatch and hid their gear in a safe compartment below.

"Is anybody out there?" Shumuti asked as she rejoined Sara.

"It's deserted," Sara said.

"They haven't made it."

"Do you think we should go up to the Lyrian Citadel?"

"I think that alarm sounded for them."

"All right. Aztec, stay. We'll be back soon."

The wolf pup lay down on his front paws with his ears pinned back and let loose a small whine, but surprisingly, he stayed put. Quickly, they disembarked the boat and ran off once more into the city.

Running light and fast, they reached the Lyrian Citadel within a few minutes and crept towards the path at the base of the hill. Sara glanced up at the walls, surprised to see them empty. A feeling of uneasiness grew as they drew close to the Citadel doors. They were ajar.

"Why aren't they guarded?" Sara whispered to Shumuti, "this feels like a trap."

"The plan already looks to have gone wrong," Shumuti said, "it's up to us to get the others out now. The only way we can do that is by going in."

Sara turned back to look at the hall and shook her head.

"We're playing right into their hands."

"Aurielle and Gabriel got caught in there," Shumuti said, "we need to get in now. We are wasting time."

"This is mad," Sara said quietly.

"True. Maybe you should wait here," Shumuti said, "I'll go in alone. Go back and find Wyn, tell her what happened."

Sara took a deep breath. "There's not a chance I am leaving you."

Before Shumuti could reply, Sara moved past Shumuti and ran through the doors into the courtyard of the Citadel. She heard Shumuti follow close behind and draw level with her after a few seconds. Like the gates, the gardens were also deserted, with the attention of the soldiers seemingly held elsewhere. The doors to the Lyrian Citadel itself stood open invitingly. Faintly, ahead of them, the sound of clashing metal could be heard inside. Sara slowed as they approached, but Shumuti did not, and instead, she drew her sword. Sara followed suit more slowly and came to a halt next to Shumuti as they reached the doorstep of the main hall.

Where outside had been calm and silent, inside was chaos. Soldiers swarmed everywhere and to Sara, it looked like almost every soldier in the city. Far in the top corner of the hall, she spotted the only group of figures not dressed in white and red. The guards had succeeded in surrounding the group of three and had disarmed all but one of them.

"Gabriel!" Shumuti cried, running forward.

"Shumuti, wait!"

Not wanting to get separated, Sara raced after her, following the path that Shumuti had begun to barrel through the throng of soldiers, her sudden appearance taking them by surprise.

After a few seconds, they registered that there was something new happening. With a thud, a trio of shields threw themselves up in Sara's path. She cried out and covered her face as her outstretched sword came into contact with the wall of shields, bouncing her back and throwing her to the floor. Her sword spun away across the stone floor and under the feet of dozens of more guards.

Amongst the confusion, arms appeared all over her. Sara had no time to recover before she was hauled back to her feet, surrounded by nothing but helmeted faces. Through the crowd, she saw the top of Shumuti's head. She had reached Gabriel, and together they were facing a line of guards, her sword held out in front of her, not knowing which would attack first.

"Give it up," one of the guards called, holding Sara.

Shumuti saw that she was caught and lowered her sword slightly. At the very back of the hall, another door swung open and out filed two ornately armoured guards, who then stood either side of the door. Finally, a third figure strode slowly into the hall, and Sara recognised him instantly as the King.

"My final guests have arrived," the King said, looking down on the scene of disarray in the hall.

The doors to the outside courtyard swung shut with a resounding boom and the mess of guards instantly shifted into an orderly formation, lining the walls and the door at the end, blocking any chance of escape.

"Give them some space," the King ordered.

The guards holding Sara and those surrounding the others drew back to walls. Sara walked forward quickly to join Shumuti and Gabriel. She saw with relief that Gail was also with them, as well as the man they had been searching for in Lyria all this time, but Aurielle was missing. Together, all five of them warily turned towards the King, wondering what was going to happen now.

"You don't hold us captive," Gabriel said to the King, "not even close."

"I am well aware of the talents that you possess," the King said, "so why don't we all lay our weapons down and just speak?"

The five of them silently regarded him, still braced ready to fight if need be.

"Why don't we go through to my chambers?" the King said, gesturing towards the room he had just come from. "I have wanted to talk to you for a while now."

"You want to talk?" Shumuti asked.

"Yes."

"We shouldn't go," Sara whispered.

"Aurielle is in there," Gabriel said quietly, his attention fixed on King Pala.

"Between all of you tonight, the list of crimes you have committed is longer than my arm," the King said, "you have come here under false pretences, broken criminals free of their cell, lied to me, attacked my guards and broken into the Citadel. Oh, and you have stolen food from our kitchens. I think you should think carefully about disobeying my orders, even given what you can do."

Sara knew he was referring to Magic. Gabriel had said the King had been searching for their group for a while now. Their only hope now of getting out of here without bloodshed was the smallest of chances that they could make some sort of bargain with the King. Perhaps Shumuti thought that too because she silently took the lead and walked up to the steps at the end of the hall to follow the King as he turned to go back into the next chamber.

"Guard the door," King Pala said to his two personal escorts.

"But, my Lord!" one of them objected, "these people are dangerous."

The King silenced the man with a glacial stare. "You will stay here."

Sara caught up to Shumuti as she reached the door, and soon all of them had left the hall and the King's guards behind. The five of them entered the private rooms of the Citadel and clustered together, silently taking in the grandeur of their surroundings. This room was smaller and made a little cosier and less intimidating than the last by the sight of a large, open and roaring fireplace cut into one wall. King Pala settled in the high-backed chair at the back of the room and sitting across from him was Aurielle, at the first seat of a long table, her expression displaying a mixture of shock and worry about seeing all of them gathered in the room with her. Aurielle's wrists were still bound. The King regarded everyone carefully.

"There has been a lot of lies and deceit inside my hall tonight," he began, "here, in private, it is my command that we all be honest with each other and speak plainly. Unless you agree to that, we have nothing more to talk about."

The six of them glanced across at each other, unsure what new turn this night was taking.

"We agree," Shumuti said finally.

"It has taken me a long time to find you all," the King continued, "honestly, I did not know there would be so many."

"You were looking for people like Gabriel?" Shumuti asked.

"I was."

"I'm not one of them," Gail blurted out instantly.

The King looked at her.

"It's true," Shumuti said, "it's our fault that she got mixed up in all of this, but she shouldn't have ever been."

"I see," the King said, "then you are free to leave this room."

Gail did not hesitate to react and spun on her heel to exit as quickly as she could, throwing them all one last look before she disappeared.

"I can't use Magic either." Sara felt the need to add this information. "These are just my friends, and I travel with them. But I'd prefer to stay, if that's all right."

The King's attention switched to her instead, before he considered the group.

"Interesting. I know a little of this skill that you have. I have some sense of what Gabriel can do. I do not understand it, but I can see the powerful potential in it. Am I correct to assume then that the remainder of you have access to these abilities?"

As Shumuti visibly stiffened before her, Sara knew that every part of Shumuti had been taught all her life never to reveal any information to do with Magic. But finally, she gave the King the smallest of nods.

"Do you all control fire, as Gabriel does?" King Pala asked.

"No," Shumuti said, "we are all different. There are four elements that we can have control over; fire, water, earth and air. Aurielle controls water, I use air and your other prisoner uses earth. It's hard to explain what we can do to you, but we call it Magic."

"I do not need to know the specifics," the King said, "you might wonder why, considering your actions here tonight, I have been so lenient with you. I only need to know one thing from you, and that is whether or not you will help me. In return, I am prepared to forgive all of your conduct tonight in the Citadel."

"What exactly do you want from us?" Shumuti asked.

"I am a strong King, and my armies have never yet seen defeat in battle, but something new has come to challenge me now and threaten my people. I have never encountered an enemy like this before, and it has power beyond what I can fight. From what I have seen of Gabriel, I have come to hope that perhaps you may stand a chance of succeeding where I fear I cannot."

"Gabriel described to us the threat that you are referring to," Shumuti said, "we faced these creatures on our way up to Attaching. Aurielle, Sara and I managed to fight them off, but we did not defeat them completely. We have never seen anything like them before either and know hardly anything about them."

"All I can offer you is a name," the King said, "during one encounter, they called themselves Atabra. It means nothing to me, and I have spent hours researching its meaning and origin."

"Perhaps there is no information on them because they have no history," Shumuti said, "we were worried that perhaps there was someone in Attaching who had a hand in their creation."

She glanced over to the man who had been imprisoned with Gail, and he stared back at her with wide eyes.

"But now, I'm not so sure."

"No," the King said, "these creatures originate from Nimaz."

"You know it is Nimaz specifically, and not Boctor?"

"I do. My patrols have confirmed it."

"Nimaz." Sara repeated the name under her breath.

"I began to grow interested in Nimaz a while back," the King continued, "ever since the disappearance of your parents, Gabriel, into that region. I never knew anyone or anything to get the better of my finest Guard Captain. Their disappearance, I could not shake from my head. I began to think there was more happening in Nimaz than I realised. We had thought it was almost a dead region.

"In the years following their disappearance, everything returned to normal and none of my scouting patrols came across anything out of the ordinary. I learnt precious little, until earlier this year when one party came across these creatures. Only one of my men returned from Nimaz to tell the tale, but since then, these Atabra have begun to roam on our side of the Winterburn River."

"You have no idea why they are here?" Aurielle spoke up.

"Other than to kill, none," King Pala answered.

"They have hunted us fairly relentlessly," Shumuti said, "we thought they might also be searching for people that can use Magic, but maybe not if they are attacking you as well."

"Are there any more like you out there?" the King asked, "if I know one thing, it is that there is strength in numbers."

"There may be," Shumuti replied carefully, "we don't know for sure. My father has the same abilities as me, and there are others among our parents who did, but where most of them are now, or if any more had children, we're not sure."

The King sharpened his eyebrows into a frown. "Gabriel, did your father have the same talents and kept them secret from me all this time?"

"No," Gabriel said, "it was my mother."

"Then that is why she left with him." The King closed his eyes for a second, as some information seemed to click into place in his memory.

"My father always impressed on me the importance of keeping Magic a secret," Shumuti said, "he was worried what might happen if too many people knew of its existence and misused it."

"People like me, you mean?" King Pala asked.

Shumuti blushed slightly.

"I'm sorry. It's the reason we sneaked in here. With you imprisoning people, we didn't know what your intentions were."

"Gabriel could have told you my intent," the King said.

"It was more your methods that I was uncertain about," Gabriel said, "I didn't like the way you were going about trying to find Magic users."

"I see," the King said, "and you felt unable to tell me this."

Gabriel fell silent.

"But if I may," Shumuti said, "now that we have a few things cleared up, it does seem like we're working towards the same goal, and we might be more successful together. These Atabra are linked to Magic somehow, so it's our responsibility to deal with them. My father and Sara's mother are looking into this now, back in Merrywater."

"Then why did you come to Attaching?" the King asked.

"To find Gabriel, initially," Shumuti said, "we thought something here might be connected to what has been going on. That was before we realised there was a second person that could use Magic here as well. We want to bring them both back to Merrywater to train them properly in Magic. Gabriel, at least, is a little out of control of his abilities at the moment."

"Putting it lightly," Aurielle muttered.

"I will admit," the King said, "that my earlier methods may not have been the best to ally with you. I think I could say the same of you. To tell the truth, with my lands at risk, I was becoming desperate. Therefore, I am going to ask you plainly, will you fight with me to put a stop to whatever is challenging us from across the river?"

Sara wondered what Shumuti was thinking. This was not the situation they had expected they would find themselves in tonight.

"And would you sign it and swear it?" King Pala continued, "in return for your service, I would pardon your actions tonight and grant you the help of my guards and access throughout the city, unhindered."

Tentatively, Shumuti glanced over to Aurielle, who shrugged her shoulders in reply, with a look of disbelief etched onto her face.

"I will give you a moment to talk."

King Pala rose and exited the room, his robes billowing out behind him. The door shut behind him with a snap, and simultaneously, everybody felt a weight drop from his or her shoulders as the tension broke in the room.

CHAPTER 4
FAREWELL

~SHUMUTI~

"Seaglen warned us that we didn't want to get entangled in the King's business," Aurielle said.

"My father knew the old King," Shumuti said, "but we have the same goal as King Pala, and it seems foolish to not work together, especially now that things are more serious than we realised. Seaglen is not going to leave these vultures, these Atabra, to roam around unchecked. It is the same as we were going to do anyway, except now we have the backing of the King, and his aid."

"He wants us to swear fealty," Aurielle said, "that doesn't necessarily stop once the vultures are no longer a threat."

"It's true that if his interests change, he could try to force us to do things we don't want to," Gabriel said, "but he was more the King I remembered today, so perhaps he has thought things through. Just remember though, that he will stop at nothing to defeat an enemy."

"If he's right, and we have to go to Nimaz, we might need all the help we can get, and so would the King," Shumuti said.

Slowly, Aurielle nodded. Gabriel considered a moment before he too agreed.

"Sara." Shumuti turned to her. "What do you think?"

"It feels wrong to go against what Seaglen advised," she said, "and I still haven't forgotten the way the King's soldiers treated Astrid back in Silverspring, but I don't think the King means us harm. After all, he's had plenty of opportunities to hurt us if he wanted to."

Finally, Shumuti turned to the one stranger in the room. The man in brown robes they had been searching for, for weeks now. The expression on his face reminded Shumuti that he must not have a clue what was going on. It felt unfair to ask him to be a part of this when he had not even agreed to join them in the first place. Shumuti realised she didn't even know his name.

"This is Alejandro," Gabriel said, almost as if he was reading her mind.

"I remember you from the inn," Alejandro said.

"We've been looking for you," Shumuti said.

"I know." He laughed quietly. "I've been searching for you for quite a while as well."

"This is not the way I'd imagine we'd finally meet," Shumuti said, "I didn't mean to get you involved in this before agreeing to it first."

"I will admit, I'm not entirely sure what is going on, but if you're going to be leaving Lyria I want to come with you, and not just because it seems like I have no other choice. There is much I would like to learn from you."

"We are taking Gabriel to my father to teach him about Magic, and we can do the same for you, if you'd like."

The door to the hall swung open once again, and the King re-entered the room.

"Well?"

Shumuti turned from the group and spoke up. "We will offer you our help."

The King gave a small nod and walked over to a side desk, bringing out a scroll of parchment. He took the time to add a few lines to it before signing and adding his seal.

"Add your names below then."

He slid the scroll across, and they gathered around to read.

In the name of King Pala of Attaching, I acknowledge the sworn alliance of these persons. They declare in the name of the King to fight and to use their unique talent to aid against the threat arising in Nimaz. In return for their sworn allegiance, I, King Pala, pardon them and grant them equal ranking and rights to my personal guard. This includes unrestricted access throughout Lyria and the aid of the King's guardsmen, wherever they are. May their names be recorded below as proof of their agreement.

King Pala of Attaching

There the King had added his seal. One after another they each signed their names. Shumuti slid the parchment across to Sara to add her signature along with the rest. Even if she did not have the same Magic skill as they did, she was no less involved than they were. The King stood back and watched, saying nothing until they had signed. Then he nodded with satisfaction and rolled the scroll up, before sliding it back into the desk and locking it away.

"I will keep the nature of what you can do private, as you wish," the King said, "though I do not know how long you can hope to keep it a secret. I trust you not to betray me, and I hope you will trust me the same way. For now, I will continue to gather what information I can on what we are facing. What were your steps going to be from here?"

"We need to return to Thayll, in Merrywater," Shumuti answered, "there is a chance that my father might have learnt something new while we've been away, and Gabriel and Alejandro won't be much use to you at the moment. They need some training. If you need us, that is where we will be for a while at least."

"Well then," the King said, standing up, "you are free to go. If you encounter anything unusual, be sure to send word to me. Any new information from my end shall find its way to Merrywater. I will grant you some time to train, but be aware that I may call on you soon and remember, you have a duty to answer."

They hesitated and followed Shumuti's tentative lead as she gave a small bow to the King.

"When next you return, look forward to somewhat more gracious hospitality," the King added.

"Next time we promise not to sneak our way in." Shumuti grimaced slightly.

One by one, they filed out of the room and back into the main hall. It was almost empty now, with only a handful of guards patrolling the walls. Shumuti could still feel them being watched and increased her pace towards the front door of the Lyrian Citadel. A guard blocked her path as she got there. She saw the bundle in his hands and took back her sword gratefully, as the guard moved on to hand out weapons to the rest.

Gail was waiting for them just outside the doors.

"Is everything all right?" she asked them immediately.

"Somehow, I think it is," Shumuti said.

"What happened?" Gail asked.

"We'll explain later," Shumuti said, "we ought to let Wyn know you are safe."

"Gabriel?" Gail turned to him shyly as they walked. "I never thanked you properly for coming to rescue me."

"Oh, it was nothing," he answered.

"I'm glad you're all right," she continued, "the other guards told me you had run away from the Citadel."

"It's a long story," he said, "it's good to see you again though."

She smiled. "I'm glad you came back, even if just for a bit."

Shumuti saw Aurielle sneak a raised eyebrow in her direction, but at the same moment, Shumuti was distracted by figures hiding in the street ahead. Wyn and Isa had been lurking in the shadows with a gathered selection of horses, evidently prepared for a quick getaway.

"No need!" Shumuti shouted as they approached, "don't worry. We're free to leave."

"How on earth did you manage that?" Isa asked.

"Gail can give you the full story," Shumuti said, "but I think we need to be on our way. We need to get back to Merrywater as soon as we can."

"The marina gates will be shut at this time," Wyn said, "they only open again at dawn."

"Why don't you come back and stay with us for the night?" Isa said, "we'd like a final chance to say goodbye."

Suddenly realising how tired they were, they all agreed and trudged across the open ground to where the three women lived. Once inside, Aurielle and Sara fell asleep almost immediately, but Shumuti had so much to think about that she no longer felt tired, and she could see that neither did Gabriel or Alejandro. Alejandro left for a short while to gather a few items he owned from the chapel and returned an hour later with a satchel and a bag that looked as if it contained a musical instrument.

The house was still the same as when they had left it last. Shumuti looked around at the strange items and the cupboards filled with little metal boxes and sealed bottles with faded labels. Whispers of a sweet fragrance drifted by in the air but the scent was indefinable. Soon Isa and

Gail went off to sleep as well, but Wyn looked as wide-eyed and awake as Shumuti and the other two. When everybody else had gone, Shumuti, Gabriel and Alejandro sat down at the table.

"Why don't I go and make us a drink?" Wyn offered, getting up.

They agreed gratefully, and once she had gone, Alejandro turned to Shumuti.

"I cannot believe I managed to find you all at last. Are there any more like us out there?"

"Two others are waiting for us in Merrywater," Shumuti said.

"But what about Sara?" Alejandro asked, "she said that she could not use Magic."

"No," Shumuti answered, "her mother could, but for some reason, Sara cannot."

"But still, you've brought her into this world," Alejandro said, "how did she react when she found out about it all?"

"It was a surprise, obviously," Shumuti answered, "but she took it well."

"Oh," Alejandro said, "I thought other people would not react kindly to us if they knew what we could do, but perhaps I was wrong."

They were interrupted then by the sound of a muffled, recognisable clink of stone on stone. Wyn had set a familiar velvet pouch on the wooden table along with the drinks. Shumuti looked up apprehensively as Wyn brought out her runestones.

"As I did with the others," Wyn said quietly to Gabriel and Alejandro, "I want to offer you a chance for me to read the runes for you. Sara's mother told me that these stones held more meaning for magically talented people, but the choice is yours entirely."

"Why do you offer this to us?" Gabriel asked, with a frown.

"Because Shumuti's father and his generation of Guardians knew their runes. You have the right to also. He hinted that the stones could be used to enhance your power, in a way. Of course, you will have to ask Seaglen for the specifics."

"Guardians?" Alejandro asked.

"My father's term," Shumuti said, "it's his name for who we are. It's so that we don't forget that our first responsibility is always to protect Magic and not just use it."

They turned her attention back to Wyn. She had not mentioned enhancing their abilities the last time she had offered this. Next to her, Gabriel's eyes glinted with curiosity.

"I would say yes."

"Alejandro?"

He frowned, staying silent.

"Think for a while," Wyn said, "Gabriel, you can go first. Each rune has a certain meaning that is personal to you and can relate to many things. It may give you insight about yourself or help with a decision in the future. Now, take one rune out of the bag. Take your time to find one that feels right for you."

Gabriel gently dipped his hand into the bag and drew a rune out, closed inside his palm.

"Lay it on the table."

Gabriel set it down. There was a simplistic symbol etched into the smooth, white surface: ↑.

"That one is Teiwaz," Wyn said, "it's a symbol of the warrior. You have courage, Gabriel, and determination to see things through to the end as long as you can find your strength inside you. You have the virtue of patience, which I believe shall prove useful."

He leant back in his chair, looking a little bemused and uncertain.

Wyn turned to Alejandro, who was still eyeing the bag of stones with mistrust, and he slowly nodded. Alejandro reached into the bag and drew out his rune with an uncertain hand. He set it down on the wood, face-up: ᛖ.

"Ehwaz," Wyn said, "its symbol is the horse and one of movement, which in turn signals new beginnings. Your progress in this new life will be steady, so do not expect everything to fit into place at once."

"So this new life of mine may turn out for the best, in the end?" Alejandro asked.

"This is no prediction of the future," Wyn said, "but keep your character true to your rune, and you may see it unfold this way. You may keep the stones."

Wyn was silent a moment, then she nodded. "I think you should try to sleep, all three of you."

She reached back into the bag and drew out the three stones that Shumuti, Aurielle and Sara had picked on the previous occasion. Shumuti turned the smooth, oval stone in her hand, tracing the imprint of its symbol with her thumb and inspecting it again for any sign of Magic. Once again, she found nothing, but still, she pocketed the stone. Gabriel and Shumuti stood, and Alejandro followed. The three of them went to the beds that had been set out by the corner of the room.

"What has happened to others that you have read these runes for?" Gabriel asked Wyn.

"They have used my advice well."

Wyn blew out the candles and the two of them left Gabriel and Alejandro in the room. Shumuti walked with Wyn down the corridor to the room where Aurielle and Sara were sleeping.

"Why do you think you have listened to the readings of all the Guardians found so far?" Wyn asked her.

"Just because I happened to be there at the time?"

"No," Wyn said, "Shumuti, your father knew the readings of all his other five Guardians in his time too. He needed to know the strengths and weaknesses of their character before he could lead them."

"I feel like I will learn that by being with them, over what a stone can say."

"The stones have also allowed you to see what their reaction to hearing what I tell them," Wyn said, "and listen to what they believe about themselves. It is all part of helping you understand their character."

Wyn and Shumuti stared at each other by the candlelight. She handed over a small velvet pouch, which clinked as she moved it.

"Give the stones to Seaglen. He will know what to do with them."

Shumuti tucked the pouch into a small bag attached to the sword belt around her waist that she reserved for valuables.

"Why didn't you tell me last time that a rune could be used to enhance our Magic?"

"I assumed Seaglen had already told you."

He had never said any such thing, but Shumuti had wondered for a while now what else her father might have failed to mention regarding Magic.

"Well goodnight, Shumuti." She turned and walked with her candle down the corridor, leaving her in darkness. In the room with the other two, Shumuti pondered over what Wyn had said to her. It was not until a faint grey glow lit up the eastern sky through the window that she finally managed to get a few hours of rest.

"No doubt we'll meet again," Wyn said, as she hugged them goodbye one-by-one the next morning.

"I hope so," Shumuti said.

Isa passed Aurielle a bundle of food and supplies.

"Thank you for everything," Aurielle said.

"It's the least we could do." Wyn waved her words aside.

The five travellers lingered in the doorway for a moment. Alejandro and Gabriel looked as though they had barely slept, but Aurielle and Sara were bright and awake in the dawn of the new day. Shumuti knew that she must appear in a similar state to Alejandro and Gabriel. The eight of them stood silently for a while until Shumuti knew they could loiter no longer and quietly spoke up.

"It's time we were on our way."

The sound of her voice roused the others, and they left the house for the last time. Nobody was stirring at this hour of the morning, and they passed through the streets like ghosts in the early morning mist. There was still a light winter chill in the air, and their breath misted in the air before them. Shumuti led the way down to the quay where their boat, Stannair, was moored ready.

Aboard the prow of the boat was a large, floppy-eared silhouette, whose ears pricked up as they approached. Gabriel greeted his companion enthusiastically. As they climbed aboard, Stannair gently swayed, sending ripples echoing out lazily along the surface of the water. A few fishermen looked up from uncoiling their ropes as the ripples rocked their boats. One of them sat back against his mast again, blowing out a trail of smoke from his pipe that circled above the mist.

Aurielle, Sara and Shumuti readied the boat as a sudden wind vibrated the fabric of the sail and further ashore, tinkled a wind chime set far into the fog. The echoing notes pealed out across the water and changed pitch as Shumuti subtly altered the wind direction to suit their needs. Everybody on the boat except Sara glanced up as they felt her Magic, before continuing with their jobs.

They sailed silently out of the harbour and Shumuti turned back a final time from the bow of the boat. A small figure decked out in the livery of the King stood in the basin. He nodded once and turned away, back to the Citadel.

"So, he knows we have gone," Aurielle said, from her side.

Sara had taken her rightful place at the tiller, so Aurielle and Shumuti took Gabriel and Alejandro down into Stannair to show them around inside. The day was spent explaining everything that they needed to know to live on and look after the boat. The putting up and dismantling of the sail was the most important job to get right. If they did not take care of it and it became damaged again, they were stuck. Shumuti, Sara and Aurielle knew what it had cost to obtain the one they had now and had no wish to go through anything similar again.

The midnight blue sail of indescribable material fluttered now high above the boat. As smooth as silk, but durable as steel, the colour of it altered continually, capturing the attention of all on deck. More than once, Shumuti caught Alejandro stop in the middle of a task merely to stare up, mesmerised at the fluid square of material shifting in the breeze.

Both of their new companions gradually got used to life on a mobile home, but Aztec took to living on the water a lot slower. The wolf spent most of his time at the centre of the boat on the raised section above the cabin where he had decided it was the least rocky, with his body pressed to the wood and his ears back. Any opportunity to moor Stannair resulted in Gabriel taking Aztec immediately overboard to spend time on some ground that did not sway underneath paws or feet.

The journey back ought to take less time than it had taken on their trip out, Shumuti calculated, provided that nothing went wrong. Winter was now settling in, and though no amount of frost or ice had ever been strong enough to freeze the Winterburn River, the weather would soon become worse, and they had no wish to be exposed out here in it when that time arrived.

Each night, they tied up in the centre of the river and steered clear of the banks. Occasionally, there was an island in the middle of the river by which to moor the boat. This deserted home for the night almost made them feel like kings and queens of their own island. The messages that had been sent to the real King about danger from Nimaz heightened their sense of caution, but every night they saw and heard nothing out of the ordinary and continued on their journey unhindered.

On the eighth day, they awoke to snow. Living by a volcano all his life, Aztec was even more bewildered by this than he had been by the boat. His first encounter with snow on the grass had him try his best to avoid touching the freezing substance with as little paw as possible, before leaping back to the now comparative safety of Stannair. Shumuti knew the weather would only get worse once they left the boat and the further south they journeyed into the mountains of Merrywater.

White dust now sprinkled the ground on both sides of the river, and the tips of far off trees in Elmdale had also become dusted with a layer of snow. Stannair had become enveloped in a thin mantle of frost, which Gabriel and Alejandro set about removing before they could get ready to sail, while Shumuti and Sara brought out the sail and Aurielle raised the anchor from the depths of the riverbed.

"My hands are numb," Aurielle said, "this chain is freezing!"

"Oh, stop moaning," Gabriel said.

"You do it then."

Gabriel considered her proposition for a moment.

"No, you're doing a good job," he said, before hastily walking away.

Aurielle continued to grumble as she gathered the remaining links up, wrapping her cloak over her hands so that they didn't freeze.

"It's all a bit sudden, this weather," Sara said, as she hoisted the midnight blue canvas up against the mast with Shumuti.

"Might be an omen," Aurielle joked, coming to join them and rubbing her hands together.

"It seems natural enough," Shumuti said, "at least it should put a halt to anything that is happening on the other side of the river."

"So when the weather turns good...then we should start worrying?"

"Perhaps."

Stannair's sail unfurled and caught the wind, and they drifted off once more back down the deepest channel of the wide river, following the path of the fastest water currents. Shumuti and Sara took turns to steer the boat for as long as they could bear. Alejandro and Gabriel offered themselves to help, but all of them were reluctant to let either one navigate Stannair yet. The tiller was like ice, and with only one pair of gloves between them, it could only be held for a certain length of time before one person had to swap.

Sometime during the morning, Alejandro arrived with three steaming mugs, which they accepted gratefully. Gabriel appeared not long after with cups for himself and Alejandro.

"You know, I could try to warm the tiller a little with my Magic," Gabriel said.

"Knowing you, you'd probably set the whole thing alight," Aurielle said.

"I would not." Gabriel frowned in objection, before taking a second to reconsider. "...I might."

"Thanks, Gabriel, but I'm all right," Shumuti said, with a smile, "a little use is fine, but there is a line. You have to understand that Magic is energy contained in the environment. Your problem at the moment is you don't know the point where your Magic use starts damaging things around you. That will be one of the first things Seaglen will teach you. For now, I can get by with gloves."

Wrapped in several layers of cloaks and blankets, it was impossible for travellers up the river to distinguish their true appearances. No glimmer or sparkle of sunlight penetrated the gloomy granite skies all day, but no more snow fell either, which was a blessing. Huddled up as they were, it took Shumuti a few minutes to notice a thin snaking tributary river in the distance. The border of Merrywater warmed their hearts as it increased in size all day. It was the first sign that they would soon be arriving home.

More snow fell that night, and the temperature dropped. Shumuti realised it was quite daunting to wake up in the morning and discover that she only had about ten seconds in which to acquire enough layers so that she did not freeze. Gabriel was most troubled by the cold, with his magical element being fire. He had lived in the volcano previously and had never experienced these kinds of conditions before in the north. Aurielle found this an inescapable opportunity to tease him and from the expression on his face, Shumuti would not have been surprised if Aurielle had ended up overboard. But it was still all five of them who made it together safely into Merrywater territory on the last stretch of their journey. The trip coming back had not taken long at all it felt, compared to the trip out.

They anchored at the border that night, and as the sun was setting, Shumuti looked out to the east, towards Boctor. Imposing mountains loomed up over there, and she thought of their journey up and the woman they had met called Xeylia. Shumuti was sure that was her mountain range, and if there was a spare moment she would like to take the chance to return there.

"Shumuti! Come and help!" Sara interrupted her musing, currently swathed in the sail.

She laughed and went to aid her. Together they got the sail rolled up and locked safely away in case of more snow before they went inside for the night.

Chapter 5
Riding Lessons

The next day, sunlight broke through at last, and it was a blue and crisp morning. Everybody felt hopeful as they set sail for the day and Aurielle even managed to shed a few of her layers.

"I'd forgotten what you looked like," Gabriel commented cheekily, as he watched her drop one of her three cloaks onto the decking.

"Wish I could say the same about you," Aurielle said, gathering up the cloth again and throwing it accurately over his head.

Gabriel smiled as he removed the covering and hummed tunefully, setting about scrubbing the deck clean with an old mop he had found. Today was the day they had to return the boat, so everything needed to be neat and clean, ready to be handed back over to Ed, the boat-keeper.

Aurielle and Shumuti tidied the cabin, setting everything back in place and packing away all their gear. Alejandro was busy polishing the mast, ducking quickly every time they went about, until Sara yelled at him to stop before he got knocked overboard. They were an efficient team, and the hard work warmed them up considerably, so it was with heavy hearts that they rounded the bend to Ed's boat shed.

Sara gracefully sailed Stannair into the small wooden jetty, while Aurielle and Alejandro leapt ashore to tie her off. The boat-keeper trudged towards them with a greasy rag in his hands and a stare of disbelief on his face. He whistled softly as he noticed the two extra passengers.

"Well, you girls have been busy," he remarked.

Aurielle gave him a wilting glare.

"They've come to see Seaglen."

Ed said nothing. His attention had roamed up to the midnight blue canvas attached to the mast.

"Whatever have ye done to my sail?"

"I'm afraid it got damaged," Shumuti said, "but you can have this one as a replacement. It should do."

He stood and stared at the sail, transfixed. "Well, it certainly is a beauty, and of good make. At least the rest is in good condition. I feared my vessel might not come back at all."

He eyed Sara for a moment before giving her an appreciative nod.

Shumuti, Sara and Gabriel then climbed overboard with their gear and set their packs over their shoulders.

"Thank you for the use of the boat," Shumuti said to Ed.

He nodded dumbly, still staring up at the sail.

"We will miss it," Sara said.

"I saw you coming in," Ed said, "you make a good sailor, lass. My offer still stands if ever you want to work on the water."

Sara gave him a grateful smile.

They looked back sadly at the boat before setting foot on the final leg of the journey back home. The midnight sail waved in the wind in the distance as they turned away.

The five of them topped the hill that showed the view of Aurielle and Shumuti's village, Thayll, in the darkening light a couple of days of walking later. The remote settlement lay nestled in a valley overshadowed by towering peaks, and smoke spiralled from many rooftops, where the cosy glow of lit fires could occasionally also be seen within. Snow coated the mountain summits permanently already, and it would not be long before the same would happen to the village. Each house appeared to be adequately stocked for winter, with large stores of wooden logs collected with remarkable care and neatly stacked in sheltered piles next to every building.

They strode along the main street, past many villagers who were finding their way either back home or out for the night to the tavern. Gabriel gave it a hopeful glance as they passed, but Aurielle, Sara and Shumuti pushed on through. Aurielle recognised a few of the people that they passed and exchanged a small greeting, but soon they were out of the village and away from the crowds, ascending the twisting path up the hill to find Shumuti's father and Sara's mother.

The parlour room was softly lit as Shumuti gently pushed the door open and poked her head around the frame. Nobody was there. Undaunted, she discarded her pack by the door and strode forward down the corridor into the next room, drawn in by the reflection from a crackling fire on the open door. Two people were occupying the snug. Seaglen sat in the chair next to the flames reading a book, with the light flickering off his craggy face. His sister, Astrid, was also there. She was mending a tear in the shoulder of one of Seaglen's cloaks with a slightly exasperated expression on her face.

He looked up as the group sidled their way around the doorway and set his book down with a soft thump. Astrid put down the cloak instantly as well, and her face lit up with a broad smile. By this time, Aurielle and Sara had managed to elbow their way through into the room properly. Astrid saw her daughter, and they went to greet each other, laughing and talking happily. Aurielle went over to join Sara and Astrid, while Gabriel walked a little nervously into the room and Alejandro shuffled behind. Aztec zigzagged his way to the front, between many pairs of legs and sniffed curiously at Seaglen, before settling comfortably by the fire. Seaglen turned from the wolf to the two strangers in the room and regarded them with interest.

"This is Gabriel and Alejandro," Shumuti said, "and this is my father, Seaglen."

"Welcome to my home, both of you," Seaglen said, walking forwards to meet them.

Aurielle was surprised to note that both Alejandro and Gabriel met Seaglen with a little uncertainly. Even when they had stood before the King in the Lyrian Citadel, Aurielle did not remember seeing Gabriel look so unconfident. Seaglen then introduced them to Astrid, who took them both aside and greeted them with a hundred questions about themselves.

"Well done," Seaglen said quietly to Shumuti, Sara and Aurielle, "I must admit, I did not expect to receive two visitors."

"Neither did we," Aurielle said.

"It's a long tale," Shumuti said, "and I'm not sure we did everything for the best."

Her father's eyes sharpened.

"What do you mean?"

"I think there is more to the whole story than we realised when we left," Shumuti said.

"It would be easier to explain if we started at the beginning," Aurielle said.

"Then let's sit down," Seaglen said.

They went and joined the others as they began to relay what had happened since leaving Thayll. Aurielle and Shumuti started with the tale of the journey up to Attaching, which Gabriel and Alejandro followed with interest, as they had only heard parts of it before. Sara was content to contribute bits now and then and correct minor details. Astrid's face brightened in surprise when she learnt they had met Wyn and Isa in Lyria.

"I had no idea they still lived there," she said, "I am glad they are well."

"Oh, that reminds me," Shumuti said, "Wyn told me to give you these. She said you would know what to do with them."

Shumuti handed over a velvet pouch to Seaglen that looked suspiciously to Aurielle like the one Wyn kept her runestones in. Seaglen drew it open curiously and proved her guess right by drawing out a white stone.

"Ah," he said, "yes. These items are unique. Each one can be used to store a concentrated portion of Magic inside. I will teach you how to use these stones."

He paused and considered each of their faces around the room.

"I take it she also offered some words with each one she gave out?"

Shumuti nodded.

"These runes do have a link to Magic, it's true, and in that way, you have a connection to these objects. In time, I will show you how they can be used. But it is unwise to blindly follow a stranger's interpretation on how to live your life."

They nodded, and Seaglen tucked the bag away safely as Aurielle continued with their story. Gabriel joined in once they had reached the volcano and Alejandro gave his account of how he came to be held inside the Citadel. Seaglen became more attentive at this point, so when they reached the part about the escape from the King, Shumuti took over.

"This is what I fear we might have done wrong," she said, "there was no other way for us to get out without fighting our way with Magic."

"You met with the King," Seaglen said, "what did he ask of you?"

"He let us leave the Citadel with Alejandro if we agreed to sign a contract to fight for him," Shumuti said.

Seaglen sat back in his chair, saying nothing, and closed his eyes.

"We had no other choice," Aurielle said, "they had me, Sara and Alejandro. There was no other way we could escape, except by destroying the Lyrian Citadel and then fighting our way through the city as well. Besides, the King already knew about Magic, Gabriel had told him years ago."

Aurielle shot a glance over in Gabriel's direction as he sheepishly backed up against where he was sat by the fireplace.

"It's my fault really," Alejandro said, "I drew the rest of you there. I was stupid to get caught."

Seaglen opened his eyes.

"What were the terms of this contract?"

"We are to fight for him," Shumuti said, "against these creatures. He offered us the help of the King's soldiers as well. I mean, it's the same thing as we were doing anyway, isn't it?"

"I warned you to stay clear of the Lyrian Citadel," Seaglen said, "at the moment our goals are aligned with the King, yes, but do you think that once this is over, he will let such powerful allies walk away freely?"

Shumuti looked down at her feet.

"But if there was no other way," Astrid said, "perhaps this will turn out for the best. We only knew the old King, Seaglen. King Pala is not his father."

"But he is King Eric's son." Seaglen stood up.

"I'm sorry," Shumuti said.

"I cannot tell the outcome of what you have done." Seaglen looked down at his daughter. "Perhaps it will work out well, but then again, perhaps not. The King will only see you as a tool to him, not as a person."

Aurielle was surprised to see the touch of anger in his face.

"A few years before I would have disagreed with that," Gabriel said, "but I'm no longer sure."

"Perhaps if you had not kept information from me, like your knowledge about the old King and what happened in the past, I would not have made any mistakes," Shumuti said, lifting her head.

Aurielle thought she saw the fire in the hearth intensify for a split second as the pair of them regarded each other silently. Aurielle glanced at Astrid, suddenly aware of an uneasy tension in the room. Astrid sat up, and her gaze alternated between Shumuti and Seaglen.

"They should get some sleep," she said.

"I wish to speak to my daughter, alone," Seaglen said, not taking his eyes from Shumuti.

"And I wish to speak to my father." Shumuti replied in the same tone.

Everybody else around the fire simultaneously stood up in an unspoken agreement. Worriedly, Aurielle filed out after the others as they left the room. The last thing she saw before the door closed was deep shadows from the fire dancing across Seaglen's face.

Aurielle led the four of them up to Shumuti's room in silence. Sara detached herself from the group to catch up with Astrid, so Aurielle, Gabriel and Alejandro set out a makeshift camp on the floor of Shumuti's room, much the same as they had done in Gabriel's cave.

"Is he always that terrifying?" Alejandro asked.

"No," Aurielle said, "I haven't seen Seaglen like that in years. He's usually the calmest person you'll ever meet, but tonight, I don't think Shumuti will join us for a while."

"I'd rather not get in the middle of that," Gabriel said, "I'd take King Pala over Seaglen any day."

"They both unnerve me," Alejandro said.

"They'll be fine by the morning." Aurielle frowned. "I think."

Aurielle made up her bed on the window seat. She nestled under the blanket and looked out of the window, watching clouds drift across the stars and wondered what would happen now. By the time she looked back into the room, both Gabriel and Alejandro had fallen asleep, but there was no indication of Shumuti's return, so she settled down to rest herself.

Both Shumuti and Seaglen were at the table when Aurielle went down for breakfast the next morning. They seemed to still be in the middle of a deep conversation as Aurielle walked in, so she hesitated by the door. At least both of them seemed calmer than the night before. Seaglen spotted her and gestured for her to sit down. Shumuti was looking tired, but a lot more cheerful than she had been that previous night.

"Did you even sleep?" Aurielle asked them.

"There was no time," Shumuti said, "there was too much to say. I've just been telling him about Xeylia."

Aurielle remembered the strange woman they had met on their journey up to Attaching and how she appeared linked to their Magic but different.

"Do you know her?" Aurielle asked Seaglen.

"No." Seaglen furrowed his forehead. "I don't remember the name, but names can change."

"Could she be one of your old Guardians?" Aurielle asked.

"I don't know why she would have kept that information from you," Seaglen said, "your description does not match anyone I remember, but perhaps when there is some free time I ought to visit Boctor myself and see."

"Do you think she is a threat?" Aurielle asked.

"Shumuti said that she was unable to leave her domain in Boctor except for at night," Seaglen said, "I do not think she is a danger to us. She had her opportunity to interfere with you and instead let you go. I do not think she is involved with these vultures we are searching for. She is perhaps a mystery for when we have more time."

"What happened here while we were gone?" Aurielle asked, "did the vultures reappear?"

"There have been several small raids, mainly on Ashtom and Saltguard, the two villages closest to the border," Seaglen said, "our Thayll patrols were sent to give aid to the ones in Ashtom and things have been quiet now for a few weeks. The vultures returned only once. Astrid and I drove them off and pursued them right to the banks of the Winterburn River. Unless they were misleading us, they flew directly back towards the heart of Nimaz."

"That's also where the King believes they are from," Aurielle said.

Seaglen grunted gruffly.

"How much have you learnt about Gabriel and Alejandro? Can they fight? Can they ride?"

"Well, Gabriel used to be a soldier for the King," Shumuti said, "but Alejandro was living alone in an old chapel. I think he might need more fighting training than Gabriel, but Gabriel definitely needs more Magic training. Alejandro at least has some natural control of what he can do."

They heard a creak on the steps and a minute later it was Alejandro who poked his head around the door frame.

"Ah," Seaglen said, "good morning."

Alejandro sat down a little timidly.

"Do you want anything to eat?" Shumuti asked.

Aurielle realised she had not yet had anything either, and they both took some bread and a slice of cheese to eat.

"So, can you ride?" Seaglen asked him after a minute or two.

Alejandro looked up. "No, I can't. I can fight a little, though. I am some good."

"We never said that you weren't," Seaglen said.

"You can start to learn to ride today," Shumuti said.

As they were speaking, Astrid entered the room, closely followed by Sara and Gabriel.

"What are we doing today?" Astrid asked.

"Riding lessons," Aurielle said.

Gabriel sat down across from Aurielle. He seemed relatively unperturbed by this information and casually helped himself to breakfast. Alejandro also seemed fine with the idea, but then Aurielle pointed out that they could not all go out riding together because there were not enough horses.

"We will share," Seaglen said, "you are all fairly light, and the horses can carry two for a short length of time."

Sara offered to take Alejandro on her horse, but no offers were made to Gabriel. He caught Aurielle's eye, and the corner of his mouth twitched, but she glared back with a look that said, don't even think about it. Breakfast was cleared away, and Aurielle set out with Shumuti and Sara to ready the horses. The sun was peering through the clouds this morning, but the air was still icy, so Seaglen produced a selection of blankets for the horses to wear under their saddles. They were unwilling to step foot out of the comfort of the warm, dry stables until Shumuti came by and bribed them with a handful of apples.

Seaglen then appeared in a heavy grey cloak, flanked by Astrid, Gabriel and Alejandro, all enveloped in brown coats. Aurielle was tossed a black coat, which she donned gladly, and so they were ready to go. Seaglen and Astrid each mounted their horses, while Sara and Alejandro rode together on Arrow. Aztec danced around the horses' feet, excited to explore a new location for the day. Hesitantly, Shumuti mounted Fynne while Gabriel turned to Aurielle with a probing look in his eyes. She looked resolutely down at him from her horse.

"You need to have a reason not to take me," he said, "you can't just refuse."

"Hmm," Aurielle said, "you abandoned me inside the Lyrian Citadel in Attaching. How about you give me one reason I shouldn't leave you here now?"

"Otherwise you'll miss me making a fool of myself all day."

The other five rode steadily away, with the wolf charging ahead, and Aurielle made to follow after them. After a few paces, she halted her horse and looked back over her shoulder. Gabriel stared up at her with one eyebrow raised.

"Get on," she said.

He grinned and leapt up lightly behind her as they trotted forward to draw level with the others. Shumuti glanced at them as they met but said nothing and fixed her attention ahead on the road. They rode east through the village and out onto the grassy plains, heading down towards the direction of the two lakes, as the horses' hooves crunched over the frosty ground underfoot.

White Lake was the first lake that they saw, but they did not stop there and headed further into the valley until the second lake came into view. In the winter months, the higher elevations near Snapper Lake and the mountains were almost permanently devoid of any other people. Crystal clear water, tinted with a vibrant blue and green hue reflected the pale mountain peaks above. They stopped short of the slope down to the water's edge and dismounted the horses. Sara continued to offer Arrow for Alejandro to learn to ride, but Shumuti quickly stepped in and allowed Gabriel to train on Fynne.

"Now," Seaglen said, "have either of you two ever ridden before today?"

Gabriel and Alejandro both shook their heads.

"Then we'll take this slowly. Can you both mount?"

Sara and Shumuti held their horses steady while they both swung one leg over the saddle and slowly sat upright.

"Good," Seaglen said, "now, we'll walk you for a few hours so that you can get used to it."

Astrid, Seaglen and Aurielle all got back on their horses while Shumuti and Sara each led Fynne and Arrow. Gabriel's posture was rigid in the saddle, and he was unable to relax, as the horses walked steadily forward adjacent to the lakeside. Fynne tossed his head twice as they moved along.

Aurielle leaned over curiously to Gabriel.

"I thought you would have learnt how to ride at the Citadel?"

"I hardly ever left the city," Gabriel said, "and any patrols were on foot. There was never a need for me to learn."

Alejandro was calmer, but he too was a little unsteady with the novel experience of riding a horse. They walked for about twenty minutes before breaking the horses out into a trot. Alejandro coped well with the change of pace, but Gabriel almost lost his grip on the reins. Shumuti and Sara slowed the horses once more and steadily, Gabriel calmed as the horses drew to a halt.

"How do you feel?" Shumuti asked.

"Good," Alejandro said, "I enjoyed that."

Gabriel did not reply. Slowly he unclenched his cramped fingers from the saddle. They had turned white.

"We'll take a break for a while," Seaglen said, "then you can have another go."

Gabriel leapt off Fynne as if he were coated in hot iron. The horse snorted and shook his mane in distaste and Gabriel steadily backed off. Seeing the look on his face, Aurielle bit back a selection of remarks she could have made in his direction. The winter air had warmed to a slightly reasonable temperature, so they went to the lake for lunch and lit a small fire while the horses grazed. A small wooden jetty overhung out over the water, and that was where they sat.

"The Magic in this area is strong," Seaglen said, as they ate, "can you feel it? It flows down from the mountains all around us."

"Does Magic make a place visibly more beautiful?" Sara asked, "because it seems to."

"I always thought so," Shumuti answered.

Gabriel shifted uncomfortably next to Aurielle.

"Are you all right?"

"I'm fine," he answered back quickly.

"Gabriel," Seaglen said, "the amount of Magic inside you is building."

"You can tell?" Gabriel's eyes widened in shock.

Aurielle noticed a bead of sweat gathering on his forehead. Suddenly, she was on edge, remembering the last time Gabriel had lost control of his Magic.

"Yes." Seaglen was regarding Gabriel carefully.

"It's all right," Gabriel said, "I can control it at this stage. It will die down in a minute."

"No," Seaglen said.

"What?"

"You must use it."

"Use it? But everybody has told me not to."

"It is safe to use Magic here." Seaglen looked up to the mountains. "To a point. Below the hill behind my house, the use of Magic is almost unlimited. It is not the same here. There are still consequences, but the boundary is higher, so a little can be used without worry. You cannot keep bottling up the energy inside of you. In time, you will learn to master it, but for now, you need to release it before it grows too powerful and you do even greater damage. Don't worry, I won't let you harm anyone."

Gabriel looked around nervously, trying to decide the best way to do as Seaglen was asking. Eventually, his focus settled on Snapper Lake.

"All right. In that case, I have an idea."

"Go ahead," Seaglen replied, intrigued.

Aurielle's eyebrows shot up in surprise as Gabriel took off his cloak and shirt until he was naked on his top half. She then had to suppress a shout as he decided to take a running jump straight into the lake. He emerged a second later, with a grin on his face, seemingly unaffected by the freezing waters. Steam curled up from the water around him from the once freezing lake and Aurielle realised he must be heating the water surrounding him with Magic. Shumuti dipped a hand into the lake and confirmed her theory.

"It's warm!"

Steam continued to drift lazily from the surface of the water immediately around Gabriel, transitioning back to cold further away from him.

"Do you think you could heat the whole thing?" Sara called over to him.

"Doubtful," Gabriel said, "it's working, though! The pressure from the Magic is receding."

He continued to tread water in the personal hot water springs he had created.

"I don't think I can keep this up for much longer. Is anyone going to join me?"

"Join you?" Aurielle asked.

"All right, then," Alejandro said.

Alejandro copied Gabriel and took a running dive into the lake. He aimed a little too far out and immediately swam back towards Gabriel with a yelp, his teeth chattering. Shumuti turned to Aurielle and shrugged, removing her cloak and Sara followed suit. Admittedly curious, Aurielle followed them, risking a leap directly into the lake.

"It's freezing!" Sara cried as she and Aurielle emerged at the surface of the water.

"Come further over here," Aurielle called to her, "you must have jumped beyond his range."

"No chance." Sara's teeth chattered uncontrollably. "I'm getting out."

Before Aurielle could convince her further, Sara scrambled to the edge of the shore and went to seize her cloak. As long as they circled Gabriel, the water was almost hot. It was a bizarre experience, Aurielle thought as she looked around, to be in this patch of heated water and look up to the surrounding mountains covered in snow in their private thermal pool. She immediately felt refreshed. Seaglen, Sara and Astrid watched them from the shore in amusement. Up on the jetty, Aztec whined and hesitated on the edge of the platform.

"Come on, Aztec!" Gabriel called.

"What? No!" Aurielle cried.

Too late, as the wolf took a running jump the same as Gabriel had and body-slammed his way into the lake, showering them all with fresh, icy water. Aztec swam over, tongue out, trying to keep his head above the surface. Aurielle heard Astrid and Sara laughing from where they sat above. The four of them swam with the wolf pup for a few minutes before Gabriel informed them that he could not sustain the heat much longer, and they dejectedly climbed out of the water, cocooning themselves in cloaks as they remembered what the natural temperature was again.

Once they were all dry, Seaglen continued with the lesson. Alejandro seemed fascinated by the horses and wanted to learn as much as he could about them. Sara and Astrid happily obliged with everything they knew about caring for them and riding techniques before Seaglen took over, describing in detail the importance of horses during a battle.

"Fighting on horseback can be a little difficult when you are new to it," Seaglen said, "but in time you will adjust. It is a completely different style to fighting on foot."

"What could I do about getting a horse for myself?" Alejandro asked.

"The traders come to Merrywater in early spring," Seaglen said, "you may have to work to save up some of the money for one, though. It depends on which horse you want to buy."

"Where could I work to save the money?" Alejandro asked.

Seaglen looked impressed by his interest. "I am certain there will be work in the village if you wanted."

Alejandro nodded.

After their break, Alejandro and Gabriel were back in the saddle. Seaglen decided to see if they could ride without being led, so Shumuti and Sara handed the reins over altogether and walked away from their horses apprehensively. For a moment, the animals did nothing, and despite the look of horror on Gabriel's face, they both seemed reasonably calm.

Satisfied, Seaglen moved his horse into a walk, and after a few seconds, Alejandro persuaded Arrow to follow. It took Gabriel almost a minute to make any progress, but with some help, Fynne began to stride gently forwards. A wash of sincere relief flowed over his face, and he relaxed in the saddle, looking back at Aurielle to give her a small smirk of success. It was at that moment that Fynne abruptly decided to bolt.

Shumuti realised what would happen a split second before it did, and she lurched to gain a hold on Fynne. Her fingers slipped from the reins, and she flung herself aside, narrowly avoiding being trodden by hooves. Aurielle watched Gabriel's eyes as they widened in shock and dismay, but then his face became a blur as Fynne whisked him off across the plains. She heard a fading cry echo from his lips as he held on for his life. After a second's hesitation, Aurielle broke her horse into a swift gallop and sped after him.

Fynne rode at full speed along the entire length of Snapper Lake and was about to turn the corner at its top end when Aurielle caught up. She drew level with Gabriel and galloped alongside for a few moments.

"Help!"

Aurielle considered what would be best to do.

"Hold on."

She moved her horse as close as she dared to Fynne. Then she reached out and on the first attempt, grabbed hold of the reins. At the same time, she drew in both horses. They whinnied and drove their heels into the rocky ground for a few terrifying moments until eventually, they were both under her control. Fynne slowed down to a trot and finally to a walk. Aurielle reached a shaking hand over to stroke the horse's neck and found that it was wet to the touch. She kept Fynne's reins in her right hand and her horse's in her left as they walked back. Next to her, Gabriel let out a long shaky breath.

"Thank you."

Aurielle nodded numbly in reply, focusing on keeping both horses in check.

"That's twice now you've saved me and prevented me from causing damage," Gabriel muttered, "I don't seem to have as much control over anything as I thought. I'm lucky you've been around to save my skin, and yet I still left you alone when you needed help most in the Citadel. I'm sorry, Aurielle."

He glanced at her.

"You'll get better with practice," Aurielle said, unable to think what to say. For once, he was being genuine.

Silently, they rode on the narrow path between Snapper Lake and White Lake. Submerged deep in thought, it took Aurielle a while to realise that the others were riding towards them. Astrid hailed them as they met and congratulated Aurielle for what she had managed to do, but all she could manage was a small smile in return.

Shumuti scrambled back up onto Fynne in front of Gabriel, soothing the horse gently. Gabriel apologised to her in a hoarse voice, but Shumuti cast his words aside, reassuring him that he was not to blame. The seven of them rode swiftly back over the plains with Seaglen at the head, all the way to the village.

Gabriel was silent that night, hardly speaking a word, and neither did Aurielle. She studied him until he noticed, and then she immediately turned away. Gabriel confused her. He had nearly killed her before. He was arrogant, he had tricked her, annoyed her and laughed at her, and yet she still saved him and helped him out of trouble. She did not know what to think of him, and couldn't keep a clear head around him. The only way to think properly was to stay out of Gabriel's way, she decided, for a little while at least.

CHAPTER 6
AN OLD FRIEND

~SARA~

"I need to share with you what my father has told me," Shumuti said to them all in the training cave, a few days later, "at the moment it is mainly theories, but even so, I think it's still important for you all to know."

The five of them sat cross-legged in a circle, resting after a hard day of training.

"The fact that the threat of these vultures, these Atabra, has also reached the attention of the King is troubling Seaglen," Shumuti said, "it's not just us that they have been targeting, and as they carry traces of Magic in them, he is worried that someone who also has Magic is controlling them. We had originally thought this had something to do with someone in Attaching, but now that we've found you two, we know that is no longer the case."

"Does Seaglen have any idea who it could be?" Alejandro asked.

"No," Shumuti said, "but whoever they are, it seems they are no friend to us."

"The only new information we know is that they are working out of Nimaz," Aurielle said.

"But who can it be?" Sara asked, "there are so few people who can use Magic."

"That we know of," Shumuti said, "but up until a few weeks ago we had no idea about either Gabriel or Alejandro."

"What was it that Seaglen and Astrid faced before?" Gabriel asked.

"It was a threat far beyond the Merrywater mountains," Shumuti answered, "to the east, further than the border of Meteorath. From what he described to me, they fought something that wasn't human, more like a manifestation of Magic that had got out of control, not commanded by anyone. They took it out, but not before it killed one of their group. Seaglen and the others fought to protect Magic and prevent its misuse. If someone is exploiting its power now, the responsibility falls to us to do something about it. At the moment we need to put all our energy into getting stronger to be ready to face whatever is out there. If something else is behind the Atabra, then my guess is it will be more powerful than they are, maybe even more so than any of us. That is why we need to train."

Over the next few weeks, Sara hardly saw Alejandro and Gabriel. Seaglen and Astrid concentrated on mentoring the pair of them, and they spent every day inside the training rooms below the hill behind the house. Two separate, underground caverns formed the central base of the Guardians of Magic, one for fighting practice, and the other for using Magic away from prying eyes. So while the two boys were away, Shumuti, Sara and Aurielle interspersed their own training routines with short scouting trips away from Thayll to search for any signs of the Atabra's reappearance or anything else that seemed amiss.

On one of those mornings, they had ventured further away from the village and spent the night in one of several mountain refuge huts scattered around the higher elevations of the Merrywater mountain range. These small wooden cabins provided much needed overnight shelter and allowed the mountains to be patrolled during the winter as well as summer.

Sara awoke just as the sun had begun to slide above the hills and after failing to fall back asleep, she silently got up and rescued their fire from its embers. She left the warmth of the hut to scan the view of Merrywater from the observation balcony that overlooked almost the entirety of the north of the region. At their high elevation, it was easy to pick out the glint of shining metal against the snow-covered plains, flared with red. A company of soldiers were riding evenly down out of the forest towards Thayll with a banner held high. These were soldiers from Attaching. Sara was frozen by a sense of déjà vu for a second, but then she turned around to wake Shumuti and Aurielle and relay the news.

The other two woke quickly and came to see the sight for themselves. After closing the hut back down, they descended back along the icy track as quickly as they dared to find the horses that they had left in the tree line beneath them. The three of them rode back to the village around the southern side of the mountains and spent the day travelling back to Thayll in an attempt to reach the village before the soldiers arrived.

After dropping off their horses in the stables, Sara, Shumuti and Aurielle burst into the kitchen as the others sat eating. Aztec leapt up from beside Gabriel with a growl. The four of them halted whatever he or she was doing to hear what had happened. Then Shumuti composed herself and leant on the door handle to catch her breath. She spoke like a messenger.

"There are soldiers from Attaching. We've seen them, dressed in red and coming down from the north, out of the Elmdale Forest. Only a small company of nine or ten, I'd say."

"Are they coming this way?" Seaglen asked.

"They looked to be heading for the village."

"Why are soldiers from Attaching coming to Merrywater?" Astrid asked.

She had turned to Seaglen for an answer, but he had set his face into an enigmatic expression.

"There is but one way to find out," he said.

"They had to circle the other way around the mountains still, so my guess is they will be here by tomorrow," Shumuti said.

The next morning, they made their way down into the village to find that the soldiers had indeed now reached Thayll. There were now ten weary horses dappled with snow picketed outside of the Boar Tavern. Coming to a halt, they stepped inside and the smell of musty ale invaded Sara's nostrils. In the dim light, the first thing they noted was the burly figure of the innkeeper bustling towards them with a rag in one hand, arms outstretched.

"We are closed!" he announced, "go on, out! If you were so keen to drink, then you would still be recovering from what you consumed last night. Can't you wait another few hours? Out, I said, now!"

"You have no trouble with them remaining here." Seaglen pointed out, gesturing to the group of soldiers who were stretching their feet and removing their mail in the corner.

"They are soldiers of the King," the innkeeper answered, "I know who you are, Seaglen, even in this light, and I do not need all of your rabble clustering my tables while I attempt to clean. You do not drink here nearly often enough to ask any favours of me. You have no business with my guests, and I doubt they would want your company. Now, leave!"

Seaglen sighed. "Well..."

"Sara?"

She jumped slightly and turned to see who had called her name. In the dull light, one of the soldiers had stood up. The figure moved around the table and stepped into a patch of light. Sara's breath caught slightly as she recognised the face of the soldier. It was Stephan, who she had known so well in Silverspring and who she had left behind when she had fled from Elmdale.

The face of the boy who she had grown up with was the same as it had ever been, but his soldier's uniform made him look entirely different. Stephan seemed to stand up straighter than she remembered and his light-brown hair had been cut shorter to just behind his ears. But the smile was still the same, and his eyes were still as bright as they had ever been. Sara also took a step forward to meet him and both their faces broke into expressions of disbelief at meeting each other again here.

"You look different," he said to her.

"So do you." Sara wondered what observations he had just been making about her. She knew that both of them were not quite who they had been a season ago.

"Hey, Stephan," Astrid said, coming forward. His eyes widened in surprise again as he noticed her. For a moment, it felt like the others were not there, and it was just the three of them back in Silverspring together. Then another voice butted in.

"I suppose this means that you're staying," the innkeeper said.

Seaglen cheerfully tossed him a coin in recompense, and they went to sit at the table next to the soldiers. The innkeeper considered for a second, pocketed the money and walked away around the bar and into the back, shaking his head. The group of seventeen sat in silence for a moment before Seaglen leant forward.

"I think drinks are a bit out of the question, but perhaps stories will do for the time being. I take it this soldier is a friend of yours, Sara."

Sara nodded.

There was a small cough from the corner, and Stephan sprang up slightly, remembering his manners. "Marshal, these are villagers from Silverspring. Well, these two are, but I'm not so certain about the others. Sara, Astrid, this is my head Marshal, Garrin, and the rest of our company, on an errand by order of King Pala III."

"Quiet, soldier," the Marshal ordered, "our errand is only for the ears of who we were sent to meet here."

"And who might that be?" Seaglen asked.

"That information is held secret by us, sir, until we find the person we are looking for." He paused for a second. "Or in this case, group."

At these words, Shumuti, Sara and Aurielle sat upright.

"Dœs this have anything to do with a contract with the King?" Shumuti asked.

Garrin frowned and looked at them carefully.

"What are your names?" he asked.

One after the other, they answered.

"You have been to Attaching before, correct? To the city of Lyria and the Citadel?"

"We have sworn allegiance to the King," Shumuti said.

Stephan's mouth opened slightly at this, and his face bore a somewhat baffled expression.

"Then I fear," the Marshal said carefully, "that I may have been too hasty.

"So, were you looking for us?" Shumuti asked.

"First, confirm one thing for me. How did you travel to Lyria?" Garrin asked.

"By boat up the Winterburn River," Shumuti answered, "Lyria's port logbook will have the name recorded as Stannair."

"Then I believe you may well be who I am looking for."

Shumuti shifted slightly.

"But I cannot talk here. It is too open to prying ears that might have already heard too much." He looked towards the doorway the innkeeper had disappeared into.

At a signal, four soldiers got up and moved towards the door. Stephan also stood up, but Garrin motioned him to stay where he was. The soldiers reappeared holding the innkeeper between them, and he was shouting in protest.

"Listening at the door, Marshal," one reported.

"This is my tavern! You can't treat me like this! What are you doing here, eh? Tell me that!"

"Good sir," Garrin said, "we are discussing private, royal matters of the highest importance. I am commandeering your building for an hour while we talk. You can go and sit with my men and relax for a little while. Then we shall be gone, I promise you."

"You can't hold me prisoner in my own inn!"

"I'm afraid we must."

The innkeeper made no attempt to hide his disapproval but did allow himself to be taken into the back by the soldiers. He glared suspiciously back at the unusual crowd before disappearing. Garrin stared after them for a few seconds before nodding in satisfaction and turning his attention back to the table. At a signal, four more soldiers rose, two to guard the back door and two at the front, until only Stephan and the Marshal remained seated, and Garrin relaxed for the first time.

"Now we can talk," he said.

"That was perhaps not the best tactic," Seaglen said, eyeing the empty doorway where the innkeeper had stood.

"And why is that?"

"The innkeeper is the largest storyteller in the village. All of Thayll and beyond will hear an exaggerated tale of what just happened here and the way you treated our villagers."

"I do not concern myself with rumours and gossip. I am here to deliver a message, and I intend to do that with no further delay."

The seven of them gently leaned in to hear what he was going to say.

"My unit and I were ordered to travel here by the King fourteen days ago. An envoy met me and sent us to Merrywater with an important message. We rode south immediately to find a small village by the name of Thayll, and in that village, we were sent to search out five young men and women going by the names you have given me. You have answered the question that was set, so I presume I am correct in thinking that my search is over. You are who I was meant to find."

"You've found us," Shumuti said.

"Is it true?" the Marshal asked, with a trace of disbelief in his voice, "that you have access to abilities other men could not dream of?"

"Who told you this?" Seaglen asked, his voice edged by anger.

"I receive my information directly from a messenger of the King," the Marshal said.

"And how many more has he shared information with?" Seaglen asked.

"The King swore he would keep our secret," Shumuti said, folding her arms in irritation.

"I am to pass on his apologies," Garrin said, "my company is now also sworn to silence, and they know less information than I. Knowledge of it will spread no further than this room. By the King's honour, I promise you that.

I have little trust in relying on strange talents and unnatural skills. Battles are won with soldiers, not sorcery."

"Get on with your message," Seaglen said.

"Well then," the Marshal continued, "it is a warning. King Pala fears there is to be an attack on our borders. More specifically, on yours."

"What?" Sara gasped, before silencing herself.

"There is going to be an assault on Merrywater?" Seaglen asked, "from where?"

"King Pala believes it will come from the direction of Boctor, but that the order has come from Nimaz."

"How dœs the King know this?" Seaglen asked.

"He sent scouts undercover on the other side of the river," Garrin said, "no word had been heard from them in a while, but recently a letter and a soldier found their way back to Lyria."

"Even if the warning is true, the border between Boctor and Merrywater is long," Aurielle said, "that's a lot of locations they could attack from."

"Yes, but there is only one crossing point," Seaglen said.

"What do you mean?" Garrin asked.

"The Lifthayll Bridge," Shumuti said.

"There is a bridge between Merrywater and Boctor?" Gabriel asked, "dœsn't that seem unsafe?"

"It is barely still a bridge," Seaglen said, "and has been unused for decades. The structure lies almost abandoned, but it still spans the water. It is a narrow bridge and not much good for a large army to invade by. But even if the Lifthayll Bridge were not there at all, that remains the weakest point in Merrywater's defence from Boctor, as it is where the distance between the two regions is at its shortest, and there are always other ways to cross water."

"We should take it out," Gabriel said, "if it's unused anyway, why don't we destroy the crossing so that there is one less option for invaders to attack Merrywater by?"

"No," the Marshal said.

Everyone around the table turned to him in surprise.

"My orders are to send a message back to Nimaz not to challenge this side of the river. I intend to allow the invaders to cross and then destroy them so that Nimaz will think twice before attacking us again."

"You are prepared to risk your own lives to achieve this?" Seaglen asked.

"I am confident that we can push them back."

"How large do you think this party crossing from Boctor will be?" Astrid asked.

"Not that great, we believe," the Marshal said, "what their goal is here in Merrywater, I don't know, but I'm sure it's nothing that we won't be able to handle."

"We?" Seaglen asked.

"Yes," Garrin said, "these five have pledged themselves to the King's service. Now he is calling on them to fight, along with the help of my company."

Seaglen regarded the Marshal inhospitably for a moment.

"We will take care of it," Shumuti said, "I was expecting the King to ask something like this of us. When do you expect the attack?"

Garrin shook his head. "We cannot say. It depends on how quickly Nimaz or Boctor can gather their force. It could be months, or it could be within weeks, but we will keep a watch out and be forewarned either way."

"What will you do in the meantime?" Aurielle asked.

"I'll send two of my men back with word to the King. The rest of us will stay and fight when it is needed."

"Where will you stay?" Astrid asked.

"Here, I hope," Garrin answered, "the innkeeper mentioned he had rooms spare."

"Then we will leave you for now," Seaglen said.

"I will need to know the location of this crossing point so that I can set up a rotating guard watch, as well as boats to organise scouting into Boctor. We will talk again soon when I have decided on the defences to put in place and laid our plans. Where can we find you if we need to?"

"Come with us, and we'll show you."

"I'll send one of my own. Stephan, you seem to be acquainted with this party. Show him where we can find you, and he will relay the information back."

Seaglen nodded and got up to leave. He led their group out of the tavern and Stephan followed closely behind. A covering of grey cloud had suspended itself in the sky above the village, and light snow was now falling on the muddy ground. Seaglen and Astrid led the eight of them, while Stephan and Sara trailed at the back.

"So how did you end up joining the King's guard?" Sara asked.

"Honestly? I thought it was my best chance of finding you."

"You were looking for me?"

"I was worried something had happened to you. You and Astrid had just disappeared. There was no trace of either of you, but then the soldiers came back to Silverspring after the Carnival. It was attacked again you know, the Carnival, on their way back to Attaching. That wasn't you, was it?"

"Stephan, we were running the other way."

"Yes, of course, you were. Sorry, but a lot of strange things were happening that day. The soldiers were recruiting, and I decided to go with them as there wasn't much left for me in the village. I thought it would be my best chance at coming across you again. Sara, what have you become involved in, and who are these people? The orders to find you came directly from the King himself.

The Marshal told us that you all can use some strange powers, but that you're fighting for us, is all of that true?"

He looked at her with slight trepidation.

"It is," Sara answered, "but I'm not like them. They call it Magic what they can do, but I can't use it, I don't know how. Don't worry, I'm still the same as I ever was."

"Oh," Stephan said, "I'm glad. That you're all right, I mean."

"I'll explain it all properly to you some other time, but what happened to you since you left Silverspring?"

"I spent over a month out in Elmdale and Attaching, gathering more recruits from other villages and training, before there was word from the King to visit Merrywater. I never actually made it to Lyria, which is a shame because I've wanted to see it, but I learned a lot in the wild. The Marshal taught me how to fight and how to survive. I'm still not that good, but I'm improving all the time."

"I've been trained to fight too, here, by Seaglen. It's a shame you didn't end up in Lyria, I might have seen you there."

"You were in Lyria?"

"It's a long story."

"Tell me."

"Soldier!" Seaglen called from ahead. They had reached the house. "This is where your Marshal may find us."

That broke their conversation as they looked up.

"Thank you," Stephan said, "I'll pass the information back."

"Tell your Marshal we look forward to seeing him soon."

"I shall." Stephan turned to Sara. "I'll see you soon too? You owe me a story."

Sara nodded. "It's good to have you back."

"You too."

Stephan turned and ran back down the hill and the others entered the house. Sara followed the progress of the retreating figure down the slope for a moment, before turning and walking back to the others.

Chapter 7
The Lifthayll Bridge

~Alejandro~

Not much altered after the visit from the King's soldiers. Compared to the ones Alejandro was used to seeing around Lyria, these recruits looked young and inexperienced. Alejandro wondered how useful they would be if they were called to fight and why the King had chosen to send them instead of the experienced fighters he kept in the city. He supposed the King preferred to keep his best soldiers close. From the sound of it, this company had not fought a battle before, but then he realised that neither had he.

The realisation that he hardly had more experience than these soldiers forced Alejandro to double his training efforts with Seaglen. Gabriel appeared to be thinking along similar lines, and they continually tried to impress Seaglen with the amount of work they were putting in. Each night, the pair amassed a new collection of aches and bruises, and although Alejandro felt like he had aged sixty years in a matter of weeks, Seaglen assured him that it was a good pain and soon he would become stronger.

He had also come to realise that the two of them had become locked in an unspoken competition with each other. Gabriel far outmatched him with a sword because he had trained with the King's guard before coming here and had much more experience. In terms of Magic, Alejandro had been in the lead, in the beginning. But now that Gabriel was getting his power slowly under control, Alejandro feared that Gabriel would soon become better than him at that too. The same could not be said of his riding skill, and with Alejandro's natural talent in that, he was confident he could at least continue to outshine Gabriel in one respect.

In the minute amount of free time they were not training, he had found a job at the small blacksmith's in the village and learnt a new skill there too, spending his time beating metal and also leather into shape for the pieces to be put together into saddles. He was gradually saving money for the small spring market that came to Thayll each year. Alejandro hoped to be able to buy a horse of his own at this fair. Gabriel often joined him as well, as Seaglen believed they would both need a horse soon, and he wanted to work for it as well, although personally, Alejandro felt that there were other things Gabriel would rather spend his money on.

The weather reminded Alejandro that the spring market was still a while off. Substantial amounts of snow fell almost every day, meaning that each morning the first task was to fight the way out of the door with shovels and beat a path through the garden to the road. It was a relief to get into the blacksmith's fiery workplace and the almost volcanic heat was a blessing after spending the morning frostbitten and blue. Gabriel seemed to feel this even more than Alejandro and the blacksmith was greatly impressed to learn that Gabriel had spent time living on the volcano in Attaching, asking him for endless descriptions of his old home.

"I have had a large request for my steel to be sent to Attaching," the blacksmith, Erdic, told them one day, "I hear the King is recruiting soldiers from all over Meteorath. From now on, we will be making armour, not saddles. I know the signs, this means that peace is coming to an end. Do you two intend to fight?"

They both took a minute to slowly nod.

Erdic stood in front of them with folded arms as if he was measuring them up. Alejandro found the blacksmith slightly intimidating, although he admired the man greatly. Like Seaglen, he was one of the older men in the village. He was broadly built and immensely strong still, and the only sign of his age was the fact that his dark hair was sliced by a knife of grey above each ear.

Erdic sucked in his cheeks and then finally beckoned them into a darker room behind the work area. Inside was a locked chest that he went over to and opened with a creak. Arranged within the chest was an impressive array of finely wrought swords, axes and spears, as well as shields and plates of armour.

"This is my private collection. The best pieces I have ever made, in my opinion. These weapons and armour I cannot let go, not knowing who will wield them. Each one deserves to belong to individuals with proper skill. I was able to forge armour and weaponry of the finest quality ever seen before using a small shipment of ingredients mined from the mountains above Elmdale. I have never used anything of the like, ever. This gear will be a great aid to whœver wields it."

Gabriel eyed the selection in awe. "They're beautiful."

"They are," Alejandro agreed.

"I want you to take one each," Erdic said, gathering up the most exquisite pieces of armour in the chest.

"What?" Gabriel said.

"You both know how to fight, do you not?"

"Well, yes, but..."

"Then I'd rather have you two wearing my gear. Perhaps one day it may save your lives."

"Are you sure?" Alejandro asked.

The blacksmith bristled. "Would I offer them if I didn't want you to have them?"

They exchanged a glance and took two shoulder pauldrons from Erdic. Experimentally, Alejandro lifted the armour onto his shoulder and the metal slotted into place over his clothes. He was amazed at how light it was, given the size, and he could easily still move his arm. The metal was covered in intricate designs, intermingled with leather.

"It is both strong and light. My armour will not let you down."

They thanked Erdic again before carrying on with their work, and Alejandro could not help wondering what other treasures the blacksmith kept hidden away.

With the few hours that he had left to himself, Alejandro made sure he fitted in the time to practise with his music. The instrument had been his life back in Lyria, but here he had to find time to include it, otherwise he would soon start to forget. Seaglen's garden was the best place to practise without getting in anyone's way, so Alejandro made sure to spend an hour or two there a few times a week.

"I've never heard music played so well." A voice interrupted his playing, one day by the tree. Sara wandered over to sit on the swing beside where he was standing.

"Aren't you cold?" she asked.

Alejandro uncurled his fingers tipped with callus marks. "I'm used to it."

"Do you mind if I'm here?

"No, not at all. Would you like a go?"

"Me?"

"Go ahead."

"What do you do?"

"Rest it here, on your shoulder. Then you put the fingers on one hand here. Try that."

He moved Sara's hands to the correct place on the fiddle, and she plucked a few notes.

"I have no idea how even to begin."

"It takes a while," Alejandro said, "you need to spend a lot of time practising."

"You must have done so much."

"I practised on the streets of Lyria almost every day, for hours. You quickly learn if you are any good or not from the reaction you receive."

"Hmm," Sara said, carefully handing the instrument back over, "I had better not try it then. Why don't you try playing in the inn in Thayll? I bet they would love to hear some music from Lyria in there."

"I would if we had a moment spare. I don't think there is time to be spent on things like music at the moment."

"There's always time if you choose to make it. Even Seaglen draws, as a hobby."

"Well, when I get to be as experienced as him at Magic, fighting and riding then perhaps I can take up music again."

Sara crossed her arms. "Well, I don't agree with that."

"How about I teach you how to sing, and then you can perform at the inn with me?"

"Hold on now." Sara raised her hands. "Let's not get carried away."

Alejandro laughed.

"Ironically, though," Sara continued, standing back up, "I was sent out here to stop you from playing and call you back into the house. Seaglen wants to speak to us."

Alejandro and Sara had just met Gabriel, Shumuti, Aurielle and Astrid in the kitchen when Seaglen walked in from outside, swathed in a thick cloak dusted with snow and accompanied by the Marshal from Attaching.

"The frost has lifted slightly," Seaglen said, "and the day is bright. Perfect for travelling."

"Where to?" Alejandro asked.

"The Lifthayll Bridge."

"To investigate the area," Garrin said, "and work out a plan of defence for the area."

"Remember that it will take a few days to get there and back," Seaglen said, "so pack accordingly."

Together they gathered what might be needed and all were out of the house and ready in no time at all, as five horses stood prepared and waiting on the road. Two of the Marshal's party had offered their horses out for Alejandro and Gabriel to ride. Four of his soldiers were mounted as well, including Stephan, the horses flicking their ears proudly.

The company moved off in pairs down the other side of the hill to bypass the village. Their party amounted to a total of twelve, with Seaglen, Astrid and Garrin riding at the head of the column. Once they were out onto the open plains, the order disintegrated with most of them and Alejandro found himself riding in a line with Shumuti, Aurielle, Sara and Gabriel behind the leading three, while soldiers filled in the back. They did not have a single rest stop all day, and barely any over the next two as they made their way to the bridge, so it was reached in good time, even if it did remind Alejandro's legs that he had been out riding almost every other day that week.

The landscape in the west of Merrywater was different from the mountains around Thayll. Here, the terrain was made up of undulating hills, formed from hard ground and shallow valleys and composed of soft grass that was only sprinkled with a covering of snow. Alejandro rode over the last hill to look down on the river below and saw the Lifthayll Bridge spanning the banks between Merrywater and Boctor on the other side. The Marshal looked around with a satisfied expression on his face.

"This is a good defensive site for us."

The bridge jutted up high out of the water. It was constructed out of a series of arches across the river and connected from the hill they were standing on with a point of elevation in Boctor on the far side.

"We can use the hill as a post for our archers," the Marshal said, "the enemy will be funnelled already, so it should be easy to pick them off before they can reach us."

"We have a good chance then," Gabriel said, "as long as their numbers are not too large."

"Are you sure there is nowhere else along the Winterburn River they could cross?" the Marshal asked.

"There is nowhere else on foot," Seaglen replied, "perhaps by boat. But wood is hard to come by in Boctor, so there are only a few watercraft in the region. I believe this location is the most likely option, but if scouts are placed along the river to check for boats, we will have all possibilities watched."

"I wonder why they have chosen Merrywater to attack?" Stephan asked.

"It is strange not to select Attaching as a target," Seaglen agreed, "perhaps we will get the opportunity to find out. If nothing else, capturing Thayll would form a good base in the south if the plan was to later advance north on Lyria."

"My soldiers and I will set about the best plan of defence," Garrin said, dismounting his horse, "you lay your own as you see fit."

Seaglen nodded. "In that case, we will remain here."

The Marshal shouted orders and took his company down and back up to an adjacent hilltop, while the seven of them remained at the start of the Lifthayll Bridge, where they could overlook the scene.

"I do have a suggestion of the reasoning behind an attack here," Seaglen said, "the Atabra knew that Shumuti, Aurielle and Sara were headed north the last time they encountered them, so what if this attack was meant to take out the remaining Guardians in the south?"

"You think it is to do with us?" Astrid asked.

"Perhaps. If our enemy still believes that these three are still away in Attaching, that only leaves me and you, Astrid, in Merrywater. If the two of us could be taken out while our group is separated, it would be a huge blow to our side."

"But that sounds like the plan of someone who knows who we are," Astrid said.

"It is just a theory," Seaglen said, "once this is dealt with, it will be time to begin some investigations of our own, but for now, we had best organise our defence here."

The seven of them dismounted and walked to the edge to survey the bridge and the path from Boctor. Sara seemed unsure whether to stay or go to help the soldiers, and Alejandro thought he could understand some of this, in part. He saw the look in the soldiers' eyes before they flitted their gaze away, and he recognised it from the prison keep in the Lyrian Citadel. They were wary of the rumours of Magic and wanted little to do with people who could wield the stuff. Yet Sara was not like the others, she stayed.

"Why don't I raise the level of the river?" he heard Aurielle saying, "I could flood the invaders and wash them away downstream before anyone even gets hurt."

"Do you think you have the strength to control the entire Winterburn River?" Seaglen asked her.

"I don't know. Maybe for a time." Aurielle faltered. "Is it worth a try?"

"Not alone," Seaglen said, "you have not become that strong yet, and as for now, you're the only one amongst us who can control water. Alejandro!"

"Yes?"

"I want you to work with Astrid on a plan to slow down anyone who makes it across the river." He pointed down at the valley between where they stood and the next hill where the Marshal was busy assembling his soldiers.

"Does it involve the earth?" Alejandro asked.

"Yes. If you two can churn up the ground there and make it likely to collapse, those who make it ashore will be slowed down considerably, and the archers can pick them off from above."

"I think I can manage that," Alejandro said.

"As for the fighting," Seaglen said, "keep Magic use to a minimum, for emergencies only. It should not be necessary to overuse it. It worries me that the King intended for us to deal with this threat with a display of Magic to show our strength to Nimaz. This should be a test of what other skills you have learned, and it is not a justification to forget that the main purpose of our ability to use Magic is our duty to safeguard it."

The Marshal climbed back up the slope, and Seaglen quickly turned to greet him.

"We have laid plans and defences," Garrin told them, "I will keep two guards stationed here, but the rest of us may ride back to Thayll. In addition, I will begin to organise crossings into Boctor to position more scouts into a relay so that we will have forewarning of the attack. If you have more business here, then we shall see you again some other day."

"We have one ambush left to set," Seaglen answered, "it will halt the progress of any who make it across the river first."

"Very good. I think archery will be our best weapon in this fight."

"There are many able-bodied villagers in Thayll who would gladly offer their bows to help us," Seaglen said.

"I am under orders to deal with this threat myself," Garrin answered, "I will decide whether more fighters are necessary. The King told me that this group of yours is more powerful than a whole village of warriors. I will not risk more lives than I have to."

"Then why not let the seven of us deal with it on our own?" Seaglen asked.

"The agreement was made to fight this threat together," he answered, "while I will not risk involving others, neither can I allow myself to stand idly by and do nothing."

Seaglen sighed. "Then you can count on us."

The Marshal turned to his soldiers, who were standing waiting beside their horses. Then he strode down the line to his horse at the end. Once all four were mounted, Garrin rode forwards at the head towards Seaglen.

"I shall meet with you again soon. I need to ensure that you understand that anything extra you put in place must be declared to me. I am in control of this operation under the King's direct orders and do not forget that. My word is final, before and during the battle."

"Your horse," Seaglen replied, "a Lyrian Stallion is it not?"

"One of the finest ever bred in Attaching," Garrin said.

"Take care not to fall from his high back," Seaglen said.

The Marshal stiffened slightly as he turned and rode away, leading his patrol. Stephan gave Sara a small wave before following the others.

"Remember we need to fight with him against Boctor." Astrid nudged Seaglen gently.

"I know." Seaglen's shoulders slumped wearily. "I guess I am not used to receiving orders."

Alejandro wondered if that fact had contributed to Seaglen's reluctance for them to get involved in dealings with the King initially, but he was not confident enough to voice his opinion aloud.

"Right," Seaglen said, as the group vanished from sight, "now we can get down to business. Alejandro, tell me, what do you think would happen if you released your Magic on the earth now?"

Alejandro blinked at being put on the spot and tried to think.

"In winter," Seaglen prompted.

"In winter," he repeated slowly, "the earth would be hard and cold. So if I broke it up now, the weather would freeze the ground again, and it would return to the way it was before. There would be no point."

He glanced at Seaglen.

"Right, and what could you do to prevent that?"

"Well." Alejandro thought back to his training. "If I only set the Magic down here and didn't trigger it, it would stay dormant in the earth until I activated it."

He glanced at Astrid, who was looking on in approval.

"I'll help you out with it," she offered.

"Is this all right?" he asked, "you warned me about using Magic away from the training room. What if I cause unintended effects?"

"I did, and I still do," Seaglen said, "Magic is never a thing that should be used carelessly and I stand by what I said earlier. But in this situation and in this way, planting a trap of Magic here will prevent greater damage being done and maybe save some lives. That is a worthwhile cause. It is in situations like this that we must decide between creating small amounts of harm ourselves to protect Merrywater from larger destruction. Not an easy choice, but either way, the damage won't take effect today. It will lie dormant until you choose whether or not to activate it."

Reassured, Alejandro joined Astrid as they walked down beside the riverbank, to the stretch they were going to infiltrate. Alejandro stood downstream of Astrid, as they both knelt and focused on the energy around them that they would need to draw on. Planting one hand on the ground to reinforce his connection to the earth, Alejandro sent the gathered Magic slithering into cracks in the ground, concentrating it in a layer beneath the surface, collecting in weak points in the soil structure, ready to break it up from beneath. As the energy shifted position beneath his will, he was aware of Astrid working her way to the centre from the other side until gradually they had cast an invisible net across the whole valley, a trap ready to be activated and ensnare whœver he wished. He stood up as he and Astrid completed their task to see Aurielle sliding down the slope to join them.

"Astrid? Alejandro? I have an addition to the plan. If the weaknesses in the ground run all the way to the river, I can easily direct water to enter into the cracks and flow across this valley, giving these intruders little more than a bog to fight across."

Alejandro nodded, and they added Aurielle's idea into the Magic net. The three of them climbed back up the hill once they had finished.

"Then we are finished here for now," Seaglen said.

The group mounted their horses to set off back towards the village. Alejandro looked beyond the bridge as they moved away. This was the furthest south he had ever been in Meteorath. After this point in the river, it widened and in the distance, there was a glimmer of something vast and blue, but there was no more time to look as Alejandro directed his horse down the slope to catch up to the others, and the view was snatched from sight.

Chapter 8
The Spring Market

~Gabriel~

The colder temperatures lingered for longer than expected in Thayll that year. By now spring would have usually been on its way, but this year it was still inadvisable to venture outside without a large cloak. This meant that the five of them had more time than they had first thought to train, although the Marshal and his company were maintaining a keen watch on the border.

Gabriel believed that he was finally becoming confident in Magic now. After months of Seaglen's training, he believed that he was finally getting the energy under control. The fact that he and Seaglen shared the same element had helped Gabriel hugely, and he had learnt things about using fire that he never dreamt he could have discovered on his own. Astrid was able to offer the same help to Alejandro, and so the two of them had leapt ahead in their progress.

Alongside the Magic preparation that Gabriel was receiving, his preferred training was still sword fighting, and his mental textbook of fighting moves grew by the day. He had also been able to offer some techniques to the others from his time in the Lyrian Citadel. Most of them shared his enjoyment with the physical training, especially Sara, but Aurielle and Alejandro still seemed to relish any chance to use Magic, whereas Shumuti showed no preference either way.

A snout pushed at his leg, interrupting his musing, and Gabriel looked down to pat Aztec on the head. The young wolf had grown considerably since they had left Attaching and his feet and ears no longer appeared too large for him. Aztec had accustomed to life in Merrywater entirely now. He had identified every new scent and was finally comfortable with these extended members of his family. The wolf had begun to disappear for a few days at a time, as he had on the volcano, to explore the mountains, but Gabriel was no longer worried like he had been the first time Aztec had run off. Even here, it seemed that the wolf would always return to him.

Aurielle stood next to him, wrapped up in a winter cloak and woolly hat so that only her face was visible. He realised this was the first time he had spent time alone with her since the first riding lesson at the lakes. The wind lifted her hair slightly and wafted a floral scent in his direction that he could not place. His own hair had started to grow out, and he had begun tying it a half bun at the base of his neck.

"What?" Aurielle asked, turning her head towards him.

"Nothing."

Gabriel returned his attention towards the riding field, where he had been all morning. Sara and Alejandro were there on two horses at the far end, and he could just make out that they each held a bow in their hands. Gabriel's mouth twitched, and he focused on the pair more attentively. Ever since Sara had managed to pull off this manœuvre successfully, she had been enthusiastic about showing it off to everybody.

Sure enough, Sara suddenly straightened up and broke Arrow into a canter down the field. As she reached the beginning of a series of wooden poles dug into the ground, she drew an arrow out and affixed it to her bow. Thundering down the middle of the poles, she reached the shortest one, turned in the saddle and let go of the reins, sighting down the arrow to fire. The shaft sunk deep into the centre of the pole a moment later, quivering slightly.

Sara thundered to the lower end of the field and pulled up triumphantly beside Gabriel and Aurielle. Gabriel clapped and turned back to Alejandro.

"Is he going to try it?" he asked.

"Yes," she said, looking back with interest.

At the far end of the field, Alejandro set off at a slightly slower pace but sped up as he reached the poles. He fumbled slightly at the drawing of the arrow and Gabriel winced. Then, straightening up, Alejandro suddenly moved in a fluid circle around to a pole. He fired and met his mark. The second arrow thudded into the pole next to Sara's, and Alejandro calmly rode up to them with a slightly surprised expression on his face.

Sara froze in shock and indignation.

"Was that what you meant?" Alejandro asked her.

"Your first time, how on earth did you..."

Gabriel broke into laughter at the expression on Sara's face and Alejandro joined in.

"Nice work," he said to Alejandro.

"Yeah," Sara agreed, still slightly bemused.

"You too." Alejandro smiled at her. "Fancy a go, Gabriel?"

"Ah, not right now, no," Gabriel said hastily, "Seaglen wanted me to meet up with him and Shumuti in the Guardians of Magic room."

"That place looks almost as good as new since we've all been busy cleaning it," Aurielle said, "the dust has all gone, you can nearly go in without sneezing now."

"See you later." Gabriel turned with a wave.

Leaving the other three in the field, he strolled back up the hill and turned along the torch-lit corridor at the back of the house. Gabriel took a flame from its bracket and walked through the wall at the end into the tunnel. Following it, Gabriel entered a circular cavern and looked down the concentric stone steps to the bottom arena where Seaglen and Shumuti stood. Below them, on a freshly cleaned floor, now shone the emblem of the Guardians of Magic, a silver circle with a large swirl that faintly resembled a number six at the centre, surrounded by six smaller spirals around the edge and three lines that dissected the circle equally from the centre, before extending out to the walls of the room.

"Gabriel!" Shumuti called.

He descended the steps to the bottom.

"You said you wanted to see me?" he said to Seaglen, hooking his torch onto an empty bracket.

"Yes," he replied, "if you don't mind, I'd like to test your Magic control against a real target. I thought you could try it against Shumuti."

Gabriel turned to her in surprise.

"Shouldn't Aurielle be here, just in case things get out of hand?"

"She won't always be nearby," Shumuti said, "I have complete confidence in you."

More than he had in himself, Gabriel thought, but still, he knew he had improved. He strode to the opposite segment of the room to Shumuti, while Seaglen positioned himself midway between.

"Now remember," Seaglen said, "I want to see how much you've learnt. Try to impress me."

Gabriel nodded and noted the lit torch he had brought in with him, ablaze on the wall, along with several others. Good, he thought, this ought to make things easier. He could focus on enhancing fires that were already burning rather than having to deal with creating a new one entirely. Gabriel had been reluctant to admit to Seaglen how much he had been struggling with that. He turned to face Shumuti.

"Ready?" she asked.

"Are you?" he replied.

As if she had guessed his strategy, the room suddenly darkened as a breeze whipped up from nowhere, and the fire of the torches diminished. Before Gabriel could react, the room was plunged into darkness, and his plan was snuffed. Shumuti vanished from view, and Gabriel wondered wildly what she was going to do next. Then suddenly he realised that one of the torches still contained some buried embers under the ash. Hopefully, it would be all he needed.

Gabriel concentrated a flow of Magic toward the torch, and a second later it ignited into a fireball, streaming high into the air. He realised he might have slightly overdone the flame, but it was nothing he couldn't handle, as the fire spiralled high and aimed towards where Shumuti was now illuminated. The blaze rushed towards her until at the last minute it was divided into two streams, passing her harmlessly by on either side.

As his fire flew by her, Gabriel realised the rush of air she had created could be turned to his advantage and the breeze she was creating could intensify his flames. Without him barely needing to do anything, the fire exploded in size, forcing Shumuti to shield herself from the heat. Realising he was reaching the limits of his control, Gabriel just about managed to shape the torrent of flames into a circle on the ground, trapping Shumuti inside a cylinder of fire. From here, even though she was barely visible, he could tell the heat was affecting her. There was little she could do to extinguish the fire now. He relaxed in relief, thinking he had won.

Then suddenly Gabriel felt light-headed. For a moment, he thought it was exhaustion from guiding the Magic that was affecting him, but that was not right. He was still controlling what was happening. Gabriel took in a deep breath to steady himself when he realised that was impossible. He coughed and started to panic, suddenly aware that he couldn't breathe. Realising that fear was making the situation worse, he tried to steady himself.

Falling to his knees, Gabriel felt a strange sensation, as command over the magical energy he was still directing around Shumuti was snatched from him. Weakened, Gabriel did not fight against Seaglen as he elegantly swept the fire away from Shumuti, amalgamating it once more into a floating sphere, before dispersing the crackling flames to the torch brackets around the room once more.

The obstruction around his mouth and nose receded suddenly, and Gabriel took in several ragged breaths, still on his knees. That was unlike anything he had ever experienced before. He had never come so close to believing he had taken his final breath. Shakily, Gabriel got to his feet, and Shumuti did the same across from him. Still taking in deep breaths, Gabriel ran an unsteady hand through his hair and looked across at her. Shumuti was wearing a similar terrified expression to his own. Seaglen stood between them, his face unfathomable.

"You fight with skill, Gabriel," he said eventually, "and you have learnt well."

Seaglen turned to his daughter.

"Shumuti, what did you do?"

"I don't know," she answered, "I panicked and did the first thing I could think of to get out of there."

"That was you?" Gabriel could not hide the trace of fear in his voice. "You made it so I couldn't breathe?"

"I've never done that before," Shumuti said, "I've never even thought to try something like that. I'm sorry, Gabriel."

"When I was training with my Guardians," Seaglen said, "one of them, Dagaz, used the air element, as you do Shumuti. For a brief time, he experimented with a similar style of assassin-like techniques to take out his enemies. The others used to tell me that I was lucky to have fire as my element because it had to be the strongest, but I disagreed. The power that air can have is extraordinary, but there were dark undertones to what Dagaz was doing. At times, I think he relished in the influence and control that he could have over someone else's life. Be careful if you walk this path, my daughter."

"I will."

"Then let's leave this place for today."

Gabriel and Shumuti did not speak of the events in the training room to the others. Gabriel could tell Shumuti was troubled, but he did not know what to say to her, so for the moment, he kept silent on the matter.

The next few weeks flew by until the spring market came to Thayll. With snow still piled all around, this felt like a slightly inaccurate name, but nevertheless, Gabriel and Alejandro gathered all of their money together, ready to go out in search of their very own horses. Eager to have as much choice as possible, Alejandro had dragged Gabriel down to the village on the first day that it had arrived to have a look around. Shumuti had also decided to come with them to see what else was going on at the market. It was immediately obvious where the horses were being kept from the distinct smell and a choir of neighing, so they parted ways from Shumuti and went to see what was happening.

As the two of them looked around, a large light grey horse caught Gabriel's eye, and he walked up for a closer look, leaving Alejandro beside a group of bay horses, his eyes full of delight. Gabriel smiled at his newfound interest.

"Can I help you?"

A girl was looking at him. She was a little younger than him and had an inquisitive expression on her face. Her hair was tied back under a narrow brimmed felt hat, which was grey and adorned with twine and a black and white feather. She carried a selection of reins in her hands and slung over her shoulder.

"I was just searching for a horse," Gabriel answered.

"What kind?"

"How do you mean?"

"All right, what would you need one for? Travelling? Farm work? Or a warhorse?"

"Do you get many requests for warhorses?"

"More and more recently. Lots of young men who want to enlist in the King's army."

She glanced Gabriel up and down.

"What about you? Which category do you fit under?"

"Travelling mostly, but maybe a bit of fighting."

"I thought so. Maybe I'll see you on a battlefield someday."

Gabriel glanced sideways at her.

"I'll keep my eye out for you."

"Oh." The girl looked caught off-guard. "You're serious? Sorry, I'm used to my family laughing off the idea that I could be a soldier. They want me to stay at home to keep this whole business going."

"Completely serious. I travelled here with three girls not much older than you, and they are some of the best fighters I've ever seen."

Her eyes widened. "Really? I'd like to meet them."

"One of them is around here somewhere," Gabriel said, failing to spot Shumuti.

"Gabriel!" Alejandro jogged over. "Have you found one?"

"I'm just listening to some advice," he replied, pointing out the girl.

"Oh, right. Hi, I'm Alejandro."

"Tina."

"And I'm Gabriel."

"Isn't that a bit of a girl's name?" Tina asked him.

Gabriel opened his mouth in objection before he noticed her grin. He snapped it shut with a frown. "No, not one bit."

"If only Aurielle were here," Alejandro said, rolling his eyes upwards.

Gabriel ignored him. "So what do you think? Which horses would you pick for us?"

Tina looked around thoughtfully. "Well, these over here would probably be the type you're looking for."

They followed as she led them through the gathering market crowd towards a group of horses clustered in the shade next to a wall. There was a mixture of black, roan, grey, chestnut and bay horses of different sizes, and they all stood attentively, flicking away the flies with their long tails.

"My father raised these," she said, "they're the best horses we have ever had. They'd serve you loyally, I know it."

Alejandro was immediately taken, and he moved forward. Tina went after, enthused by his eagerness.

"Do they have names?" he asked.

"Most of them do," Tina answered, "this spotted one is Oz, and that light grey one over there, she's called Mist."

"What about this one?" Gabriel asked.

"Now, that one is Lightning."

Gabriel looked up at the dark bay horse he was standing by. He turned his solemn brown eyes towards Gabriel.

"He's a Lyrian Stallion," Tina said.

"But I thought Lyrian Stallions were only bred for King Pala," Gabriel said.

"They are. Our family are the ones who raise the horses to sell them to the King."

"Really?"

She nodded.

"Gabriel?" Alejandro said, "I think I've found the one for me."

He was standing beside the patterned chestnut horse, Oz. Gabriel looked again at Lightning.

"Yes, me too."

"Great." Tina looked pleased.

They counted out their treasured savings and handed over the right price. Gabriel noted with a sigh that he was giving away considerably more than Alejandro. She put the money away and released the reins that tied the two horses, before handing them to each of them.

"Take good care of them," she said.

"We will," they promised.

"Maybe I'll see you again," she said.

Hopefully, it would not have to be on a battlefield though, Gabriel thought to himself.

"Goodbye." Alejandro waved cheerfully.

"Thank you," Gabriel added.

They led their new horses away from the bustling crowd, back to where they had arranged to meet Shumuti. She was already waiting and gasped when she saw the horses.

"Wow, they're beautiful."

The animals tossed their heads.

"Did you get anything?" Alejandro asked her.

"No," she replied, "I thought perhaps there might have been some news from the traders. But there isn't."

"Nothing from Attaching?"

"No, the only thing I heard was that a giant flying shape was spotted in the sky above the Winterburn River, between Elmdale and Nimaz."

"The Atabra?"

"I'm not sure." Shumuti frowned. "The man I talked to said that what he saw was gigantic, that was the one thing he could express. The vultures are big, but I wouldn't describe them as gigantic. Then again, I don't know what else it could have been, and people do tend to exaggerate."

They set off walking back through the village, leading the horses. Tina had given them each a bundle of useful tools to take care of Oz and Lightning. Gabriel looked across at his large horse and wondered whether the animal had been named accurately. Gabriel would certainly be at the same height as Seaglen when they were riding, and it felt strangely fitting to him that as an ex-member of the King's guard, Gabriel now owned the same breed of horse that they were entitled to.

As they reached the house, Sara and Aurielle came running out with Aztec sprinting at their heels, their eyes wide, as they took in what Gabriel and Alejandro were bringing and rushed forward to meet the newest members of their ever-growing team.

Chapter 9
Reunion

~Sara~

"Where is Seaglen?" Sara asked Astrid one morning as she came downstairs, "I thought he was meant to train me today?"

"He told me to apologise to you," Astrid answered, "but he had to do some extra work with Gabriel and Alejandro."

"You mean I have a day off?" Sara faltered in surprise.

Astrid smiled. "I suppose you do."

Sara sat down, unsure of how to use this new information. "What about Shumuti and Aurielle?"

"They've joined one of the patrols out from the village today," Astrid said, "I should have thought, you could have gone with them. They left about half an hour ago."

"No, it's all right," Sara answered quickly. She had decided on a potential use of her time today. A way to spend the day that she already knew she would enjoy.

"What are you doing?" she asked.

"Ah," Astrid answered, "I have big plans. Spring is heading our way, and I have a mind to begin tending properly to Seaglen's garden. It shames me to see what condition he has let it get into. This year I intend to have actual vegetables growing there, for us all. I'm going to make a start preparing. You can help me, if you like?"

"Maybe later," Sara said, "I thought I might go and see Stephan."

"Of course," Astrid said immediately, "go, go. Then if you like, you can bring him back here and you both can help."

"Perhaps." Sara smiled. "I'll see you later, then."

She flung on a cloak and saddled Fynne, leaving the house before any more chores could be thrown her way on a day off. The inn was the natural place to try first, and it was early, so there was a high chance he would still be there.

All was quiet when Sara arrived at the door of the tavern. She counted the number of horses picketed outside and recognised Stephan's from Silverspring. With slight hesitation, she swung open the door to see who was sitting inside. In the second it took for her eyes to adjust to the gloom, she was almost ambushed where she stood.

"Sara!" Stephan's hug almost swept her off her feet. "Do you have a message for us?"

A couple of other soldiers looked up from behind him, seeming eager that they might have something to do.

"Oh," Sara said hurriedly, "no."

They looked away again, and boredom spread back across their faces.

"I came here to see you," she told him quietly, "I wondered if you were busy today?"

Stephan laughed. "Sara, we haven't been busy since we came to this uneventful little village. There is nothing for us to do here if we are not on watch at the border, except prepare for a fight that may or may not happen."

Sara looked across at the faces of the others in the inn. At least three looked like they were still drunk from the night before. Two others were sleeping where they sat, still dressed in their mail.

"It is hard to remind yourself to always be alert for a threat here," Stephan muttered to her, "I am used to a country lifestyle, coming from Silverspring, but most of these others are from Lyria, the largest city in Meteorath. This is a big change for them."

"Have they thought of taking up a hobby?" Sara joked.

"Yeah, they have," Stephan replied, "drinking."

"Perhaps I should go back and tell Seaglen how unprepared these soldiers from Attaching are," Sara said, "why don't you spend the time getting ready for whatever might be coming our way?"

"We do, Sara. But for most of them, they lack the motivation to train all day long. Why would they, when this atmosphere in this village seems so far removed from any danger?"

Sara sighed. "Well, perhaps if you have nothing better to do, you'd like to spend the day with me?"

"With you?" Stephan asked, and his expression lit up, "that would be great."

He turned to the other soldiers. "Howell, if the Marshal returns, tell him I've gone to train with Sara here."

The soldier on the bench gave a noncommittal grunt.

"It seems fine." Stephan winked.

Stephan grabbed a pack by the door as the pair of them exited the inn and Sara immediately felt better, away from the sullen atmosphere inside. Stephan seemed to as well and the same smile that Sara remembered on his face for most of their time growing up suddenly re-emerged. As infectious as always, Sara could not help mirroring him. She felt genuinely happier and more carefree than she realised she had in a long time. Then it struck her to wonder if it was because for the first time in months she was with somebody who could not use Magic, who was the same as her.

"So what do you want to do?" he asked her.

"I have no idea," Sara said, "get away from the village, perhaps? We could ride south. I haven't really been in that direction before. Plus it will be warmer."

"Sounds good to me."

"What's in the pack?" Sara asked, noticing how significant the bulky weight was on his back.

"You'll see."

They scrambled up onto their horses and cantered out of the village. Soon nothing but snow-covered grasslands spread into view around them and the village was lost from sight. Slowing to a walk, they travelled south for about an hour before Sara dismounted Fynne beside a small stream, and Stephan appeared behind her. They let the horses drink, and Stephan finally opened the pack that he was carrying. It seemed that the contents were food and lots of it.

"Looks like there are some advantages to living in an inn," Sara said.

"A few," Stephan agreed.

She took off a bundled blanket attached to her saddle and spread it on the snow for them to sit on, and then they searched through the ingredients to make a very extravagant lunch of crusty bread, cheese and smoked ham, with various homegrown vegetables from Thayll.

"I think there's meant to be about five people's worth of food in here," Stephan said.

"I don't think I've ever seen a grander picnic, in a more bizarre setting," Sara said, as she observed the winter landscape all around.

She offered an apple to Fynne and lent back with her head on the pack, looking up at the sky.

"This almost feels like being in Elmdale again," she said.

"As if the last few months never happened."

A long white cloud obscured the face of the sun temporarily up above them. "I almost ran away back to Silverspring to find you, you know."

"Really?"

"You wouldn't have even been there." Sara laughed. "I can't believe you joined the guard, though. You know you're in it for life now, don't you?"

"I'll admit it wasn't one of my most carefully thought through decisions."

Sara shook her head in disbelief. "Well, thanks for still having time to spend a day with me."

"It was hardly the worst thing in the world to do. I did come here to find you, after all."

"All this? Joining the King's army, just to find me?"

"There's nothing in Silverspring for me anymore."

"Do you like it? Being a soldier?"

Stephan grimaced. "Not especially. I'm glad I've learnt how to defend myself, but if I had something else to do, I would do it."

Sara looked at him in surprise.

"Well." Stephan turned to question her instead. "Can you finally tell me what happened when you and Astrid left Elmdale? As far as I can tell, it is hardly much different living here. Though some of the company talk. They wonder who this Seaglen that you're staying with really is. Why is it that our Marshal would ask him for strategic advice? Is it just because of this power you say they all have?"

"You don't believe what they can do?"

"We have been told a little, but it's a hard thing to believe when you haven't seen it with your own eyes. Most of the soldiers do not think there is anything special about them. But after the events that day at the Carnival, I'm not sure what to think."

"It is a hard thing to understand," Sara said, thinking back, "it was Astrid who was behind what happened at the Carnival."

"So I saw Magic then?"

Sara nodded. "If there is a battle, I daresay you and the soldiers will see more."

"I've never fought in a battle before."

"Neither have I."

Stephan fell silent, looking out over the grasslands.

"I'll watch your back if you promise to watch mine," he said with a small smile.

"Come and practise with me. Bring those who are interested and try out Seaglen as a teacher instead."

"I might do that. Or, we could just ride off back to Silverspring and escape all of this."

He chuckled.

"Stephan, we can't do that."

"Why not?"

"You want me to abandon the others? Even Astrid?"

"But this shouldn't be our fight, both of us just got caught up in it by accident. This is way larger than either of us."

"No, we didn't." Sara frowned. "You chose to swear allegiance to the King. I chose to help Shumuti and Seaglen. We both made promises, and we can't back out of them now."

"My only goal was to find you again." Stephan sighed. "I didn't plan for what would come after."

"I don't know how much you and I can do to help," she said, "but we can do more here than by running away."

"But what use are we? Astrid knocked those two guards in Silverspring out of the way with little more than a thought. Why should we risk our lives as well when they can take out any threat so easily?"

"It's complicated," Sara said, "they explained to me that using Magic has consequences. It's tied into the environment. I saw it when Shumuti used too much trying to save me and damaged almost a whole field around us."

"So they would rather put your life in danger than risk what, a few trees?"

"They are not putting my life in danger." Sara corrected him. "I chose to help them."

"Because you didn't have another option." Stephan moved closer to her. "Now you do. I don't want to see you get hurt, Sara. Let the real fighters and the King's army deal with the attack from Boctor."

"You don't think I can defend myself?"

"I've never even seen you hold a sword," Stephan said, "and you just said Shumuti had to save you once before."

Sara stood up indignantly. "I didn't ask you to come and find me, Stephan. To join the King's army, come to Merrywater, any of it. I am happy to see you again, but I won't leave now and run away. I am going back to Thayll. I'll see you on the battlefield if you're still around then."

She gathered up Fynne's reins and swung up onto his back before Stephan could say another word.

"Wait!" She heard him shout, but Sara ignored him and angrily sprung Fynne into a canter, following the stream back up towards the village.

CHAPTER 10
BATTLE AT THE BRIDGE

~SHUMUTI~

A break in the weather of several days where no new snow fell and the sun shone through to warm their faces did not lift Shumuti's spirits the way that it normally had, with the promise that spring might finally be on its way. They watched the plains to the west with apprehension for signs of a rider because all seven of them knew what it might mean. For the next few days, everything continued as usual, until one bright morning while they were eating breakfast outside, a figure rode up the hill.

Shumuti recognised him almost immediately as Stephan. He was riding with haste and leapt from his horse to come running towards them. With a flurry of dust, he skidded to a halt, and they waited uneasily for him to speak.

"The Marshal sent me," he said, "it's the Lifthayll Bridge. There's a crowd from Boctor making their way towards the crossing point."

Seaglen stood up with alarming speed. "Everybody prepare yourselves."

Quickly they stood up and ran inside to get ready.

"Stephan, have something to eat," Seaglen ordered, "you'll need it today."

Aurielle, Sara and Shumuti rushed into their room to grab their fighting gear and swords. Shumuti considered for a moment before bringing out her bow as well. When they got back to the kitchen, Seaglen was there, offering out two sets of leather armour to Gabriel and Alejandro. Shumuti recognised the design as the same that she wore, the same that had once belonged to Seaglen's Guardians.

Then it was back outside to the stables. They brought out their horses and were joined by everybody else. Stephan stood with a piece of uneaten bread in one hand and the reins of his horse in the other. There was a worried expression on his face. Aztec came running out and danced enthusiastically at Gabriel's feet.

"No Aztec, not this time," Gabriel said, "I don't want you getting hurt."

He shut the young wolf inside the house to make sure that he could not follow and Shumuti saw a crestfallen pair of ears rise at the window. The party then mounted their horses and immediately cantered away around the back of the house by the cliffs, bypassing the village. Shumuti looked up briefly as they passed under the overhanging cliff of the training room. Faintly, she made out sections of the route of the stairs, but it was impossible to pick out unless you knew it was there.

They jumped one of the small streams that came from the underground waterfall and galloped on over the plains, riding parallel to the river. The distance from Thayll to the Lifthayll Bridge felt like too long in Shumuti's head to get there in time, but the Marshal had assured them there would be enough forewarning. Whœver was coming from Boctor had not reached the border quite yet.

On arrival at the Winterburn River, it was not long before they heard shouts from ahead. Quickly, they pushed forward to the crest of the last hill where the Marshal and the rest of his company stood, arranged in formation. The eight riders reached the summit at the same time and let out a single gasp.

Standing before them, on the opposite side of the river, was quite a crowd indeed. The group who had travelled to Boctor's border looked to be almost a hundred, assembled on the far side of the river. The first unit had made their way to the edge of the bridge on their side, while the rest fanned out along either side of the riverbank. Above their heads flew flags of Boctor and Nimaz; dark bats on a sandy background and a winged snake on a banner of grey. Shumuti looked around at their allies, silently counting up. They were seventeen.

"Did you know?" Astrid asked the Marshal, "did you know there would be so many?"

"We had no idea."

"We should send word to Thayll," Gabriel said, "there are at least some there who might be able to help us."

Shumuti shook her head. "It will take too long."

"We have little choice but to fight," Seaglen said, "you have all trained for this. By the time they reach us, their numbers will be far less."

"Soldiers," Garrin ordered, "assume your positions."

Half of the Marshal's company gathered on the adjacent hill, along with Seaglen, Astrid, Sara and Gabriel, to overlook the battle, while the Marshal rode his horse down the slope they were on and back up the next so that he stood alone before the bridge. Shumuti, Aurielle, Alejandro and five of the Marshal's archers lined up behind him. The figure at the head of the Boctor army, Shumuti thought it was sufficiently large enough to be called one, took a step forward onto the bridge. The Marshal of Attaching approached him on their side.

"If you step one foot on Merrywater soil with the intent to do harm, know that it is our duty to prevent you."

His voice rang with authority, but the opposition took one look at their numbers and openly laughed.

"You have no way to stop us!"

The man took a further step onto the bridge on his side and raised an arm to signal his followers. Wasting no time, the rest cried out and followed him, charging straight forward across the stone. There was a ringing of steel as they drew their swords.

"Archers!" the Marshal commanded, "loose your arrows!"

Sixteen arrows, shot headlong and perpendicular to the bridge, sprung out towards the oncoming tide of invaders, but they seemed to have little effect, as any that fell were just as quickly replaced from behind.

"We need to stop them!" Aurielle cried, turning to Shumuti.

Shumuti knew what she was thinking, Aurielle still wanted to try and control the Winterburn River. With the force standing before them larger than expected, Shumuti did not immediately say no to her.

"Let me help," she said, "if I can create a wind at the same time it might increase your chances at directing the river where you want."

Shumuti dropped her bow and joined Aurielle at the edge of the bridge. Like she always had done to help her concentrate, Aurielle raised one hand, and the waters in the river began to churn. The water level dropped even less around the pillars of the bridge, but the Boctor army charging above barely noticed. Shumuti felt a trill of Magic down the back of her neck as two mirrored waves rose threateningly from both upstream and downstream of the battlefield. The group on the bridge halted as they took in what was happening. The crests of water shimmered, suspended in the air. Shumuti focused on billowing additional wind behind each of these magically formed waves. The army on the bridge looked up fearfully as water towered up on either side.

Aurielle held her hand there for a moment before rotating it over, palm down. As she dropped her arm, the waves crashed down on the army below, one after the other, tearing into the bridge and flinging many that stood on it into the river far below and tearing out chunks of the stone at the same time. The waves plunged back into the river, flooding the grass on both sides and swirling deep into the valley that Astrid and Alejandro had prepared.

More had managed to hold on to the bridge than Shumuti had thought, and they shakily got back to their feet, using the sides of the bridge as cover against anything else that might be thrown their way. Beside Aurielle, Astrid suddenly appeared and Shumuti almost stumbled at the surge of Magic that she directed towards the Lifthayll Bridge. A shuddering earthquake struck the bridge and cracked the stone, so that a portion of the crossing between two arches on the far side fell into the river below, splitting the army into two and cutting off the retreat for those on the bridge. The Marshal glanced worriedly in Seaglen's direction, knowing that these attacks had not been part of the original plan. A couple of his soldiers moved as if to flee from the battleground before Garrin forcefully shouted to remain.

Those from Boctor who had held their ground by clutching to the sides of the bridge and swimming back to the surface of the water below held their ground but dared to move forward no further. Aurielle stumbled slightly next to Shumuti, her face pale. Shumuti caught hold of her friend and supported her while Aurielle recovered. She eyed the slope below them. The once green grass had withered and dried up and deep cracks had opened up in the muddy riverbank.

Between the two opposing forces, there was now a tense stalemate and a sense of uncertainty over what had just happened. Shumuti watched the leader of the Boctor army, thinking that if she were in his shœs, she would order the immediate retreat of her fighters after what they had just seen. Whether the Marshal had wanted a fight or not, the sheer numbers from Boctor meant that they had had to do something. But the leader from Boctor hauled a pair of men beside him back onto their feet and thrust weapons back into their hands. Turning back to face Merrywater, he screamed at his soldiers to move forward. The remaining forces behind him obeyed and followed their leader over the bridge into Merrywater. Even those that had been cut off by Astrid's attack began making their way down the riverbank to swim across.

"Regroup!" the Marshal cried, wheeling his horse around.

Shumuti dived for her bow and leapt back onto her horse with Aurielle as their unit galloped back to the far hill where the others stood. Seaglen's archers covered their retreat and held the enemy off their backs.

"They're still coming?" Sara asked, watching the army below in disbelief, as Shumuti came to a halt beside her.

"Alejandro," Astrid said, "I think now would be the best time to activate our part of the plan."

With the plains already soaked in water, Aurielle's job was complete, so Alejandro and Astrid walked their horses forward to the crest of the hill.

"Wait until the first ones almost reach the limit of where we worked," Astrid said.

Alejandro stood nervously on the hill as their enemy unfurled out below them. Shumuti felt the energy of Magic gathering around them for the third time in a matter of minutes as the Marshal made a move to signal his archers again, but Seaglen held up a hand for him to wait.

Suddenly, Oz reared up and crashed his front hooves on the ground with a hollow thud. Alejandro cried out, and a crack sounded from the earth by the river. The muddy ground fell apart beneath the invaders' feet, and there were cries as all who had made it across the water fell into a deep trench spread across the valley.

The army floundered in the freshly created marshland and the Marshal quickly sprung into action. The rest of his astounded company promptly regained composure and followed his commands. All of the soldiers lined up their bows, training their arrows down on the valley. Shumuti led the others in joining them, receiving a few distrustful and fearful glances from the men they stood with. In the Winterburn River, a number of the invaders had not managed to swim across against the current, but more than she hoped were now scrambling out onto the Merrywater bank to join their allies.

"Ready yourselves!" the Marshal bellowed.

Shumuti drew out an arrow and picked out a target. As she looked down the shaft she began to hesitate, remembering that this was the first tangible battle they had been a part of. Her arrow picked out an unfortunate mark below. With one movement, she could destroy this man's hopes, all of his dreams. Shumuti didn't even know his name.

"Fire!" She heard the Marshal's order.

Fifteen arrows shot down the hill and made their mark on those below. Shumuti lifted her face from the taut bowstring to discover that of the rest of them, both Alejandro and Sara also still had arrows in their bows. Down below, the fighters from Boctor assembled in formation and trained their own longbows back up the slope. Shumuti saw one take aim at Sara and that made her decision. Quickly, she picked him out and knocked him back just as he was about to shoot.

Her action snapped the other two out of the spell that held them. Two more archers fell to the ground before they could shoot back. Out in the river, those who had drowned already were slowly exiting the battleground, a selection of corpses drifting downriver. But too many more had broken through their trap.

"Ready!" the Marshal shouted, and they fitted another volley of arrows.

"Fire!"

A cluster of more archers fell to the muddy ground. Several arrows flew towards them back up the slope in retaliation, but a fierce wind whipped up out of nowhere like a barrier to protect those who stood on the hill and Shumuti smiled grimly down at the confusion on the faces of their attackers below. They kept the enemy from advancing for a good while and eventually no archers remained to fire back up the hill. Ahead of them, the first row of remaining Boctor fighters had made it out of Astrid and Alejandro's swamped trap and onto firmer ground, still unwaveringly heading towards the base of their hill. Shumuti checked her quiver and found only a couple of arrows remaining there.

"Seaglen!" Garrin cried, "I want none of your powers being used down there. I will not have my men put at risk from you. You have evened out the field, but we can take it from here. Am I clear?"

Shumuti opened her mouth in protest, but Seaglen laid a hand on her shoulder and nodded.

"We will obey, for now," he said to her, "use it only if necessary."

"Draw swords!" came the order as nine blades flashed brightly in the sun.

"Ready to charge!"

The Marshal wanted to take advantage of the fact that they were mounted and their enemy was not. Garrin bellowed, and he and Seaglen led the first charge down the hill, accompanied by Aurielle, Gabriel and five of the Marshal's men. The eight archers that remained let loose arrows as they set off. As the first charge galloped into the front line of the invaders, a second flurry of arrows took down the left and right flanks of fighters.

Then it was Shumuti's turn. Fluidly, they packed their bows, drew swords and cantered down the slope after the first line. Shumuti's charge crashed into the enemy from the opposite side just as they were recovering from the first attack.

The defenders from Merrywater were still outnumbered and further restrained by the Marshal's refusal to allow Magic. Shumuti defended herself from a flurry of blows and took a moment to see what was happening around her. Gabriel fought alone, wielding two blades together and creating a wide arc around him, barely managing to keep falling from Lightning. Shumuti found herself next to Aurielle. They worked together, fighting off the hordes that surrounded them from every angle and gradually, they made their way towards Seaglen and Astrid.

Glancing around, Shumuti noted that Alejandro had fought his way over to Gabriel and that Sara was with Stephan and two other Attaching soldiers. Her right arm ached already from the difficulty of having to use her sword at unusual angles on the horse.

"Shumuti!" Aurielle shouted, "we have to forget what the Marshal said, we need to use Magic here!"

"Seaglen said we had to wait until it was necessary!"

"It is necessary! There are too many left!"

"All right!"

They turned and focused their Magic out on the charging enemy. A jet of water and a rush of air shot down the middle of the group, throwing several onto the ground where their own side trampled them.

"Retreat!" Came the sudden call of the Marshal. "Back up the hill!"

Spurred into sudden action, they obeyed, fighting back through the smaller crowd to the hill slope. Sara and Alejandro had their bows out, and Shumuti watched as they turned together in their saddles and shot two arrows back into the throng. Sara's arrow had been aimed at a man about to launch an attack at Stephan. He had lost his horse, and Shumuti watched Sara pull Stephan up behind her and canter on up the hill.

Satisfied they were safe, Shumuti quickly moved Fynne upwards. They made it up the slope, shaking off the last of the pursuers and gathered there. Shumuti did a swift count and noticed with a sickening jolt that they had lost five of the soldiers. The Marshal had also noted this and set his face into a stony expression.

"We make our stand here?" Seaglen suggested to him.

The Marshal nodded.

"You have lost nearly half of your company," Seaglen continued, "stand back, let us do our job here and no more will die."

Slowly, Garrin nodded again.

Seaglen ordered them to retreat a little way, before turning back to see the mass that was assembling and rushing up towards the hill. Seaglen stared down at them, calculating.

"Shumuti!"

She went over to where her father was standing.

"We will make the first line and hold the enemy off with Magic. We cannot let them reach the top of this hill...whatever the cost."

"I understand," Shumuti said.

Swiftly, they moved forward to protect the cluster of Attaching soldiers and Sara, who was standing on the end. Shumuti looked across to her and tried to give her a reassuring smile. She smiled weakly back, with her bow still in one hand and blood smeared across her forehead and hair.

Facing down the slope, the six of them spread out evenly on the hilltop, with Seaglen and Astrid in the middle, Gabriel and Alejandro on the left and Aurielle and Shumuti on the right. The enemy below had reached two-thirds of the way up the hill.

"Remember everything I have taught you," Seaglen called to them, "and make it clear today that our enemies should fear us...and that our allies should trust us."

Shumuti saw the Marshal shift slightly out of the corner of her eye.

"Now!"

The force of power was stronger than anything Shumuti had felt before. She had never used Magic with so many others at once. The rush of energy that surrounded the six of them was electrifying, and it seemed impossible that the others behind them could remain unaware of it. The ground beneath the invaders' feet shook as blades of grass reached out, twisting up around their ankles and pulling them down. From the top of the hill, two spirals of raging fire blazed over the grass of the mound. Simultaneously, a precise fissure of earth rent its way down the slope behind them. In addition, Shumuti directed a cyclone, next to Aurielle's whirlwind of water, into the line of charging attackers, throwing them back down the hill.

The weakened force that remained daringly continued to charge up the hill. Shumuti quickly counted. Roughly a dozen Boctor fighters remained on their feet. The enemy was battered and bruised, and as the smoke cleared, a trail of their fallen members became visible all the way down to the river. Shumuti reeled at the damage they had caused, feeling sick. Seaglen turned to her in concern.

Out of nowhere from behind Seaglen, an arrow shot up the hill, aiming straight for his back. Shumuti saw it happen almost in slow motion and reacted instantly, holding the arrow dead in the air, as she had done once before, before letting it fall harmlessly to the ground. Her father slid her an impressed glance, before turning his attention back down the hill. Shumuti's reaction turned to anger. These attackers did not know when to quit. The eyes of the archer below widened with surprise that his attack had failed, but then his expression turned into a snarl, and he drew his sword with a blood-curdling yell.

The bedraggled group of Boctor fighters shouted in eager agreement. Next to Shumuti, Aurielle was shaking her head in disbelief. They continued to charge up the hill, and Seaglen met the leader full on with shuddering force. One of them made his way towards Shumuti, and she gripped her sword ready. They fought backwards and forwards for a minute until he fell limply to the side, with one of Sara's arrows protruding from his body.

The fighting was fierce, but it was over in a few minutes. Seaglen and Shumuti dispatched the last together, and he toppled back down the slope. Shumuti stood there, trying to take it all in. All of this destruction and for no gain, they had fought down to the last man. She could not understand it at all.

"What was the point?" Astrid asked, throwing her sword on the ground.

It was only after a few moments that Shumuti realised one of the figures on the summit was still alive. Astrid also saw the movement, and she swiftly made her way over to the unlucky survivor. The man cried in fear as Astrid stood over him and shielded his face. Shumuti recognised him as their leader.

"Who are you?" the man spluttered angrily, a trickle of blood emerging from his mouth.

"That dœsn't matter now," Astrid replied, "why did you come here?"

"I have nothing to say to you."

"Answer me."

"You'll get nothing of use out of him," Seaglen said.

Seaglen wiped his blade clean with the hem of his cloak. The man continued to ignore Astrid and turned his attention to Shumuti's father.

"Seaglen," he said, "I came here to give you a message."

Shumuti felt a tingle of unease, and Seaglen stopped what he was doing, dropping silently to Astrid's side.

"How do you know my name?"

The man remained silent, his bloodstained mouth splitting into a grin in reply.

"Why do you smile?" Seaglen asked, "you have failed here. There is nothing more you can lose. Not a single one of your allies remain alive."

"It dœsn't matter." The man laid his head back on the grass calmly. "You will all be dead soon. There is a real army headed from Nimaz to take you all out. It will start in Elmdale and spread here. You will be gone by the start of summer."

"Listen," Astrid said, "we can help you. Heal you."

"No, you stay away from me..."

"Keep your attention on me," Seaglen said, lifting the man up by his armour, "who was it who sent you? Whose orders do you follow?"

The man focused on Seaglen as if the others around them did not exist. "He is the most powerful individual in the whole of Meteorath. Do you think this is the first time I have seen sorcery like yours? Your display of power here today pales in comparison to what he can do."

"You're saying that your master is like us?"

"He is far greater than you."

"What is your message?" Seaglen said, "do your duty and deliver it."

The man's expression relaxed and his lips curled back up into a smile.

"He told me to tell you his name is Dagaz."

Seaglen let the man fall. Shumuti had never seen an expression like that on her father's face. He looked frozen. Suddenly, the man gasped and choked. Astrid rushed forward instinctively, but the man cried out in terror and shuddered before he lay still. Shumuti turned to her father, and his face was frightening. She glanced at Astrid, but she was staring at the dead man.

"Who was he talking about?" Sara asked.

Astrid turned to Seaglen and laid a hand on his forearm.

"He could be lying," she said, "it could be anybody who is in charge in Nimaz."

"Somebody with power has been controlling Nimaz for a while now I think, perhaps longer now than any of Shumuti's generation have been practised in Magic. I don't think it could be just anybody, Astrid."

"Seaglen," Astrid said, "it can't be him though, it just can't..."

"That name," Gabriel said slowly, "Dagaz. You mentioned it to me before, the other day."

Gabriel's eyes shot to Shumuti as they both remembered their fight in the training room.

"There was only one other man in our original group," Seaglen said, "me and Dagaz."

"He was a Guardian," Astrid said, "but this is not possible."

"Dagaz died years ago," Seaglen said, "in the middle of another battle."

"Then this man is lying?" Shumuti asked.

"We never found his body though," Seaglen said, "that always bothered me. We thought it had been destroyed by Magic and there seemed no way he could have survived, but we never found him."

"We need to discover if this man was speaking the truth," Astrid said, "but for now, the King needs to know the other part of his message."

Seaglen stood up. He walked over to where the Marshal was counselling the remaining members of his company and Shumuti trailed behind. As Seaglen approached, Garrin stood up with a mixture of uncertainty and relief on his face.

"It's not over," Seaglen said, "I think there will soon be another attack to the north, on Elmdale, before the spring ends and on a much larger scale."

The Marshal was silent for several minutes, taking in this new information.

"I will send one of my company to inform the King of what has happened here. If this account is accurate, you will no doubt be summoned again soon for the next fight."

Shumuti nodded wearily. "We will find out the truth and make our preparations."

"If there is a war coming, we must raise your region," the Marshal said, "ready both Merrywater and Elmdale."

"Yes," Seaglen said, "I only hope there is enough time."

"I must decide what to do," Garrin said, "come men, back to the village. Thank you for your aid today, the King will be most grateful. I will inform you of our plan. For now, we must collect the bodies of the fallen."

The Marshal turned and led his few remaining men over the hills, leaving the others to make their own way home.

Chapter 11
Travelling Through Water and Air

~Aurielle~

Seaglen said almost nothing until they arrived back at the house. Astrid and Shumuti were deathly quiet as well, which only heightened Aurielle's trepidation. They had won the battle, but nobody was celebrating. The bodies at the Lifthayll Bridge had been burned, except for the five soldiers that the Marshal and his men had taken back to be buried honourably.

Aurielle had tried to ride with Shumuti on the way back, but Seaglen set himself firmly in between, so she drew back to Sara and the pair of them rode on in confusion. Several bruises were painfully changing colour on her left arm, and Aurielle could also feel a deep cut stinging on her neck. Looking around, everybody else had been similarly damaged, but they had all been fortunate enough to avoid any real harm.

They rode back the way they had come, under the cliffs and around the side to the house. After quickly taking care of the horses, they moved gratefully inside and sat purposefully at the table, making sure that Seaglen would give them answers. Aztec rushed up from the rug by the fireplace to greet Gabriel but drew back once he smelt the blood and sweat the whole party was covered in. Gabriel tried to calm him, but the wolf retreated uncertainly away back to the fireplace, with his ears back. As a peace offering, Gabriel took a moment to clean out and relight the fire for him before joining the others at the table.

"Finally I have answers, but it leads to nothing but more questions," Seaglen muttered.

"Do you believe it?" Astrid asked Seaglen.

"It is a hard thing to accept," he said.

"But even if it is Dagaz, why would he reveal his identity to us?" Aurielle asked.

"Perhaps there is no need for secrecy anymore," Seaglen said.

"He seems to be confident enough in his strength to sacrifice hundreds of allies without a second thought," Gabriel said, folding his arms, "maybe it is also a message that he believes we have no chance against him."

"But how could an old Guardian, this Dagaz, be trying to hunt us down?" Aurielle asked, "why?"

"I don't know," Seaglen answered, "but I intend to find out."

"How?"

"With Shumuti's help."

Aurielle saw her look up in surprise.

"And yours, Aurielle."

"Mine?"

"It is some of the most complicated Magic you will ever do," Seaglen said, "but I believe that together you can manage it."

"What will we do?" Aurielle asked.

"I will explain when it is time."

"When will you need us to help you?" Shumuti asked.

"Soon, I think," Seaglen said, "but not until you've had some rest."

"And I've had a chance to heal you all," Astrid added.

"I can help," Alejandro said.

"No," Astrid said, "you've done enough today. Rest, I will do this alone."

She set about moving from one to another, closing their wounds and healing their bruises. She reached Sara last and sat down in front of her daughter with an apologetic look on her face.

"I'm sorry, Sara, but I've never been able to heal you with my Magic."

"What?" Sara asked.

"It's true." Astrid said, "Never. I don't know the reasons why, but you are unaffected by anything I've ever tried."

"But after I learnt about Magic, I thought you had always used it on me as a child," Sara said, "I assumed that was why I was never really ill."

Astrid shook her head. "I gave you herbs and ointments to heal you if needed, but I could never apply Magic directly to you like I can with anyone else."

"Why?" Sara asked.

"I have been trying to work that out ever since you arrived," Seaglen said, "you are unique, Sara, both unable to use Magic and unaffected by it. I have never heard of anything of the like before. I suppose I should not be surprised. There is still a great deal that remains unknown when it comes to Magic. It is still relatively new to us, after all."

"Does that mean that nothing any of you do would affect me?" Sara asked.

"That remains to be seen," Seaglen said, "I felt it would be unwise if I was the one to test the theory. I did not think it was worth the risk of setting you on fire in order to know, for example."

"No," Sara said, "I'm glad that you didn't."

"In any case, your wounds will have to heal on their own," Astrid said, "I'll find something to apply to your skin to help them close faster."

"Now all of you, get some rest," Seaglen said, "Shumuti and Aurielle, I may call for you in a small while."

They obediently followed his orders, feeling drained and exhausted. Aurielle's dreams though, were anything but restful, and she relived the battle a thousand times in her head. Unable to escape the nightmare, Aurielle felt herself cry out. Forcing herself awake, she sat up with a jerk, forgetting for a moment where she was. Hugging her knees, Aurielle sat there quietly in the dark, trying to remove the images from her head.

Looking down to her right, she saw Sara and Shumuti were both wide awake, staring at the ceiling. Shumuti turned her way and Aurielle knew they completely understood what the other was feeling.

"Do you want to try and sleep again?" she whispered.

"Not really," Aurielle answered, forcing a smile.

"No."

It was still dark, but a small group of birds calling from outside indicated that dawn was slowly approaching.

"Let's not wake the others if we don't have to," Sara said quietly.

Aurielle nodded her head in agreement, and the three of them silently got up. When they walked downstairs, they found Seaglen sitting there at the table, lost in thought.

"You're awake," he said, "I had thought about coming to call on you."

"We couldn't sleep," Shumuti said.

Seaglen glanced between them. "If you could do with a distraction, I am eager to try out my idea."

Aurielle swallowed and nodded. Something to do would be useful.

"Sara," Seaglen added, "you may come and watch if you would prefer not to go back to bed."

All three of them followed Seaglen as he led them down the corridors of his house that led to the Guardians of Magic cave. He lit two of the torches that fitted into the brackets on the wall and handed the second to Shumuti. Then he opened the secret entrance at the end of the corridor. Aurielle felt the well-known chill, and suddenly the underground tunnel materialised before them, allowing them to proceed along the path to the second door.

Once past that, the circular cavern unveiled itself out below them. Down the concentric steps they went, until all four stood in the centre. Then Sara went to sit on the lowest level of steps to see what they would do.

"Now," Seaglen said, turning slowly, "I would never have dared to try Magic of this level with you before, but after what I saw at the Lifthayll Bridge, I think you can handle it."

"What are we going to do?" Aurielle asked.

"As you know, the reason I was able to find Gabriel was in Attaching was that one of the skills I have developed over the years is to detect the location of Magic and those who can use it. It is an enhanced version of what you all can do at close range. Now, the only reason I was able to detect Gabriel from so far away was because of the volume of Magic he was using at the time. I have been trying to do a similar search in Nimaz or Boctor, but so far, I have been unsuccessful. This is where the two of you come in. I believe that by combining my skill with both of your Magic, I can enhance my abilities, and we can look across to Nimaz from right here in the training room and confirm whether it is Dagaz out there or not."

"How?" Shumuti asked.

"I'm going to ask you to think about Magic in a way you never have before," Seaglen told them, "Magic is everywhere. It runs from this room to all of Merrywater and all of Meteorath. When you draw on it to use, you find it around you and gather it. What I am going to ask you to do here is the opposite. Instead of making Magic a part of you, I want you to let yourself become a part of it."

"That dœsn't sound like something I can do," Aurielle said.

"All you have to do is think differently," Seaglen said, "I will show you how."

"And if we become a part of Magic, as you say, it allows us to do what?" Shumuti asked.

Seaglen indicated the waterfall that they could hear faintly rumbling in the underground cavern beyond the training cave. "It opens up a world of new possibilities. I'll give you an example of how I intend to use it today. Water and air are present from where we stand here, all the way from Merrywater to Nimaz and Magic runs through it all. By working the energy in this way, it allows us to travel mentally through wherever Magic is present.

"But there are limitations. The same way that you are restricted to only one element when you transform energy into Magic, you can only connect with that same element. I require fire to be present, Aurielle requires water and Shumuti requires air. That is why I need the two of you. I cannot undertake this journey alone, but together we can. We will travel through water from here until it runs out. Then Shumuti will take us through the air."

"You're leaving?" Sara asked.

"No," Seaglen answered, "this will be a mental journey."

"So," Aurielle said, "I have to sense out for the water running through the waterfall...with my mind?"

"In a sense. I will help you," Seaglen said, "come take a seat with me."

Seaglen sat on the central design of the floor and Aurielle and Shumuti joined him. Seaglen offered a hand out to each and so the three of them sat the shape of a triangle in the centre of the spiral.

"If you practise this technique, Shumuti, eventually you will be able to develop your own ability at being able to detect Magic over distances."

Shumuti sighed. "I know. I've just never been able to fully grasp what you mean before."

"You were not as skilled then as you have since become. I believe you can master it. Now, Aurielle, follow my lead and focus on the water. Sara, you may see us move or call out. Do not try to intervene, even if you are worried. We must remain concentrated, and besides, there is nothing you would be able to do to help us."

"I understand," Sara said, with wide eyes.

"Aurielle, reach out for the Magic within the waterfall as you would normally. Then, instead of gathering the energy to you, allow yourself to become a part of it. Do not forget to bring us with you."

Uncertainly, she reached out and felt the Magic stir. Simultaneously, she was aware of Seaglen, Shumuti, the waterfall and the heightened connection that ran between all of them. She had linked Magic with Shumuti and Seaglen before and was comforted that so far this was something she was familiar with. Aurielle concentrated on the waterfall and felt Seaglen take slight control of what she was doing and let him direct her Magic. Slowly, she made an invisible tendril reach out towards the direction of the waterfall.

"Good," Seaglen said quietly.

Heartened, Aurielle extended her reach further through the walls of the cavern until she found what she was looking for. Her Magic immediately sought a connection to the waterfall and quickly became a part of it, until she almost felt as though she was flowing down the rock too.

Aurielle felt unsteady and instinctively gripped Shumuti's hand tighter. A whole new range of sensations and consciousness ran through her. She could feel the fluidity of the water as it ran over the rocks and the churn as it hit the bottom pool, hundreds of meters down into the cliffs. Enthusiastically, she dove after the water as it moved out of the rock into the open stream. For a second, the image darkened, and she almost lost it. She felt a resistant tug behind her and fought against it.

"Aurielle!" Seaglen's voice sounded distant. "Don't lose us now. Don't leave us behind."

"Sorry!"

Making sure that she knew they were with her, Aurielle let them crash down the waterfall, and after a few seconds of turbulent darkness, they were thrown into the outside world. Merrywater opened up before them and a fast-flowing river carried them away. Disorientated, Aurielle saw the cliff that held the training room diminish in size as they were swept away. They moved under the night stars lighting the sky like a million eyes and headed in the direction of the Winterburn River.

Taking advantage of the ephemeral streams that ran across the plains of Merrywater as winter began to lose its hold on the lowlands, Aurielle kept the pale skies of the rising sun at her back as she directed the party westward. Quicker than she thought possible, they hit the main Winterburn River and sped along the border of Merrywater. Travelling along the river, or rather as part of the river was curious, to say the least. Aurielle wondered what would happen if they saw somebody on the bank. She doubted that they would be able to see them, but...

"Concentrate, Aurielle." She heard Seaglen's voice.

Aurielle snapped her focus back immediately as they found themselves travelling faster in this livelier current. She was unsure if she could control their passage as easily here, so instead, she let the river take them wherever it willed while she became accustomed to what was happening. This form of Magic was more complex than any she had ever felt and already her strength was waning rapidly. As this thought came to her mind, she felt a boost to her energy levels and knew that Seaglen was helping her.

"We must turn west at the Nimaz border," Seaglen said.

"Wait," Aurielle said, "I don't know if I can."

"I am here to help you."

"Are we nearly there?"

"I'll tell you when."

Being on the level of the water, Aurielle found it hard to tell where exactly they were geographically, but somehow Seaglen knew, and he shouted out that it was time. In her tired state, it took Aurielle a moment to realise he had spoken and act on what he had said. With his help, Aurielle managed to catch the currents and alter course to set them travelling along the border between Boctor and Nimaz.

"You will need to give me a moment to see if I can detect anything," Seaglen said.

"All right," Aurielle answered, unsure how much longer she could keep this up.

Aurielle took in the ominous landscape that blurred past on either side of them as they travelled. Boctor was well known for being little more than desert, but Nimaz somehow seemed even more barren. It was as if something had worn the region down to only its bedrock. Deep cracks ran through the rock that bordered the river, as though the area had suffered an earthquake recently.

"I have something," Seaglen said, "we can go no further on the river. Shumuti, search out Magic in currents of air above us. Be quick. I think Aurielle could do with a rest."

"I'll try," Shumuti said.

It was a minute or so before Aurielle became aware of Shumuti's request to take control. Gladly, she let her friend take the reins of this strange journey and realised that Shumuti was attempting to lift them. With a sickening jolt, Aurielle felt them rise above the water and much to her surprise, splash back down a second later.

"Sorry, sorry!" Shumuti said.

"Again, quick!" Seaglen said.

No longer having to do anything, Aurielle wondered how this whole situation looked to Sara, back at the training cave. Shumuti lifted them again and held them in place. Aurielle did not feel attached to anything and saw nothing to stop them from falling at any moment. Shumuti tugged them vertically upwards once more and with her last reserves, Aurielle remembered to stay with the others, her stomach lurching as they rose. This time, Shumuti managed to keep them airborne and with what Aurielle suspected was Seaglen's help, they floated high up over Nimaz, buffeted by air currents and drifted towards the heart of Nimaz.

"There's barely any Magic here." Shumuti gasped. "Hold on, there's more if I go higher."

"You may use the supply in the cave as well," Seaglen said, "we are still linked to that."

Below them, a giant gorge rose into view, more cavernous and extensive than the one that cut through the Elmdale Forest, so deep that Aurielle could not see the bottom of it. Jagged cuts into the earth bordered the ravine on either side, which was fed by smaller chasms, altogether forming a malformed representation of a river's catchment area.

"What is that?" Aurielle asked.

"Pinnacle Gorge," Seaglen answered, "one of many ravines that lead to the heart of Nimaz."

"Is that where we're going?" Aurielle asked.

"Yes, it is not far now. I believe there is indeed something in the centre of this region that is of interest to us."

"I am struggling to keep us in the air," Shumuti said, "I'm not sure I can take us any further."

"We need to use the source in the training room," Seaglen said, "here."

"That's a little better."

Aurielle looked down at the gorge in awe as they drifted over, but what came next fitted in beautifully with the rest of the surroundings. The canyon opened up into a circular valley, where a fortified stronghold rose directly out of the central stone, built out of a mixture of iron and the rock itself.

Ringed by a high wall, the structure looked impenetrable and very formidable. Two circular towers rose from the centre of the stronghold, one slightly taller than the other and a glow illuminated the top of the shorter one. Armoured figures guarded the walls and towers of the fortress. As they took in the sight, Aurielle had to forcibly remind herself that nobody here could see them.

"Shumuti," Seaglen said, "take us towards that light."

Obediently she flew them forwards, dodging up into a higher current of air and floating evenly towards the tower. They drifted down to the window on the breeze, and steadily the arch-shaped hole grew in size. Dropping to the left of the window, Shumuti fought to keep them in place. By gradually edging forwards, they reached the rim of the window and looked through to the room inside.

In the centre, there was a polished desk made from jet and a carved chair. Adorning the desk were several clusters of what looked like minerals and gems of all colours. What was more, someone was sitting on the chair, pouring over a map of Meteorath laid out before him. Aurielle felt Seaglen react as he took in the figure on the chair, they could not be described as human. A shadow of a male human shape sat before them, held together by smoke and ragged armour. Aurielle recognised it as the same armour that was hung up in the training room in which they sat. The figure's hands moved towards the map, and his fingers were blackened like dried volcanic lava, cracking as he elongated them. There were gaps where parts of his body should be, and grey mist twisted there instead.

Behind the chair stood someone Aurielle recognised. Chana, the Atabra they had faced on the road up to Attaching, watched on intently. Her concentration was centred on the map too, her hooked face absorbed in studying it. Aurielle noticed how she stood back from the chair, whether out of respect or fear, it was unclear.

Dark eyes flared as the figure turned and looked up, suddenly sensing something around him. He looked at them and Aurielle froze with the others. Sanguine irises stared directly back at her, and she knew instantly without a doubt that he could see them. At that moment, they were ripped from their out-of-body experience. Reverberated out of the air, they desperately clung to each other as they were blasted across the entirety of Meteorath.

"Stay with me!" Seaglen's cry distorted around them.

Shaken and jolted, Aurielle felt a shift as flames burst all around them, but the way they were travelling somehow seemed to have more direction. They were drawn downwards, Aurielle's vision was blackened, and she felt distinctly sick. Pain shot through her, and she yelled as they shot through what looked like rock, and for a surreal moment, Aurielle saw her body sitting below her before she was launched back inside it.

Her eyes sprang open, and she gasped in shock. Her body felt like it was being electrocuted and everything seemed out of place inside her. Aurielle waited, shaking with adrenaline until gradually, her body sorted itself out and normalised.

Sara hovered over them, inches away, but refraining from touching anyone. Feeling disoriented and dizzy, Aurielle slumped back against the start of the stone steps of the Guardians of Magic room and Shumuti crawled over to collapse next to her.

"Are you both all right?" Seaglen asked, with a concerned expression.

"I think so," they both replied.

"For a moment, I was not sure if we would make it back here," Seaglen said.

"He knew we were there," Aurielle said.

"Yes," Seaglen said.

"Well?" Shumuti asked, "who was it that we saw? Was it Dagaz?"

"He wore the same armour as on the walls here," Aurielle said.

"It was Dagaz in that keep," Seaglen said, "although he is barely recognisable."

"What we saw," Aurielle said, "wasn't human, was it?"

"Not entirely," Seaglen said.

"What happened to him?" Shumuti asked.

"I do not know," Seaglen answered, "something twisted. It was as if he was more Magic than person."

"You said he was dead," Aurielle said.

"I think he should be, but perhaps something has prevented it," Seaglen said.

"How is that possible?" Aurielle asked.

"He has either done it himself or been made that way," Seaglen said, "whatever happened to him, it has increased his strength. Dagaz is powerful now, more so even than me."

"He was with Chana," Shumuti said, "that confirms he is linked to them. He is behind all of this."

"We shall take things as we have done so far," Seaglen answered, "one step at a time. He sent the Boctor force to challenge us. A strangely foolish plan, but it means that he feels we are at least a threat. The last remaining question is why he is doing any of this. I fear what he has been doing in Nimaz. He was always experimental with Magic. Now he dœs not have me to prevent him from experimenting."

"Do you think there's more in Nimaz than the vultures?" Shumuti asked.

"I fear there may be."

Aurielle glanced worriedly at Shumuti.

"But it is not all bad news," Seaglen continued.

"What do you mean?" Aurielle asked.

"In regards to the attack on Elmdale," Seaglen said, "the map Dagaz was looking at. I caught a glimpse of a marked location on the Winterburn River, towards the north of Elmdale. If I am not mistaken, that could be where he plans to invade from."

"The Marshal needs to know before he leaves," Shumuti said.

"Wait, there is one final thing you should know," Seaglen said, "as we were moving towards Nimaz I detected something faint, something I have not felt since I realised there were Guardians in Attaching. Alongside the source of Magic in Nimaz, there was another in the very west of Boctor. I believe there is another Magic user out there."

Chapter 12
A Night Out

~SARA~

The next morning, Seaglen, Shumuti and Aurielle recounted the story of the previous night. The others listened intently to what they had to say, and Sara could tell that even in the warm light of day, the tale chilled each one of them. The description of Dagaz, or what he had now become, had especially shocked Astrid and none of them could come up with a possible suggestion how he firstly, was still alive and secondly, had reached the condition he was now in. Sara was secretly glad that she had seen none of it.

The rest of the day was spent in various ways. For Sara, Shumuti and Aurielle, it meant sleeping, Seaglen and Astrid moved to talk more about Dagaz, and Gabriel and Alejandro trained a little, before doing some resting of their own. One of the Marshal's men had ridden up to the house while Sara, Shumuti and Aurielle had been asleep and requested that a small meeting be held at Seaglen's house tomorrow night. Garrin seemed to want to discuss the problem of what their enemy would decide to do next. He and his company would be leaving for Attaching the day after, but before they went, he wanted to talk with the seven of them about what they were planning to do next.

Stephan would not be leaving with them, Sara had learnt, after she had awoken that afternoon. He was to stay behind as an envoy that Seaglen could use as he wished to relay messages with and as an extra pair of hands for them here. If there was any sign of trouble in Merrywater then Seaglen would be able to use him to send for reinforcements. It was agreed that as Seaglen's once quiet home had now become ridiculously overcrowded Stephan was to carry on living at the Boar Inn in the village.

That same tavern had asked Alejandro to perform for them that evening at the Wintertide festival to celebrate the coming onset of spring. Sara had been the one to arrange it a while back, after hearing about the event from Stephan. Given what had just happened, she was unsure if it was still a good plan, but Seaglen had assured her that perhaps it was not a bad idea to go somewhere where they could forget about the battle for a night. There was a dance being held, and he was to be part of the music. Shumuti had told them the whole village would turn out, and they had all decided to go. Gabriel was even bringing Aztec along. Aurielle had gone back to her home to get ready and was going to meet them there.

"Be careful," Seaglen warned, as they were all preparing to leave, "the Marshal prefers the fight at the Lifthayll Bridge to remain confidential for now, until more news is gathered, so try not to mention it just yet."

They nodded.

"Do not wear yourselves out too much either, remember you have to present and awake for tomorrow's meeting."

"We will have a full day to recover," Gabriel said with confidence, as they walked out the door.

Seaglen locked it behind them and Shumuti led the way down the hill, the wolf bounding ahead into the evening. Seaglen and Astrid fell behind the others, choosing a slower pace. Sara felt a strange relief as they walked and realised that for the first time since they had got back, she found herself not worrying about what might lie ahead and able to just enjoy the company of her friends.

"It's time to show you a night in Thayll!" Shumuti said.

"Shumuti, you seem a little too excited about tonight," Alejandro joked.

"Is there a lot of entertainment in a remote village like this?" Gabriel asked.

"I'm not sure you can compare Thayll to Lyria," Sara said.

"Perhaps you might be disappointed if you compare it to Lyria," Shumuti answered, looking back over her shoulder, "but I'll bet it beats the amusement of sitting on your own in a volcano every night for weeks on end."

Sara chuckled.

"Oh, really?" Gabriel smiled challengingly. "Well, before I left the city, I spent every night in the capital of Attaching. You will have a hard task ahead if you want to impress me."

Shumuti laughed, before turning away and linking arms with Sara as they entered the village. The Boar Inn was set in the centre of Thayll, and already a steady stream of villagers and travellers alike were passing under the swinging sign. Hovering by a nearby shop door, Sara spotted Aurielle standing with a man she did not know, but Shumuti met him cheerfully.

"This is my father, Seamus," Aurielle said.

Sara greeted him, surprised that she had been in Thayll this long and never encountered him before. She did not think she had even passed him on the streets. He gave them all a reserved nod.

"Nice to meet you all," he said.

"My own father is coming," Shumuti said, "but they fell quite far behind."

"Seaglen is here?" Seamus asked in slight surprise.

"Yes," Shumuti answered, "I was quite impressed as well that I managed to get him to come to a party. He's with his sister, and I don't think you've met her either."

Shumuti turned back, searching the crowd.

"There they are."

Seaglen and Astrid had found the blacksmith, Erdic, and were already nearly inside the inn. Shumuti and the others joined the crowds eagerly. The group entered to the smell of wood smoke, the sound of roaring laughter and the sight of a bustling, merry crowd.

A few nearer the door looked up as they entered. Shumuti lingered in the doorway for Gabriel and Alejandro to take in the full atmosphere, until an elderly man beside them slammed the doors shut to cut off the cold draft blowing in from the street and they were forced to move forward into the centre of the room.

They pushed forward through the throng to an open, blazing fire near to the bar and huddling close together, soon melted off the evening chill of outside, until they were pushed aside as a fresh group of customers hurried to take their place.

"Shumuti," Aurielle said, as they all tried to find somewhere to stand, "did you see where my father went?"

"No," Shumuti answered, looking around, "did we lose him?"

Sara stared around at the sea of faces around them, thinking that they had been lucky to keep the rest of the group together.

"Sara!"

Surprised to hear her name, Sara saw Stephan wind around the many tables to reach them. She regarded him steadily, remembering the last time they had properly spoken to one another, but he acted as though that conversation had never happened.

"Come on, I'll get you a drink. I have a free table for us upstairs if we're quick."

Stephan led the group up to a corner table on the balcony, directly overlooking the area where the band was set to be playing. They left Seaglen and Astrid chatting to Erdic downstairs and filed in to claim seats in their cosy corner. The table was illuminated overhead by a small chandelier, crafted from several intertwining deer antlers and set with small, warmly lit candles.

Stephan returned to the bar, accompanied by Aurielle and Gabriel, who were trying to remember drink orders. Sara took a second to wonder why there was so little room underneath the table when she peeked underneath and saw the long tongue and pointed ears of Aztec poking out from the shadows. As she settled in, he nestled himself next to her leg. Shumuti and Alejandro squeezed around the table on her other side, and the other three returned not long after with six deep, clinking glasses. Gabriel eyed his happily.

"How are you doing?" Stephan asked, squeezing in beside her, around the wolf.

Sara hesitated. "All right, I suppose."

He nodded and offered her a drink.

"You fought well," he complimented her quietly.

Sara was about to reply to him when she heard another conversation being held on the far side of the table.

"He left," she heard Aurielle saying, looking dejected.

"What?" Shumuti asked.

"His friend at the bar told me my father went home," Aurielle said, "maybe I should go after him."

"Hold on," Gabriel said, "you all promised me a night to remember, and you're leaving already?"

"No." Aurielle had begun to rise and faltered.

"Maybe he just didn't feel like being out tonight," Shumuti said to her.

Aurielle nodded, slowly sinking back down.

"Stephan, are the rest of the soldiers here?" Sara asked.

"Most are," he said, "the Marshal refuses to ever come down here in the evenings, though. He has kept a clear head for over twenty years. They are at the bar. We could join them, if you like."

"I don't know that they would appreciate us, being what we are, if you understand," Shumuti said.

"True, they are uncomfortable with Magic. I had noticed."

"You aren't though," Alejandro said.

Sara felt Stephan's arm freeze up slightly beside her.

"I take my example from Sara," he said, "she has faith in you, therefore so do I. Don't worry though, they can be trusted not to talk about it. Dœs anyone else in the village know what you can do?"

"No one," Shumuti said. She stared down at the group of villagers Seaglen and Astrid stood chatting merrily with below. "I don't know how they would react. There was never any reason to tell them before now."

"If things continue the way they do, people might have to find out eventually," Stephan said.

"I know," Shumuti said.

"But that is future Shumuti's problem," Gabriel said, interrupting her musing, "and if what lies ahead is nothing but gloom, we had better enjoy tonight while we can. Alejandro, when do you start?"

"In a little while, I think," he said, "they were going to prepare an area for me to play."

Sure enough, little over an hour passed before an area was cleared in the corner and a set of wooden instruments were smuggled into the space. Alejandro got up to join a small trio of musicians. A few minutes later, the sprightly notes of a flute solo struck up, ringing out high and clear above the noise of chatter. Everybody in the inn fell quiet to listen. A second later, another musician rang out a catchy drumbeat, picking up the pace of the music. Alejandro then began to play the melody with his fiddle, and the room fell silent completely. It was clear to Sara that Alejandro was the best musician of the three, and she could also hear a few others around their table ask who he was.

"I've never heard Alejandro play with other people before," Sara said, "he sounds good."

"I've never heard him play at all," Gabriel said, while Aurielle and Shumuti nodded in agreement.

After the first song came to an end, the inn erupted into applause. Alejandro smiled and bowed slightly. Sara had never seen him so confident as he looked now, and it was as if a different person stood on the stage. The drumbeat started up again, but this time it was livelier than before. Alejandro upped the tempo of his fiddle to match, and the flute played a clear, bright melody above it all.

Taking that as a cue, a dance floor was cleared in the centre of the room. Several from below, including Seaglen and Astrid, retreated upstairs and lined the balcony that overlooked the dancing. The others joined them, abandoning their table for a closer view to watch Alejandro play and not minding that it was lost almost instantly.

"Are you going to dance?" Astrid asked Sara.

"Are you?" Sara asked her curiously, thinking back to Silverspring when they had often got involved in nights similar to these.

"You know, Seaglen used to be quite the dancer," Astrid said.

"Really?"

"You don't believe it?" Seaglen's head appeared around the other side of Astrid.

"I..." Sara trailed off, not knowing quite what to say.

Seaglen offered her a raised eyebrow and silently proposed a hand to Astrid. Sara watched in amazement as he led her down the stairs and onto the dance floor. The group on the balcony witnessed the pair of them cut across the crowd below and out dance many around them. Sara turned to Shumuti, to see that she was equally taken aback.

"So, this is your idea of a good night?" Gabriel called across to Shumuti.

"It's only as good as you make it," she answered.

"Fair enough." He grinned back, before grabbing her arm and dragging her down the stairs to the dance floor. Sara and Aurielle laughed at the expression on her face.

"Sara." Stephan turned to her. "What do you think?"

"You can't dance!" Sara shouted, "but yes, after you!"

She heard Aurielle call indignantly after them. "Who am I meant to dance with? Aztec?"

Sara saw one of the soldiers appear at Aurielle's side a second later, and after a moment of surprise, she accepted their invitation to dance. The four of them jigged across to Shumuti and Gabriel, who were laughing hysterically.

"Shumuti, you are the most useless partner I have ever had!" Gabriel exclaimed, "Sara!"

He grabbed her, as she happened to be closest, and whisked her off into the crowds.

"Hey, you're not bad!" Sara shouted across the music to him.

"Neither are you." He grinned back.

Gabriel's face suddenly fell. Sara had to twist almost entirely around to see what he was looking at. He was watching Aurielle dance with the soldier. Sara turned back to him and opened her mouth.

"What is it?" she shouted.

"It's nothing," he said forcefully back.

Gabriel turned his attention back to Sara.

"We're swapping again!" Stephan whirled back into view and whisked Sara away before she knew what was happening.

They danced for several more songs, but Sara's mind was completely elsewhere. Aurielle and the soldier were still close by, but she could no longer see Gabriel. The current tune came to, and Alejandro stepped away from the stage to take a break. As a new set of musicians came on, Sara detached herself from Stephan and went up to congratulate him. A handful of girls beat her to it, and Sara hung back, watching Alejandro awkwardly accept their compliments. He noticed Sara and immediately made an excuse to leave.

"You were great," she said, "though I'm not the first to tell you that."

Alejandro glanced at the girls in embarrassment.

"Where are the others?"

"I'm not sure," Sara said.

Stephan came up to them, looking slightly affronted that Sara had just abandoned him. The music started up again and a pirouetting Astrid and Seaglen forced them off the dance floor, so they took the opportunity to head out of the inn for some fresh air. Outside was a large group of others who had a similar idea. A few braziers had been set up next to tables to provide heat and light, and a string of lanterns even decorated the sky above as well. A large group of younger men and women from the village were clustered around one of the tables, playing cards. Shumuti and Gabriel were amongst them.

Sara, Alejandro and Stephan hung back to watch the game come to a close and Shumuti beat one of the villagers from Thayll, taking the last card in his hand. A cheer rose up as her opponent flung up his hands in defeat. The next round began, and Alejandro and Stephan moved towards the table to join in. Shumuti noticed Sara and came over to her, with Gabriel. On Shumuti's way over, one of the soldiers from Attaching intercepted her and pulled her aside. He spoke with her for a few minutes and left her with a puzzled expression on her face.

"Making friends?" Sara asked her.

"Apparently I am," Shumuti said, "he was thanking me for what we did at the Lifthayll Bridge. He said without us, none of them would have survived."

"I'd say he might be right in thinking that," Sara said.

"Are you sure that was all he wanted?" Gabriel asked.

"What are you suggesting?"

"Well..." Gabriel raised an eyebrow.

Shumuti folded her arms, watching the soldier disappear back into the inn. "Even if it was something more, I have no time for that."

"Hey," Gabriel said, "tonight is about celebrating and having a good time. You wanted to make sure we enjoyed ourselves, so why not you?"

"Because whilst we're in the middle of all this, I can't allow myself to be distracted by anything," Shumuti said, "not tonight, not ever. Besides, he was not for me."

Sara admired her determination.

"That's a big commitment," Gabriel said.

"But that dœsn't mean the same for you," Shumuti said, "you all should go have fun."

"Maybe I will," Gabriel said. He gathered up Alejandro and the pair of them headed back towards the inn.

"Where is Aurielle?" Sara asked.

"Still dancing inside I think," Shumuti replied.

Sara watched Gabriel retreat. She felt the urge to confide in Shumuti what she had learnt but fought against it and instead joined in as a new round of card games began. The game disintegrated a while later and Seaglen and Astrid came out to join them.

"We are heading back up the hill," Seaglen told them, "remember what I said about tomorrow."

"But don't forget to have a good night," Astrid added.

"Right," Seaglen said.

"Goodnight," Sara said.

Seaglen and Astrid turned away to walk home, just as Aurielle finally appeared to join them. She did not look as cheerful as she had done earlier, and Alejandro trailed after.

"Did you cross paths with Gabriel in there?" Shumuti asked.

"Oh yes, he's a little preoccupied," Aurielle said.

Sara turned to see three of the girls from the village huddled around Gabriel and Aztec, smothering the wolf in attention and asking Gabriel many questions about him.

"That animal is like a secret weapon," Alejandro remarked, shaking his head as he appeared at Sara's side, "he emerged from under the table, and I was physically pushed out of the way as they crowded around. I'm pretty sure I became invisible. You three can still see me, right?"

Sara smiled. "Don't worry, you're still visible."

"What about Stephan?" Alejandro asked her, "wasn't he with you?"

"He went to join the other soldiers," Sara said, with a little guilt. Stephan had been distant with her since the dance.

Gabriel noticed them all standing together and slowly pulled Aztec away from his group of fans. He wandered over to them, looking somewhat pleased with himself. Aurielle folded her arms when she saw his expression.

"What?" he asked.

She huffed in response and turned back inside the inn. Gabriel sighed despondently, watching her go. The music struck up again from inside, and people steadily started to file back in for the second round of dancing. None of the four made a move to go back inside.

"Are you playing again, Alejandro?" Sara asked.

"No, I think I'm done for the night. The villagers seem to have taken over in there. Everybody seems to be attempting to have a go, but thankfully I managed to save my fiddle before somebody else managed to borrow it."

"I think I might head back to the house," Shumuti said, as though her mind was elsewhere.

"I might come with you," Alejandro said quickly.

"What?" Sara said, "you're all going?"

"You two stay!" Shumuti said, "I just don't want to let my father down. I need to show him that I can be relied on, and for that, I need to be awake tomorrow."

"Maybe I should come too," Sara said.

"What about Stephan?" Alejandro asked.

"He'll be all right without me," Sara said, "but you need to stay, Gabriel, to make sure Aurielle makes it home."

She looked at him meaningfully, and he turned dubiously back to the inn.

"All right. Well, I'm going. You all decide what you're doing," Shumuti said.

She began to walk away, and Alejandro followed. Sara gave Gabriel a nod of encouragement before turning after them. He took a deep breath and re-entered the inn. The three of them trudged evenly away into the gloom and silence of the main street. The coolness and quiet of the night was a comfort to Sara, and the stars glinted softly overhead. They all walked on in silence, each lost in their own thoughts. As they crested above the horizon of the village, Alejandro gently breached the undisturbed quiet.

"You have so many stars down here. In Lyria, you can only see half as many, the city is so bright."

"Just before dawn is most beautiful," Shumuti said, "I have no idea what it is about that time, maybe because it is not often you see it, but if I'm awake, I feel as though I am about to set off on an adventure. Everything in the world seems bright and crisp and new."

Sara turned to the mountains far off in the distance, but they were barely visible at this hour. Moonlight faintly glinted off the snow-capped summits but the rest of the rock had melded with the night sky.

"This seems like a place that is worthwhile protecting," Alejandro said, "I never really understood that before."

"As is every place," Shumuti said.

"We should get up early one morning to see," Sara said.

"Perhaps not tomorrow though," Alejandro said, "I wonder what will happen at the meeting?"

"We shall have to wait to find out," Shumuti said.

The door creaked open as they entered the house. Sara said goodnight to Shumuti and Alejandro and watched the stars out of the window for a while from the comfort of her very own bed.

Chapter 13
Preparing for War

~Alejandro~

The thunder of hooves drew Alejandro's attention firmly away from the seeds in his hand. He and Shumuti had been trying to pass the time waiting for the meeting by planting vegetables in the garden at Astrid's request, ready for the summer. Closing his palm around the remaining seeds, he caught Shumuti's eye, and together they stood, careful to avoid trampling the soil of Seaglen's small garden.

A lone rider came into view up the hill from the village. They recognised the garb of the King's red and white uniform before walking out to greet him. The soldier was Stephan. Alejandro gauged from the dark rings shading his eyes that Stephan had not gotten much sleep last night. His words, despite that, were admirably controlled and alert.

"My Marshal sends me with a request," he reported, "he wishes to bring the meeting forward to one hour from now, for our company must ride through the night in order to reach Attaching and report to the King in less than a week from now."

"Will your company be able to make it to Lyria in so short a time?" Shumuti asked.

"They must," Stephan said, "the King's need is urgent."

"Has something happened?" Alejandro asked.

"My Marshal will reveal more," Stephan said, looking at Alejandro for the first time, "that is all I can say for now. I trust the change of time will be no problem?"

"No."

"Then, farewell for now. I will be back soon." Stephan hesitated. "Is Sara all right? You three left early."

"She is fine," Alejandro replied.

Stephan lowered his gaze. "Good. Tell her...no, never mind. I have to go."

He wheeled his horse around and cantered back down the track. Alejandro stared after him for a minute.

"I had better tell my father," Shumuti said.

"What?" Alejandro had not been listening. "Oh yes, we better had."

Inside the sunlight-flooded house sat Astrid, pouring over a gigantic old book bound in leather, but which looked remarkably untouched.

"Ah," she said as they entered, enthusiastically slamming the vast volume down on the tabletop, "have you finished planting?"

"Almost," Alejandro replied, "but then Stephan rode up to the house with a message. The meeting is being brought forward to one hour from now. We need to tell Seaglen. Is he at the training cave?"

"Yes," she answered, "but he might be on his way back now. You'll have to go down the cliffs if you want to be sure of meeting him."

"Right. You don't mind if we take a break, do you?"

"No." Astrid sighed. "The future of Meteorath ought to be put before potting Seaglen's garden. I'm almost confident he would agree."

Unsure if she wanted them to dispute that, they carefully placed their remaining seeds onto the table, before sprinting out of the house and up the hill towards the cliffs. Alejandro could not help wonder whether any of them would be in Thayll in the summer anyway to reap the benefits of what they had planted this morning. At the same time, he decided against pointing that out to Astrid. She was planning for a future that could be altered so easily.

Thinking about the future was pushed from his mind as they climbed onwards. The path was steep and left them out of breath as Alejandro and Shumuti jogged out of the copse of trees and into the buffeting air currents on the cliff-top, confirming that Seaglen must still be inside the training cave. Alejandro felt his stomach tighten as they approached the edge. He had done the descent a few times before, but it left him feeling no easier about traversing the fragile steps to the cave halfway down the rock face.

Shumuti went first. She walked to the edge of the crag and carefully swung her legs over the edge before standing up. The sight of her from this side of the cliff appeared almost quite comical, and Shumuti seemed to be hovering in mid-air. Alejandro walked forward, and the slim staircase that was carved into the side of the cliff came into view, treacherous and deadly if they put so much as a foot out of place. Moss and lichen gripped some steps and the side of the rock. Even as Alejandro picked his way after Shumuti, he heard the fierce pounding of the underground waterfall that crashed down inside the cliff.

Thankfully, they arrived at the small platform unscathed and quickly ducked into the darkness of the cave. Immediately unable to hear anything at all, except for the power of the cascade before them, Alejandro followed Shumuti. His eyes adjusted as they walked around to the blank rock face on the opposite side to the entrance. Placing a hand each on the stone, Alejandro and Shumuti each felt a tingle as the door absorbed a stream of their Magic. A flash of green and silver radiated from under both of their palms, and the door began to grind open.

The figure in the room rotated as he felt the change. Alejandro thought for a moment he saw a flare of red fire, but then he blinked and the light vanished. Seaglen relaxed as they stepped inside, and he sheathed the blade he was holding.

"What were you doing?" Shumuti asked.

"Simply practising," he said, "I too must keep my skills sharp. Now why am I graced with your presence, may I ask?"

"The Marshal has requested that the meeting be moved forward an hour," Shumuti said.

"It's almost midday now," Alejandro said.

Seaglen gazed up at the light holes, far up in the roof of the cave. The sun shone almost directly down. "Come on then, we had best get prepared for our visitors."

Seaglen led the way as they exited the training room and climbed back up onto the cliffs.

"Where is everybody else?" he asked, beginning the descent to the house.

"They're still asleep, except for Astrid. She enlisted us to help with the preparation of your garden. She is determined that it will be put to good use."

"Astrid has always cared about it more than me. This year of all years, it seems to have little point."

"I think it comes from having your magical element as the earth," Alejandro said.

"Yes," Seaglen said, "it dœs not help that my own is fire."

*

The seven of them sat in the parlour, waiting for the Marshal and his company to arrive. Aurielle and Gabriel were slouched over mugs of steaming tea, supporting each other to remain upright and awake, both suffering after staying out all night at the inn. Alejandro had no idea what time they had returned home. Aztec lay curled up at Gabriel's feet, the only one allowed to catch up on sleep missed out on the previous night.

Shumuti, Seaglen and Astrid kept their eyes fixed on the road out of the window, waiting for the soldiers to materialise on it, each lost in thought. For his part, Alejandro wondered what their role would be after today and what they would be required to do next. A spot of rain hit the glass on the windowpane and the sky outside turned grey as the sun was blotted out.

"They're here!" Shumuti said, with evident relief in her voice.

Alejandro sat up and saw the company, headed by the Marshal, canter by the window. He left his soldiers and brought only Stephan and one other to the door. Astrid welcomed them inside.

"My men will stay out there," Garrin said, "I must be quick, and there is much to decide. We must ride once we are done here."

The Marshal placed himself on the opposite end of the table to Seaglen. Seaglen had Astrid on his left and Shumuti on his right, while the Marshal had Stephan on his right and a soldier Alejandro did not recognise on his left. The rest of the Guardians filled in where there was space and Sara and Alejandro were left to stand.

"This is Ramin," the Marshal said, "it is because of his message that we have to depart in haste. The best way to inform you, I feel, is to let him give an account of it himself."

All attention focused on Ramin.

"There has been a report of trouble on the eastern bank of the Winterburn River, in the north of Elmdale," the messenger said, "the account was unclear, but it was suggested that a wide area of forest had been destroyed overnight, and the trees removed."

"Do you know who is responsible?" Seaglen asked.

"No, and it unsettles me," Ramin said, "deforestation on that scale should have been noticed, but the event was observed by no one and the report states that no tracks lead away from the forest. It's as if the trees have simply vanished."

"But why?" Astrid asked.

"I will be looking into it," Ramin said, "the attack from Boctor at the Lifthayll Bridge was unsuccessful and King Pala thanks you for that. It is unlikely our enemy will attempt something else in the same location. Therefore, the likely options left for Nimaz are attacks to Elmdale and Attaching."

"We have sent a messenger ahead of ourselves already to relay what we learnt from the dying man on the battlefield," the Marshal continued, "this attack further backs up proof that what he said was accurate. Now, you said you had new information for me."

"We have gathered details on the location of the attack from Nimaz," Seaglen said, "here. Take this to King Pala."

He handed over a bound scroll to the Marshal, who pocketed the document immediately.

"I won't even begin to ask you how you got this information," Garrin said.

"Best if you do not," Seaglen said, "but I don't think we can attempt something like that again."

"Was this everything you discovered?" the Marshal asked.

Seaglen did not answer immediately. Alejandro could tell how hard this was for him to say aloud.

"We saw the Atabra in Ringstone Keep, at the centre of Nimaz," Seaglen began, "that they come from Nimaz is confirmed beyond any doubt now, and the Keep appears to be the base of operations in that region."

He paused.

"There is something else," the Marshal said.

Seaglen did not speak.

"The Atabra are not alone in Ringstone Keep," Shumuti said, "they are working under someone else's orders."

"There is someone else behind them?" the Marshal asked, "who?"

Shumuti glanced at Seaglen, unsure if she should be the one to speak.

"We thought that the vultures were linked to Magic," Seaglen said, "and we were right. Someone who can use it, someone like us, is leading them. I knew him. He once fought by my side, but something evil has happened to him in Nimaz. He gœs by the name of Dagaz, and he is a large threat to us."

Seaglen looked up across the table sadly. "I suppose, Marshal, this means, in the end, you were right to mistrust Magic."

The Marshal sat back, and for a moment, Alejandro saw his hand reach for the hilt of his sword before it dropped to his side. He took a deep breath.

"I thank you for your honesty. This information will be passed on to the King and I know he will need to call on you for this next fight. He suspects that the next assault will be the largest yet, and I know now we will have no hope of prevailing without the skills that you here possess.

"But it is not just you here who the King wishes to command, the entire region of Merrywater must be warned of the forthcoming attack. There have been suspicions for a long while, but now the time has arrived to stir the region. Merrywater must prepare itself for war, and following the ancient agreements set down, aid King Pala in defence of our borders. This is his law. You say this enemy in Nimaz was once like you. This is your chance then to prove your loyalty to Attaching and help us lead the charge against him."

"Prepare for war," Alejandro whispered, so that only Sara heard.

"I have already begun this momentous task," the Marshal said, "and Ramin will continue to travel Merrywater, spreading news and gathering troops. You should remain here for the time being and help prepare Merrywater. Time is short, and you will be of great help establishing a force here in the village. I am putting you forward as the representative for Thayll. You are a natural leader, Seaglen, and the time has come to prove it. You can no longer hide in the shadows."

"I understand the need to motivate Merrywater into a state of readiness," Seaglen said, "but you must understand that we need time to make preparations of our own as well."

"What do you need to do?"

"We need to learn why Dagaz is doing this if we are to defeat him," Seaglen said, "I knew him. He is clever and there will be a reason behind his actions. There is no sense in running blindly in to face him. I have discovered another who has the same talents as us. I intend to recruit them, or if they are against us, then it is our duty to deal with them as well."

"Where?"

"Boctor."

"Boctor! What madness is this? I cannot allow you to travel such a great distance when our three regions stand on the edge of war. Boctor is enemy land, and this is too much of a risk. You dealt with the force at the Lifthayll Bridge well enough as you are. There is no need for this."

"I will not take orders from you on matters you know nothing about." Seaglen's tone suddenly sharpened. "The force at the Lifthayll Bridge held no more than humans. The force that rides from Nimaz will hold, at the very least, the same creatures that attacked Lyria. We would be fortunate indeed from what you have said if Dagaz himself did not choose to ride out with his army. If you wish to win this fight, I suggest you listen to what I say."

"Is that a threat?" the Marshal asked.

"It is the truth, something that you have failed to see. You have no idea what you are up against. How could you? I do not say this to offend, but you are ignorant of Magic, so please don't think this is like any other fight you have trained for. If you treat it like that, Dagaz will destroy you."

Garrin sat back, considering his words.

"How do you know you will return from Boctor?" he asked, "it is a dangerous place as well."

"That is not your concern. There is time to travel there and to return. I only intend the journey to take a few weeks. Now, is there any more business that you must share with us?"

"I told you that Stephan would remain here. That still holds, but he will also be spreading the word about Merrywater with Ramin. We have given ourselves a month to ready ourselves, and I pray that it will be enough. I fear that I have no authority over your actions, Seaglen, but I appeal to you not to venture into Boctor."

"I will consider what you ask," Seaglen said.

The room fell silent as the Garrin wrestled with what to say.

"Then we must go. I wish you luck."

"To you as well," Seaglen answered.

"Seaglen." Garrin stood. "I know how fiercely you have endeavoured to keep your Magic a secret from the outside world. But I fear now that time has passed. Farewell, for now."

For once, Seaglen did not answer. Stephan and Ramin stood up on either side of the Marshal. Seaglen, Astrid, Shumuti and Sara all accompanied them out, and after a moment's hesitation, Alejandro followed as well.

It was a silent farewell outside in the rain, which by now was falling rapidly. Stephan exchanged a brief embrace with Sara, looking once more like he was attempting to convey a message to her, and failing. Then Stephan said goodbye to Astrid and mounted his horse before the Marshal signalled the departure. Their horses' hooves kicked up mud and rainwater as the red and white livery of Attaching faded to grey. The gloominess of the air pressed down on the group huddled by the door until they soundlessly filed back into the warmth of the house.

Walking back through the parlour, Alejandro moved to go to the room that he and Gabriel shared.

"Wait," Seaglen said, "we still have things to discuss."

Obediently, Alejandro fell back and seated himself alongside the others at the table, waiting for Seaglen to speak.

"I had not prepared to share the news about Dagaz today," he said, "but it is done. Even if the King counsels against it, we must journey into Boctor in search of this Magic user, whether they are a friend or fœ to us. We know so little of the motives behind what Dagaz is doing. This is an opportunity to perhaps uncover some reason as to why Nimaz is attacking us and I do not want to be unprepared, marching into this next battle. This individual is the only potential lead we have."

"If this Magic user comes from Boctor, do you think they are allied with Nimaz?" Shumuti asked.

"In Boctor it is never easy to tell," Seaglen said, "but that region has a long history with Nimaz and it intrigues me that there is someone with Magic residing there. There is a chance that whœver is there is connected to Dagaz. Boctor is where Dagaz originally came from."

"You sound as though you have an idea of who we might find there," Gabriel said.

Seaglen did not answer immediately but Alejandro had the impression that there was something he and Gabriel were unaware of. Beside him, Shumuti had linked arms with Aurielle.

"Well, there is one original Guardian we know of who did indeed travel into that region," Seaglen said, "there is every possibility that it might be Aurielle's mother out there."

"One of your group went to live in Boctor?" Gabriel asked.

"After the fighting was over in our time, I settled in Thayll," Seaglen said, "Astrid was in the south of Merry-water, and Annah and Jemina had moved to Attaching, but it was not long before I received a letter from the final surviving member of our group, Lyria. She asked me what I thought about travelling into Boctor now that the fighting was over. I remember telling her blankly that I did not think it was a good idea. Boctor had become a wilderness and there were no safe places there anymore. The land was beyond our skills to repair. I never received a reply in return from her. Now I wish that I had not written so bluntly and asked why she was considering the idea at all. At the time, I must confess I had other things on my mind."

He looked at Shumuti.

"I had just been told I was to become a father, and I was distracted. Not long after that, I detected that someone with Magic had come to Thayll, but it was not Lyria, it was Astrid. She stayed here for a short time before moving to Elmdale but I never heard from Lyria again. I can only assume that she went through with her plan."

"You never found out why she went there, or if she is still alive?" Gabriel asked.

"No," Seaglen said, "but out of all of us, she was always the closest with Dagaz, and I wonder now if she may be linked to this in some way. I never found out the reason why she wanted to travel into Boctor, but this discovery that Dagaz still lives makes me begin to wonder again."

"Aurielle." Sara turned to her. "Wouldn't you want to go to Boctor to find out?"

She regarded them stonily and folded her arms. "I have no interest in going."

"None of us should go," Gabriel said, "the Marshal is right to be worried. If we are needed to fight, then we should be here. We've given an oath. We don't know how long we have before the next battle."

"We need to learn Dagaz's plan," Seaglen said, "if we don't go now, there may not be another chance. I am wary of how powerful he has become in Nimaz. Even in a fight of six of us against one, I am not certain we could defeat him. Dagaz has abilities none of us have encountered before. We must gain every advantage possible before the next encounter. But you are right, Gabriel, you have made a promise to the King, which is why only two of you should go."

"Only two?" Gabriel said.

"I don't like the idea of separating us," Shumuti said.

"Time is pressing, yes," Seaglen said, "but a journey into Boctor and back should take no longer than a couple of weeks. That is more than enough time to be back before spring arrives fully. A smaller group would have easier access into the heart of Boctor and would be less noticeable than all of you going. Also, it means that there will be some left here to fight in the worst scenario that you do not return in time."

"I'll go," Sara said.

Everybody turned to her. Seaglen nodded gently in approval.

"If I go," she said, "the majority of you can all stay here. I'm not as much use to the King as you four are, I can only provide the help of a soldier. If I go, then your force here will be stronger."

"I don't know, Sara," Astrid said.

"It makes sense. You know it dœs."

"Yes," Alejandro said, "but I'll come with you."

"What?"

"You shouldn't go alone," he said, "none of us should. Besides, you wouldn't know how to find who we are looking for. Shumuti and Aurielle are the most experienced at Magic and Gabriel is the strongest fighter. They should stay."

"No." Seaglen shook his head. "I agree that Sara should go and her reasons make sense, but Alejandro should not be the one to accompany her. Both you and Gabriel still have your training to complete. Aurielle, perhaps this is an opportunity you should take up."

Her face remained blank as all attention in the room flickered her way for a moment.

"Aurielle has said she dœs not want to go," Shumuti spoke up quickly, through the silence, "I will go with Sara. We will not be away for long."

"Very well," Seaglen said.

"But if Aurielle reconsiders, I would not be against taking her as well," Shumuti said, "the three of us have proved an effective team before."

Aurielle still did not speak up in agreement.

"The majority of Guardians must remain here," Seaglen said, "in that case, I see no better pairing than Shumuti and Sara."

"We had thought that the Magic in Attaching may be related to an old Guardian," Astrid said, "and instead found Gabriel and Alejandro. True, the last we heard of Lyria was that she had headed into Boctor, but that was many years ago."

"It could still be a relative of hers," Gabriel said, "just as I am to Annah. Aurielle, what if you have a brother or a sister out there?"

"We should not jump to conclusions," Seaglen said.

"Anything is a possibility out there," Shumuti said.

"Aurielle, what about your father? Dœsn't he know anything more?" Gabriel asked.

His words snapped Aurielle out of her silence.

"I have to go," she said, "I'll leave you here to discuss my family, while I have questions of my own to ask."

"Aurielle, wait!" Astrid called to her back, but she was already out of the door.

CHAPTER 14
QUESTIONS

~SARA~

"I'll go after her," Shumuti said, immediately after Aurielle had left, "Sara, would you come with me?"

Sara nodded, unsure what help she would be, and the two of them ran off after Aurielle. They caught up with her halfway down the hill.

"Let me go. I want to speak to my father alone."

"Aurielle," Shumuti said, "we don't know what the truth is to all this. It might not be Lyria or anyone related to her at all who is in Boctor."

"That is what I intend to find out."

"Will you at least let us come with you?"

"Do what you like."

Shumuti waved a hand to Sara, ushering her on, and the two of them followed a step behind Aurielle as she headed into Thayll. She reached a door near the end of the village and finally halted before the entrance to the house, for the first time considering her actions. A second later, she charged on in, bouncing the door wide open against a table on the other side. Sara recognised Seamus from the previous night, and he looked up with evident surprise as they entered. Shumuti took a step after her friend and Sara lingered on the doorstep, before deciding to close the door behind her, deciding it would be best to try and prevent the other villagers from overhearing.

"Aurielle, what is the matter?" Seamus asked.

"Have you lied to me all this time?" she asked.

Sara saw all of the colour drain from his face as he stared up at his daughter. He seemed unable to speak.

"Do you know more about Lyria that you never told me?" Aurielle asked.

Seamus' face contorted into a slight frown. "What are you talking about? Aurielle, what has happened?"

Aurielle paced the room, deciding how to attack next.

"We found out some information," Shumuti said. She fell silent immediately after a glare from Aurielle.

"Do you know what happened to Lyria after she headed into Boctor?" Aurielle shot an accusing glare in Seamus' direction. "Do you know why she went? Tell me the truth."

"I don't know." Seamus' face was still a deathly shade of white. "I've told you everything I knew about her."

Aurielle fumed silently, in front of him, but gradually Sara noticed that she was calming down.

"You promise me?" she asked him.

Seamus closed his eyes and nodded. "I promise."

Aurielle seemed to have run out of questions and accusations. Seamus stared up at her, with a distraught expression on his face. Aurielle turned back to Shumuti and Sara.

"You can leave now," she said, "it's safe. If you don't mind, I'd prefer to be left alone."

"Seamus." Shumuti turned to him. "Can I ask one question? Lyria, before she left, did she ever mention the name, Dagaz?"

"No," Seamus said, in a hollow voice.

"I will ask the questions, Shumuti," Aurielle said, "alone."

Shumuti stared at her, still unwilling to leave. "Come to the house tomorrow."

"I might."

Sara took hold of Shumuti's arm, gesturing that it was probably best to leave. Shumuti nodded, and they left the house, shutting the door firmly behind them. Shumuti took one last look at it before they turned away.

"She'll be all right," Sara said.

Shumuti nodded, but Sara did not believe she was listening.

"Perhaps we should convince Aurielle to go Boctor in my place," Sara said.

"I'll let her decide what she wants to do," Shumuti said.

"Do you think we're likely to find Lyria there?" Sara asked her.

"It is strange that she would have been there for so long with hearing no news from her unless she is indeed allied with Dagaz. I think there is still a lot that we don't know. It seems to me that the best way to learn the truth is to go to Boctor and find out for ourselves. Lyria sounds like the only person with all the answers."

"Everything is speculation until we get to Boctor."

"Yes." Shumuti frowned. "I almost wish, for once, that Seaglen had kept his theories to himself."

"Perhaps you're beginning to understand his reasoning behind keeping some things secret."

Shumuti turned to her with a slight smile, but it was quickly masked by a troubled frown. When they arrived back at the house, they went back inside to find the scene much as they had left it.

"What happened?" Astrid asked immediately.

"Seamus says he knows nothing more. Aurielle is talking to him more now, so he may tell her something extra. He has no notion of why Lyria would have left for Boctor.

He is either oblivious to the whole thing or an excellent liar."

"He was bothered by something though," Sara said, "maybe it is just a painful subject, but I don't know."

"I'd like to talk with this Seamus myself," Astrid said.

"It's probably best to leave it for tonight," Shumuti said, "Aurielle said she might return tomorrow."

Seaglen said nothing from the far end of the room. Perhaps she had assumed correctly, Sara thought, maybe Seaglen did regret his decision to disclose his ideas.

The next day, it took a while, but Aurielle did eventually return to them. She was silent and subdued and not herself at all. She said that she had discovered nothing else from her father. It seemed she had questioned him to the point where he had walked out, so there was no other choice other than to let him be. Shumuti offered Aurielle the option of going to Boctor to get answers again, but Aurielle was still reluctant to agree.

"I don't know if I'm ready to see Lyria, if it's her," Aurielle said to Sara and Shumuti as they sat in the garden together, "I think over the years I had come to the conclusion that she had died, so to learn that there is somebody with Magic out in Boctor dug up those old feelings for me again. But whatever the reasons, she left me, walked out. Why should I give her my time now? Why should I search for her?"

"But you want to know what happened," Shumuti said, "this is the only way."

"I don't think I would be in a good state to deal with meeting whœver is out there," Aurielle said, "I know you might not be able to understand it, Shumuti, but I do not want to go. I'd prefer to send you two to investigate for me. That way, when I do eventually meet whœver you bring back, I might be ready for it."

"We'll find out all that we can," Sara said.

Aurielle smiled at her.

"In that case," Shumuti said, "if you're truly certain you want to remain here, I want you to take my place in front of the King while I'm away. Act as our leader and make the decisions while we're away."

"Shumuti." Aurielle looked taken off-guard. "Are you sure?"

"Plus," Shumuti added, "it means that you can't spend your time over-thinking this situation too much. You need to prepare the others for the fight in Elmdale."

"I will. You can rely on me."

"I know. I'll miss you while we're away, though."

"I will miss both of you as well."

Gradually over the day, more and more people made their way outside to join their small group. Finally, with the arrival of Seaglen, everybody found themselves sat in the sun and the talk slowly turned back to the trip into Boctor.

"Whereabouts in the region do we go to find them?" Sara asked.

"When I detected Magic in Boctor it was to the south," Seaglen said, "far down to the south and west in Boctor. I am sorry I cannot be more precise, but I think the inhabited areas are few down there. With luck, you should be able to pick up on a trail."

"Then that's where we will go," Shumuti said.

"Just one more thing," Gabriel said, "I know we weren't planning to follow the King's orders, but isn't he expecting to see a leader for our group?"

"I have passed that duty over to Aurielle, for the time being," Shumuti said.

"As long as you're sure," Aurielle said.

"Absolutely." Shumuti gave her a broad smile. "Who else?"

Sara saw Gabriel glance at Alejandro, and they both cleared their throats in an unsubtle manner.

"I'm sure though that the need for it will hardly arise," Shumuti said.

"When should we go?" Sara asked.

"Soon," Seaglen said, "in the next few days. Meanwhile, the rest of us have the task of getting Thayll ready."

CHAPTER 15
A VISIT TO THE FORGE

~GABRIEL~

Over the past few days, the whole of Merrywater had suddenly become ablaze in activity. The day after the Marshal and his company rode to Attaching, Stephan and the messenger, Ramin, were also seen to speed out of Thayll faster than the northern wind. Numerous collections of riders flurried back and forth across the plains, and talk of war had exploded underneath a cooking pot that had been simmering for months.

As for Thayll, Ramin had done his job well. Apart from a few panic-stricken residents, the whole village leapt into action as though they had known all along what was going to happen. In all honesty, Gabriel thought he should have realised. From what Erdic, the blacksmith, had shown Alejandro and himself of his hoarded collection of weapons, it seemed reasonable that the rest of the village had been thinking along similar lines.

Seaglen had no real need of encouraging Thayll into action because they had taken the hint as soon as Ramin had arrived. What needed more of his attention proved to be the venture into Boctor. It had been agreed that Shumuti and Sara should enter by the Lifthayll Bridge. Seaglen had a plan to temporarily reconstruct the crossing to allow easy access into Boctor and back, and provided that all plans were set in place, Shumuti and Sara were due to set off in two days.

Alejandro and Gabriel broke away from the hasty preparations of the house one afternoon to travel down to the village. Erdic had requested their help with preparing a new order of armour down at the forge. It had initially been agreed that the pair of them only worked there until they had saved enough for their horses, but after the announcement by Ramin, the blacksmith's workload had almost doubled, and Erdic needed every spare pair of hands he could get.

They arrived at the fiery furnace to discover a flurry of comings and goings. Alejandro and Gabriel spotted Erdic and waited patiently as he drew out a white molten rod of steel from the fire.

"We might as well have stayed at the house," Alejandro muttered to Gabriel, "there's about the same level of activity here as there was there."

"But at least here we can be of more use."

"True."

"Aha! Gabriel, Alejandro!" Erdic's voice boomed out as he strode over to them, causing a few of the other workers to look up in alarm.

"We thought it best to let you finish before we spoke up," Gabriel said.

"Bah! Nonsense. I would not let a small interruption distract my attention from the fire. I could work just as effectively with a battle raging behind me. Speaking of which, both of you, I see your sword belts are scuffed and there is a rip on your scabbard Gabriel. The two of you have been in combat since we last met."

"You are extraordinarily perceptive." Gabriel grimaced, covering the tear with the palm of his hand.

Alejandro half-smiled, stepping forward beside him. "We were only practising for what might be to come."

Erdic nodded his head slowly, his gaze fixed unwaveringly on Alejandro. Then he let the matter slide.

"Well, I have need of your help here."

He beckoned them further in and turned, ushering them further into the forge. The duration of the afternoon was consumed by heat and fire. In other words, Gabriel was in his element. Countless shards of metal were moved under his fingertips as the team of twenty strong men and women bent and shaped the King's finest metal into armour for his fighters, and for theirs.

The news was spreading around Thayll that a war meeting for the whole of Merrywater was to be held in the village. Seaglen and Erdic were to be at its head, but Ramin and Stephan were also to be present, with the possibility of more messengers from Attaching. Much to the disgruntlement of the bartender, the inn was the chosen location for the gathering, and the entire the village was requested to be present. The council was to be held just over a week from now, and there was much preparation to be done before then.

Alejandro and Gabriel left the forge as dusk fell. They waved farewell to a cheerful and contented Erdic, before beginning the rush up the hill slope back to what had now become home. Auriello and Astrid were there to greet them by the door and together the four of them strolled inside, Alejandro nursing a blister he had discovered running down the side of his left thumb.

"Hmm," Shumuti commented as she saw them, "you smell singed."

"Good," Seaglen said when they entered, "you're back."

"Has anything happened?" Gabriel asked.

"Sara and Shumuti are fully prepared."

He looked across the table. The two of them were now sitting at the far end, with a pair of saddlebags clustered behind them.

"Which means," Seaglen continued, "that they will be unable to attend the council meeting in the village."

"When will you go?" Alejandro asked.

"Tomorrow," Shumuti replied.

"So soon?"

"This is turning into an urgent matter, Alejandro," Seaglen said, "we must make the best use of all the time that we have left. Now, if there are no other matters to discuss, we should be able to enjoy our final evening together."

Seaglen even went as far as to bring out a few dusty bottles of wine from a shelf, and everybody began talking. Shumuti and Sara checked their belongings for a final time and pushed them up to the side of the wall. Alejandro went over to them, and Gabriel found himself next to Aurielle.

"Just the sight of that bottle makes me feel a little sick," Aurielle muttered to him.

Gabriel chuckled in amusement as he remembered the night out in the village.

"Still?"

Aurielle wrinkled her nose.

"It was a good night, though, wasn't it?"

"You're right," Aurielle answered with a touch of surprise, "in the end, it was."

"I forgot to ask," Aurielle asked a few seconds later, "what did that girl from Thayll ask you at the end of the night?"

"Oh, she just wondered if I'd like to meet her in the village," Gabriel answered.

"You didn't want to take her up on it?"

"There are other people I'd rather spend my time with."

Aurielle's teasing grin reshaped itself into a genuine smile, and she glanced away.

"Unless they're busy with soldiers from the Citadel, of course," Gabriel added.

"I prefer the company of ex-soldiers from the Citadel."

Gabriel opened his mouth in slightly in surprise, glad that Aurielle was still facing away and thought back to the end of the night in the inn, when the two of them had met up again and had a great time, getting on better than ever before. So much so that they had not returned to the house until the first rays of dawn lit up the horizon. In fact, Gabriel realised, the two of them had continued to get on well ever since.

Across the table from them, Seaglen suddenly got to his feet.

"I think now is the time to hand over the gifts I have prepared for you," he said.

Gabriel glanced at Shumuti to see if she knew what he was talking about, but she looked just as confused as the rest of them. Seaglen left the room for a second and came back with a bundle in his arms that clanged as he set it down on the table.

He unwrapped the cloth to reveal that the parcel contained five freshly wrought swords, nestled inside the sheaths that would contain them. The hilts were wrapped in new leather and Gabriel noticed that set into the cross guard of each was the same runestone that they had pulled from Wyn's pouch in Lyria. He recognised the signature of Erdic's work in these blades immediately.

Shumuti picked up the sword embellished with the runestone she drew and unsheathed it, gasping slightly at the quality of the weapon. The others reached forward and searched for the symbols that they had each selected, to identify their sword. Gabriel examined the sheath of his first. It was dark brown and decorated on both sides by a line of different symbols burnt into the leather. Ever so slowly, he slid the cross guard away from the scabbard and revealed the metal underneath. The blade emerged effortlessly from inside, its edges gleaming keenly in the firelight as Gabriel drew it.

"They're beautiful," Shumuti said, "thank you."

"There is also a sixth for whœver you find in Boctor," Seaglen added, "just in case they are a friend. You should take it with you."

Gabriel noted the final, untouched blade on the table. The cross guard on this one remained unembellished, but it was no less stunning in its craftsmanship.

The remainder of the evening was lost in words. What they talked about was meaningless, and they would forget it all by the next morning. But Gabriel found that that was the beauty of it. Their conversations not once brought up the subject of war, or Nimaz, or Dagaz, topics that had been mentioned almost constantly during the last few days. Aurielle almost seemed like her old self again, back to how she had been before the discussion about Lyria. Gabriel was happy that she seemed more content and resolved to do everything he could to keep it that way.

However, the mood on the final morning felt like a pale comparison to the evening before. Not a single person broke into a smile or hardly spoke a word all morning. Out of all of them, Shumuti seemed the least affected, so Gabriel sought out her company, and together they walked up to the cliffs to get away from the doleful atmosphere of the house.

"You realise that there's a chance we may not return before Dagaz sends out another assault, don't you?" Shumuti said as they looked out.

"Yes," he replied, "I am afraid of that. The timing of this worries me. You must make sure that you hurry back."

"I only intend to be away for a couple of weeks," Shumuti said.

"We will deal with whatever comes until then," Gabriel said.

"Aurielle may take our departure hard," Shumuti said, "even if she dœsn't show it. Alejandro too, he's grown fond of Sara, and I know he wanted to come with us. I'm not saying you don't care, but you're strong, Gabriel. I need you to be ready to help them if it's needed."

"I'll do my best," Gabriel said, "Alejandro is easy, I can distract him with working at the forge, but I'll have to figure out how to cheer Aurielle up."

"I think you already have. I saw the two of you last night." The corner of Shumuti's mouth twitched. "Did something happen at the inn?"

"No. We just had a good night."

"That's good."

"You know, I'm glad to have met you, Shumuti. I'm grateful the three of you came to find me on top of that volcano."

"Me too. Both you and Alejandro, we all make a good team."

"You have no judgements on anybody. You know and understand the character of people. For the first time in my life, I would follow someone because I want to, not because someone else appointed them."

"Funny. I always thought that you would have made a better leader than me. You are good at making decisions."

"But they're not always the right ones, and I don't know my team as you do."

Shumuti looked at him appreciatively.

"Well, perhaps then we don't need a leader at all," she said quietly, "we are a team, and the only way we can hope to succeed is by complimenting each other and working together. That way, our strength is greater than any force Dagaz commands from his army because we choose to fight for what we believe in. None of us leads anyone else, we do it together."

"Maybe you are right."

Shumuti took a step away from the cliff side.

"Come on, I think it's time I left."

Back at the house, Shumuti and Sara walked out of the stables leading Fynne and Arrow beside them. Then all seven of them mounted their horses and rode out from the house. Once they were down the track, the party thundered around the back of the cliffs, travelling along the path that they had ridden before the battle, across shallow streams that embroidered the plains towards the Lifthayll Bridge. Fountains of water splashed up as their horses kicked the ground with their hooves, and they reached the last slope before the river after only a few days' travel.

Seaglen and Astrid, who were at the head, slowed as they ascended the embankment and walked the horses towards the edge of the bridge. As they gladly started to feed on the grass surrounding the area, the seven turned to face each other, reluctant to begin the final farewell.

Astrid broke the statues that they had all become. She went over to Sara and spoke a few words to her. Gabriel heard Sara laugh, and the two of them embraced. Alejandro and Gabriel moved forward to give their goodbyes before standing to one side. Then Aurielle walked forward and said something to both of them, spending an extra amount of time with Shumuti. Finally, Seaglen strode up to them both and placed one hand on each of their shoulders.

"Good luck in Boctor. I wish you all the speed in your journey to return to us as soon as you can."

"Hurry home," Astrid said.

"Good luck to all of you here as well," Shumuti said.

Alejandro and Astrid stepped up all the way to the Merrywater side of the broken bridge. Alejandro crouched down and laid two hands on the jutting outcrop of rock but Astrid remained standing. A second later, Alejandro's back tensed up and Gabriel heard a shift in the ground and a grinding of stone on stone. He caught his balance slightly from the reverberations around his feet and watched in wonder, as the ruined section of the Lifthayll Bridge appeared to rise again in front of his eyes.

The design of the bridge was constructed from a series of arches that linked their way above the surface of the water to the other side. The arch that Astrid had destroyed during the battle now began to rise back up from the river, propelled upward by two new pillars. He saw cracks and missing pieces where parts of the crumbling structure had been washed away downstream or eroded and reshaped by the current. Enough of the bridge remained though to form a new crossing and Gabriel watched as the stone reshaped itself slightly to reinforce and extend its foundations beneath the water's surface.

Alejandro lifted his slightly shaking hands away from the rock and accepted Astrid's hand to get back up onto his feet. Shumuti and Sara led their horses over the new bridge and onto Boctor soil at the other side. As soon as they were safely over, Astrid and Alejandro walked forward onto the bridge after them again.

Astrid removed a woollen glove from her right hand and as if they were painting with their fingers, the two of them started to trace lines on the stone at certain sections and points of weakness in the stone. As they worked, a lattice of green thinly sketched streaks overlaid the stone for a few seconds, before the intricate pattern of light flared green and the forms of Shumuti and Sara were lost in the shimmer that followed. The network of lines flashed and diminished, before vanishing entirely, but Gabriel could still sense the inert Magic running through the entire bridge.

"The trap will trigger if anybody attempts to cross," Astrid said, pulling her glove back on as she and Alejandro rejoined them, "and the bridge will collapse once more. Only Shumuti can disperse the Magic and cross this way again."

They turned towards Shumuti and Sara. From the opposite side of the bridge, they each raised a hand in farewell, and the two small figures rode away, gathering speed as they kicked up dust. Seaglen watched them for a while until Sara and Shumuti had vanished out of sight.

"Let's return to Thayll," he said, "we still have work to do."

Their numbers diminished, the group on the Merrywater bank turned silently and left the Lifthayll Bridge for the final time.

Chapter 16
Village Council

~Aurielle~

Training continued as usual after Sara and Shumuti left. Aurielle spent a lot of time helping Astrid, while Alejandro and Gabriel were working with Seaglen. Astrid still held on to her resolve to make use of Seaglen's garden, and he had given up on persuading her otherwise. She was also planting a wide range of herbs to replenish her healing stock.

In and amongst, Aurielle found time to ride and train with her sword, bow and Magic. Aurielle, Gabriel and Alejandro rode out for days at a time to nearby villages, to gather news and, more importantly, to see who was coming to Thayll for the council. As they spread the word and gathered more people, they realised the strength of the crowd that would be travelling into Thayll and wondered if the small village would be able to accommodate everybody.

"Where can they all possibly stay?" Alejandro raised the same question as they rode back to the house one evening, two days before the council date.

"It depends how long the meeting lasts as to the numbers who will have to stay overnight," Aurielle said, "but I wonder if the inn is big enough to host it at all."

The truth was that it was not, so the arranged meeting place became an open field on the outskirts of the village. Every chair and bench from each house had been taken to provide for the multitude beginning to arrive. Grumbling incoherently as he paced around the bare parlour, Seaglen commented once more on the lack of seating before heading upstairs.

Alejandro, Gabriel and Aurielle were sitting on the table.

"How long?" Aurielle asked, for the fifteenth time.

"Still an hour to go," Alejandro replied.

She sighed and slid down off the table, walking over to the window that overlooked the village down below. Ribbons of travellers were winding their way towards the fields from every direction. The three of them had been ready for hours now. Seaglen had disappeared to change, as he was to be one of the heads at this council. Astrid was also finishing getting ready.

Finally, with half an hour left to go, the two of them appeared. Aurielle, Gabriel and Alejandro took in their appearances silently. They had never seen either one looking as neat and well-dressed as they did today. Seaglen wore a shirt and black leather jerkin, covered by a long coat of light brown, embroidered at the seams with contrasting blue thread and split up the back for riding. His longsword hung from a belt across his chest. Astrid was dressed in a black and silver embroidered dress covered by a navy blue coat, but she too wore a sword at her hip.

The three of them looked scruffy in comparison, dressed merely in their training leather sleeveless coats, shirts and trousers, embellished by their swords and cloaks that admittedly, had been freshly cleaned yesterday.

"You both look amazing," Aurielle said, "I've never seen you so smart."

"Time to go, I think," Seaglen said, with a nod of acknowledgement.

Alejandro and Gabriel jumped up eagerly and led the way as the five of them exited the house and collected the horses from the stables. The ride down to the fields was quick, and they made an impression with their entrance. Seaglen and Astrid rode together, followed by the three others riding proudly and straight over to a picketing post for the horses.

They strode back across to the front of the field, where a crowd of people had gathered. Erdic was also there and gave Alejandro and Gabriel a nod. Stephan and Ramin were also present, alongside several others who Aurielle had never met, but who were dressed to a similar level of smartness as Seaglen and Astrid. Though truthfully, their glamour had become a little diminished by the dirt and dust of travelling on the road.

"Seaglen." Erdic met them warmly and clasped Seaglen's hand. "May I introduce you to the five who were selected to journey from the surrounding villages of Merrywater to represent each of their communities."

The cluster of individuals moved forward, each eyeing Seaglen with curious scrutiny. They all seemed of a similar age to Seaglen and similarly respected in each of their villages. Erdic introduced them each in turn; Beernard, Elias, Evaine, Drystan and Brayden.

"It is good to have met you all, and I am glad that all of you have come," Seaglen said.

Aurielle examined each of the five faces in turn. The man introduced as Elias had an open and honest expression, whereas Drystan and Brayden were glowering steadily at Seaglen under their eyebrows. Evaine stood regarding Seaglen coolly, with her arms folded. There could be trouble here, Aurielle thought warily, with too many heads of the villages in one place. Beernard switched his gaze to her as she passed over him.

"And who are these?" he asked, indicating Aurielle, Gabriel and Alejandro.

"They are my students," Seaglen answered.

"You are a teacher?" Beernard asked.

"To these, yes."

"Seaglen is the finest teacher you could ask for," Aurielle said.

"I see they are loyal to you." Beernard nodded.

"Others may be harder to impress," Aurielle heard Drystan mutter under his breath.

The three of them simultaneously glared at him.

"Aurielle! Gabriel!" Stephan was calling from a little way across the field. Speedily, they detached themselves from the tense atmosphere and strolled over to meet Sara's old friend.

"Thank you," Gabriel said as they met.

Stephan looked back to the group they had just left. "Oh, I see. Those five have been selected as candidates for the position of the Commander for Merrywater, and they've just heard that they're up against Seaglen now too. We heard the same, endless arguments when we were travelling, Ramin and I. There is no figure of authority in Merrywater, so everybody wants to make sure their village is the one that gets the pride of leading the region, but what we all need is the one who is going to do the most good."

"We need Seaglen then," Aurielle said.

"Unless somebody else proves to be better suited," Stephan said.

Aurielle held her tongue.

"Where is Sara?" Stephan asked, after a moment, "is she all right?"

"Oh, she's fine," Aurielle answered.

"Sara and Shumuti are away on a task," Alejandro said.

"She's gone?"

"She didn't tell you?" Alejandro asked.

"No," Stephan replied in a ruffled tone.

"We don't think they'll be away long," Aurielle said, "maybe another week or so."

"It's a shame that the two of them are missing this though," Gabriel said, "I'll bet this is one of the most memorable events in the history of Merrywater."

"Possibly in the history of Meteorath," Aurielle said.

They admired the arranged seating on the large, open field. Almost every seat was taken, and the grass had become invisible beneath a swathe of bodies. The villagers of Thayll had set out the eclectic array of furniture in a large, concentric semicircle that morning. A rectangular raised podium had been erected in the centre like a stage, and eight chairs were positioned on top, in a line facing outwards. As Aurielle gazed around, she noted on the back of the podium, three raised flags bearing the devices of Merrywater, Elmdale and Attaching; a horse on swirling water, a deer cantering through a pine forest and a wolf twisted in flames and smoke. The banners fluttered and tangled as the breeze shifted direction.

"Have you got any more news for us from Attaching, Stephan?" Aurielle turned away.

"Yes, but you'll have to wait until I announce it formally to the crowd."

"Speaking of which," Gabriel said, "isn't it time to begin yet?"

"Five minutes or so," Stephan said.

"We'd better get some seats," Alejandro said.

"Don't worry. Yours are reserved."

Stephan led them to the front row beneath the podium, which had been left clear. Aurielle recognised a selection of chairs taken from Seaglen's house, and the four of them claimed them. They were perfectly positioned with the best view in the whole field.

The four talked together, exchanging news for a few more minutes when Aurielle noticed that Seaglen and the other five were moving towards the raised platform. Astrid left the group after sharing a brief word with Seaglen and rejoined them, taking her seat next to Aurielle.

"I am to represent Elmdale," she said to them, "as a witness to what happens here. Ramin is the same for Attaching."

"Is Seaglen all right?" Aurielle asked.

"He dœsn't cope well with formality." Astrid grimaced. "But I think he's the person we need here the most. Let's hope the rest of Merrywater thinks the same."

Aurielle was about to answer when three sharp horn blasts rang out from a herald. He lowered his horn and strode down from the stage. Figures occupied the six chairs, and silence crept through the field, laced with anticipation. Gabriel stirred in his seat. Looking to the left and the right, Aurielle saw groups of people who failed to claim a chair, forced to choose between standing or sitting on their horses. The entire field was awash with people. Then her attention was brought back to the centre as Ramin, the messenger from Attaching, paced forward to the front of the stage.

"People of Merrywater!" he cried, projecting his voice forward, "today you have come of your own free will to hear decisions that could change the future of your region!"

The crowd cheered in anticipation and approval.

"Six individuals sit before you here." Ramin indicated the stage. "They stand for each area of Merrywater. But today we need to listen and decide which is suited to combine your forces and lead Merrywater, alongside Elmdale and Attaching, to a victory against Nimaz because we are at war!"

"Is it certain? Without a doubt?" someone called in the crowd.

"It is." Seaglen spoke up from the stage.

All eyes turned on him as Seaglen stood up. He shot a confirmatory glance at Ramin, who nodded, before continuing.

"For months now, we have sent scouting parties all around Merrywater, repelling all threats to this region. I have led many myself, and more and more have been needed. The enemies we have fought have come from across the Winterburn River, and they come with the intent to kill villagers and soldiers alike in our three regions. What's more, creatures from Nimaz have been terrorising the skies above our lands for months now."

"Has anyone here seen these creatures of which you speak?" a voice called from the crowd, "it is hard to believe such rumours without proof."

"The King's soldiers have sighted them in Attaching," Ramin answered.

"But has anyone here seen them?"

"I have, and there is another in the crowd here who has fought these creatures," Seaglen said, "they take on a human appearance, but they are also vultures, and we have learnt they call themselves Atabra. You may have seen them as abnormally large birds in the sky."

"I saw!" a voice shouted, "three of my flock were slaughtered, enormous talons tore their necks and I found man-sized claw marks in the trails of blood that were left behind. I would have said it was the work of a devil if I believed in such a thing."

"I've also seen strange shapes in the skies!"

"Well, I haven't!" one man objected.

"Me neither!"

"How could such creatures as these exist?"

"And where is this person who has fought one?"

Seaglen looked down at Aurielle. She shuffled further into her seat under the shouts from the crowd. Should she speak up in front of all these people? All these strangers?

"Aurielle, Seaglen needs your help," Astrid whispered, looking at her with concern.

Aurielle looked back at Seaglen. He was reserved himself, Aurielle had never known him to speak in public like this before. But for the good of Meteorath, he would do it.

"I have fought one of these Atabra," she shouted, a little angrier than she had intended, standing up. Her outburst hushed the rush of conversation. Standing taller than any but those on horseback and the seven on the stage, Aurielle shivered.

"You?"

"You fought this creature and survived?"

"Do you doubt her skill with a sword?" Seaglen frowned. "Challenge her if you wish."

"Seaglen," Elias said slowly, "I remember your name now. You fought in the time of the old King, didn't you? Helped to put an end to it. I heard stories of your bravery on the battlefield. I remember now. You were there."

"So were you," Seaglen said.

"You have fought enemies like this before?" the candidate called Beernard exclaimed, "then you ought to be our Commander. You know what will happen! You have faced Nimaz before!"

"Wait!" Drystan objected, "how could he possibly know what will happen in this war? No two battles are the same. I know, I too have fought as a soldier."

"So have we all here," Evaine said, "but this council is to search for the best leader amongst us."

"I do not claim to know the events that will occur in the fighting that is going to happen," Seaglen said, "all I know is that I have experience not to allow the same mistakes to happen again."

He spoke with a bitterness that reminded Aurielle forcibly of when he had spoken about Dagaz. Slowly, she retook her seat.

"I have heard a rumour." A bearded man on the edge of the field leaned forward from the saddle of his horse. "So I have come to hear if it is the truth. Less than one month ago, there were sounds of a battle at the Lifthayll Bridge. The man who told me this described feeling the earth move even as he stood miles away and the waters of the Winterburn charged downstream like the waves themselves were pushing the enemy back. Now I trust this fellow, but his tale does sound doubtful. What I want to ask is, did a battle happen or not, and has the war already begun?"

"The rumour of battle you have heard is true," Ramin said.

The crowd broke into hushed whispering. The man on the horse watched the stage intently.

"In part at least," Ramin continued, "a large group came through the border from Boctor, armed and determined to cross. A patrol of the King's soldiers was there to meet them, suspecting that such an attack would come. The invaders from Boctor had come to try and assault Merrywater, but they failed. The King was aware of this attack and sent fighters to protect your borders."

Aurielle glanced around at the crowd to see the villagers either shaking their heads in disbelief or nodding them in approval.

"How long do we have before the real fighting begins?"

Ramin took the centre stage. Seaglen sat back down beside Elias, who immediately held a whispered conversation with him.

"We believe we still have over a month in which we can prepare," Ramin said, "I know that at least in the villages of Thayll and Ashtom, the forges have been preparing gear for war."

"In Arlan too!" a blacksmith called from the crowd.

"Is there enough to arm us all?"

"That is the question," Ramin said, "one of the main ones of this council. You knew I would ask this of you. Will every village pledge soldiers to help our King? If so, we need the number. There will be time for you to consider this. The council will break for one hour. Use it to mull over the question we have asked and come to a decision. The individuals up here stand for each of your villages. If you decide to fight, go and inform them of your choice. We will return in one hour."

A rumble of voices grew as people began to move confined legs and dropped items, such as cloaks, onto their chairs, so nobody else could allege that the seats were theirs. Astrid, Alejandro, Gabriel and Aurielle got up and hastened over towards Seaglen, and he excused himself from talking to Elias and Evaine as he saw their approach.

"I must say thank you to you, Aurielle," Seaglen said, "for speaking up like that. I am sorry for putting you on the spot."

"It's all right. I'm glad I could help."

"Elias seems to side with you," Astrid said.

"He knew King Pala's father, Eric, well."

"He did?" Astrid said, "I should go talk to him."

"Excuse me." A group of five approached Seaglen tentatively. "We would like to put ourselves forward to fight for Thayll."

Seaglen produced a small book and handed it to the one who had spoken.

"Thank you. I hope you have considered your choice carefully. If you are certain, please write your names down here."

A line was forming steadily behind the first five. Aurielle motioned to Gabriel and Alejandro, and they left Seaglen to concentrate, seeking out Stephan instead from amongst the crowd, who was standing beside what looked like a new horse. Alejandro and Gabriel walked forward, but Aurielle hung back, deciding instead to wander and see if she could learn the general mood around the council field. Seaglen and the other five soon became invisible in the circle of applicants that had gathered around each village representative. Aurielle turned and carried on walking until she came across somebody who blocked her path.

"Sorry," the girl said, "but are you the one who stood up saying you had fought one of these creatures?"

"Yes," Aurielle answered slowly, "I did."

The girl's wide eyes peeked out keenly from beneath the brim of a feathered hat, widening with wonder. "How did you do it?"

"Well, I fought him with my sword. To be honest, I caught him by surprise."

"But how did you get the chance to face the creature in the first place?"

This girl was asking too many questions.

"We were on an errand for Seaglen and were attacked in the wild."

"You mean you didn't go looking for an Atabra?"

"No. Why would I?"

Gabriel suddenly breached their strange conversation.

"Aurielle, I've been looking for you!" he said, "Alejandro said to tell you that...wait, Tina?"

"I remember you!" the girl said, "at the spring market I sold you and your friend two horses."

"So you both know each other?" Aurielle asked.

"We've met," Gabriel answered.

"My name's Aurielle."

"Well, it sounds like you need to go. I won't keep you anymore, but I'd like to talk again if you have any free time. I have to go and find your father to enlist."

"He's not my..." Aurielle let her words fade as Tina waved and vanished into the crowd of villagers.

"What had she been saying to you?" Gabriel asked, "you seem bewildered."

"She was asking me lots of questions about my fight with the Atabra."

"When I met her before at the market with Alejandro, she talked a lot about fighting. She told me she was going to defend Merrywater and nothing could stop her going to war. I think her family have different ideas, though. Maybe she wants to be like you, Aurielle."

"Like me?" Aurielle asked in surprise.

"Why is that so hard to believe? Come on, we need to grab our seats again."

Three more notes signalled the return of the meeting. They found their places once more and waited in expectation for Ramin to begin speaking.

"We have nearly finished," he began, "I thank you all for your contribution here today. All that remains is the final decision and one concluding revelation of information, news from events in the north.

"Every village has offered fighters for combat. I shall send the news to the King, and it will ease his heart to know that there is support here in Merrywater. We are grateful. But there is still one more thing left for you to do. You must decide who is to lead your region. Some upon this stage you will know more than others, and knowledge of their character may influence your decision. After me, they shall each speak as to why they are fit to lead. Judge simply on who you feel will do the most good for your region."

Each of the six village representatives then stood and spoke a piece about why they believed they could lead Merrywater. Seaglen said little, saying that he felt he had already said most of what he had wanted to earlier. Elias then stood and, much to everyone's surprise, made no case for himself but urged the villagers to see that Seaglen was the one they should choose. Once he sat back down, a quiet chatter sprung out in the crowd as everybody decided where to cast their vote. All fell quiet once again as Ramin stood and raised his arms.

Starting at the left end, Ramin announced each name in turn. For Elias, a few stood but not a significant number. For Evaine, a few more. Then Drystan. More stood and Aurielle craned her neck to see as almost a third looked to be on their feet. Next Ramin announced Seaglen's name. Aurielle glanced furtively around after standing herself and examining who stood with her. A considerable amount, but was it more than those who had voted for Drystan? Aurielle could not see far back enough to know if it was more. Only then, the unthinkable happened, Elias, Beernard and Evaine stood up as well, and with them, a good proportion more of the field. A slight gasp ran through the crowd, and even Seaglen's face bore an expression similar to astonishment.

Ramin stood gaping for a moment before slowly gathering himself and dutifully announced the remaining names of Beernard and Brayden. But there was nobody left to stand. Seaglen had won.

Ramin's voice rang out clearly across the field. "Seaglen is your new Commander."

A roar of approval rose out of the crowd, with applause mixed in with the cheering. Aurielle grinned and let out a loud whistle, amongst the sound of Gabriel, Alejandro and Astrid crying out. Then her eyes focused on Drystan and watched in trepidation as he approached Seaglen. As Drystan met him, she saw Seaglen become slightly rigid, but Aurielle's fears came to nothing as Drystan took Seaglen's hand and clasped it respectfully.

That evening saw them celebrating. It was more an excuse for the villagers to have a party and to forge relationships than for Seaglen's benefit, as he was not interested in residing in the limelight. It did not prevent the rest of them remaining on the council field though, and the gathering continued long after dark had fallen.

Old friends from across Merrywater were reunited here, who had not seen each other in years. Aurielle and the others met countless new faces and heard stories of brave exploits from the past, though they were unsure how much of the information could be trusted as the truth. The council field had transformed into a village of tents, as nobody wished to begin the journey home so late on. The inn was also full, but between the village and the camp, everybody was provided with lodgings for the night. Even at Seaglen's house, he had agreed to let Stephan, Elias and Evaine stay the night.

It was with difficulty that they crawled back up the hill to the house. All who were present staggered through the front door, carrying one of Seaglen's chairs, unable to properly see where they were going. It had not occurred to anyone so late on in the night that a more straightforward solution would have been to leave the furniture in the field until morning, but Seaglen had also been adamant that he wanted to sit on a chair once he returned to his home.

Astrid came into the darkened parlour at the sound of the clamour they were making trying to get the chairs back in their correct rooms in the house. It was at this point that Aurielle realised how tired she was as she and

Gabriel wrestled with one chair, him inside the room and her outside, until Astrid pointed out that the arm was caught on the latch of the door. Under her guidance, everything was swiftly sorted out, and the seats returned to their rightful places. By this time, Elias and Evaine had appeared at the door frame and were watching curiously on.

"Sleep," Seaglen announced wearily, "now. Go."

Obediently, Gabriel, Aurielle, Alejandro and Stephan stumbled into Shumuti's room and just remembered to grab a cover each before dropping into a night of instant deep rest.

Chapter 17
Into the West

~Shumuti~

It felt strange to Shumuti to be travelling again on horseback. The last time she had done so was all those months ago when she had brought Sara and Astrid home from the Elmdale Forest. Shumuti remembered the thought fondly and was about to mention it to Sara when she spoke herself.

"How long do you think the journey will take?" she asked.

"To cross to the west of the region, I am hoping no more than a week," Shumuti answered.

"Have you ever been so far into Boctor before?"

"No. But I know a little of what to expect here. It will be very different from Merrywater and Elmdale, and even to what we experienced when we met Xeylia. That was only the border of this region."

"Do you think Xeylia would have been able to tell us anything useful?"

"If time was not an issue I would like to ride north to see her. But for this trip, I think we should focus on the Magic user in the south."

"We know a direction to travel in, but it could still take a while to find the Magic user once we get there, if we find them at all."

"I have been trying to practise Seaglen's technique of detecting Magic." Shumuti sighed. "But it's difficult for me. At the moment, we would have to be very close for me to notice them, but I'm going to keep trying to get better as we travel."

"I hope we can learn something useful while we are here," Sara said.

"So do I. We have to understand what happened to Dagaz and why he is attacking us."

She thought back to home and the conversation she had had with Seaglen the night before they had left. For once, he had not seemed his usual, confident self and Shumuti knew something had been bothering him.

"All my life, I made it my priority to keep Magic a secret," he had said to her, "I believed that if too many people knew of its existence, it would not be long before someone took the opportunity to use that power for their own gain and create destruction in the process. In the end, I was wrong. As it turned out, it was misused by someone who already knew all about the risks and chose to ignore them anyway."

"It's not your fault," Shumuti had tried to tell him.

"Is it not? I was the leader of the original Guardians of Magic. Dagaz was my responsibility, to understand him and prevent something like this from happening."

"You couldn't have predicted something like this."

"If I knew him better, perhaps I could have."

"He betrayed you, not the other way around. You thought he was dead."

"Yet another thing I was wrong about."

"What happened is in the past. Look at what you have achieved since, with me and Aurielle, Gabriel and Alejandro, even Sara. You taught me everything I know and now it's our turn to use that to help you. We will bring down Dagaz together, you and me."

"Shumuti, my proudest achievement in life has been to have you for a daughter."

Shumuti had never seen her father show much vulnerability before. It had felt strange to be the one offering encouragement to him, now that the world that Seaglen had known for so long was slowly beginning to change.

*

They lit a fire on the first evening of the riding, managing to gather together enough twigs and scrub to last a few hours, and Shumuti brought out the tattered scroll that served as their map for the journey. The parchment was faded and unsettlingly blank because nobody had travelled into Boctor from Merrywater for so long and even Seaglen, who it belonged to, was dubious about the accuracy of the few features listed on it. Their only sliver of comfort he had given them was that the mountains and shorelines could not have shifted a large amount of distance.

"So?" Sara asked, as she watched Shumuti ponder over the sparse map.

"We may be in luck," Shumuti said, "the path that is marked here running from the bridge is what we have been following, and so far, it seems to be accurate. As long as we follow the river and then the curve of the coast, we can't get too far lost. If we keep going, eventually we should reach one of the outer villages marked in the area Seaglen thought we should search. As good a spot to start at as any, I think."

"But what if whœver we are searching for is not in the west?"

"Then we will have to pick up a trail there until we run out of clues, or time. If we have to go northwest to search then we will, but first I think it is a good idea to explore the southern area of the region. The village that we are heading to is the closest from the Lifthayll Bridge. Lyria may, at the very least, have passed through it, if she didn't stay there."

Sara nodded.

Satisfied, Shumuti released the map and let it spring back into a coil.

"We should give ourselves two weeks maximum regardless," she said, "if we cannot find who we are looking for in time, I aim to be back in Merrywater anyway. I couldn't bear it if something happened to any of them and I wasn't there to help."

"Agreed."

Shumuti turned to her saddlebags that she had taken off Fynne and rummaged around in the closest one.

"I think we should put these on now," she said, pulling out a large bundle of tattered clothes. They had packed a disguise each to wear once they were close to the heart of Boctor. Their cloaks had served as a covering against any travellers that they had met on the road today but Shumuti was beginning to feel exposed in the foreign-looking armour she usually felt so comfortable wearing in Merrywater.

Shumuti threw Sara her outfit and pulled on her own over the top of her shirt, severing a link to home, and bundled her cloak delicately inside the saddlebags. Straightening the baggy covering she now wore, Shumuti stood up and slid a tattered, dark grey waistcoat over the top. Finally, she attached her sword belt diagonally across her body and picked up the scarves that they were both going to use as protection from the wind and sand, handing one to Sara.

"Well?" Shumuti asked, hopefully, once her transformation was complete.

"We still look pretty fresh for travellers," Sara said, "but I'm sure if we give it a few days that will change."

"Mud."

"What?"

"Mud," Shumuti repeated, "we have stayed at home for far too long. Dirt was covering the travellers we passed today from head to toe."

"I've only just got used to being clean," Sara muttered.

"Well maybe with less conspicuous faces we might be able to blend in better."

"Shall we do this now?"

Shumuti stopped. "Perhaps when we get closer to the village..."

Sara grinned.

Sleeping on the ground that night added a little grime to their faces. They rose early the next day, keen to press on. Shumuti and Sara both pulled up the scarves to half cover their faces from the wind that was already beginning to blow sand in their direction, so soon only each other's eyes were all that remained visible.

The desert plains that spread to the horizon before them were devoid of any life, so they rode on more confidently. The landscape here was wilder than the small portion of Boctor they had visited before. Still, it also seemed in better condition, and Shumuti noticed there was a slightly higher abundance of Magic around them than she had remembered from last time. Being further away from Nimaz had sheltered the south of Boctor a touch, but it was hardly alive in the same sense that Merrywater was. The hue of the land here was a mix of light grey and brown, made of shifting colours that shimmered before their eyes in the heat. The continuous sight of it made Shumuti begin to think she saw things in the desert ahead, but once they rode a little closer, it was always nothing but sand.

When they stopped at midday, Sara and Shumuti took out their swords and attempted some practice, and Shumuti was startled at the amount of improvement Sara had undergone. Where Shumuti might have gone easy on her a few months ago, it was now a challenge to hold her own. At this stage, Sara could easily rival Aurielle or herself.

"We've seen no one all day," Sara said, after they had finished.

"Everything about this land is harsh and barren," Shumuti said, her attention wandering little way over to the left, where a horse skull lay half-buried in the sand.

"The towns ought to be more alive."

"I hope so," Sara said.

Their horses tossed their heads in silent agreement.

Shumuti and Sara came across the first village on the third day of travel. A half-buried piece of driftwood in the sand named the town as Cirrus, and on first impression, the settlement did indeed contrast with the arid landscape they had been seeing over the last few days.

"Are those trees?" Sara asked.

"I think so, though not any kind I've seen before."

"And...water?"

Shumuti and Sara rode up to the outskirts of the village, past the chaotic jumble of brightly coloured tents that made up the settlement. They hitched their horses by a cluster of large trees with thick, patterned trunks and overhanging giant green leaves in place of branches. Bunches of a small, red fruit hung from the boughs high up, dangling tantalisingly just out of reach.

The tents were pitched around a central small waterhole, which Shumuti noted that despite the lack of water elsewhere, this single source of it was almost unoccupied. There was an unspoken sense of respect that the water should only be approached when there was a need to. They left the horses in the shade and wandered with interest around the ever-changing settlement, noting that as they had arrived, several of the tents were packing up and leaving, and another group was coming in from the west. Shumuti got the sense that no day was ever the same twice here.

Market stalls littered the forefront of the nomadic settlement, with travellers from presumably all over the region bringing in handcrafted, hunted and foraged wares. Exotic and unusual sights and smells littered the oasis, and Shumuti and Sara had to try very hard not to look too bewildered or fascinated by this complete change of lifestyle to back home. They stocked their bags with a series of unfamiliar supplies, asking a few questions about the road ahead as they went, and gradually made their way towards the pool.

The group that had arrived from the west approached the waterhole to refill their waterskins and Shumuti and Sara diverted their path over near to where they had stopped, taking the opportunity to get new water of their own.

"They've come from the direction we're heading in, haven't they?" Sara said.

Shumuti nodded. "I wonder if they know anything that might be useful."

She hesitantly walked forward to the water's edge and knelt beside one of the group. Underneath a layer of dirt and sand, she could see that he wore a tunic of once brightly coloured, patterned fabric and a series of metal bands decorated the upper arm that reached towards the water.

"Have you travelled in far from the west?" she asked.

"We ride from Newark," he answered, "nobody travels west of there anymore."

"Why is that?" Shumuti asked.

"Have you not heard the whispers from there? I would have thought the stories would have reached Cirrus."

"We have only recently come in ourselves, from the far north," Shumuti said, "we are heading west, but what are these stories?"

"Then I would warn you to turn back the way you came."

"But why? What is out there?"

"They say the villagers fear an omen on the border of Newark. High in the skies, a shadowy mountain range materialises in the clouds and guarantees sure death to all who lay eyes upon it."

"A mountain range in the air?" Sara asked.

A few of his companions leaned in around his side to gather water and interrupted. "Not mountains, it's an island suspended there high in the sky."

"No, it's a huge tower floating among the clouds."

"Fools. There's a shining, silver city up there. I've seen it."

"As you can see, there are conflicting reports." The first traveller's eyes twinkled. "We all share one same belief though, that it is a place to avoid."

"Then we'll be sure to take your advice," Shumuti said, straightening up.

"Beware, that it is a hard road to take."

"Thank you for your aid."

"You are both welcome to share our portion of the camp for this evening if you desire."

"Thank you," Shumuti said again, "but we have no time to rest here. It was nice to meet you."

"Then may your road be rewarding."

Shumuti was not sure how to respond and nodded her head slightly as they departed. They turned back and gathered the horses to set out once more from the oasis.

"You didn't want to stay here?" Sara asked.

"No," Shumuti said, "they seemed friendly, but I don't like the idea of people here discovering that we don't come from Boctor. Very few people from Merrywater would have need to travel here and I don't want the wrong people to become interested in us. Boctor is split between those who support Nimaz and those that don't. Without knowing, we should keep moving on."

"What do you think about this mysterious floating landscape?"

"It is intriguing, and what's more, it fits with the general location we had. All we have to do now is to find this town called Newark and try to gather more information about it there. Let's find out the reason why it is a place to be avoided."

Chapter 18
Elias and Evaine

~Alejandro~

Alejandro woke to the sound of Stephan.

"My head! I think I must have hit it on the way to the floor last night."

"It serves you right for trying to steal the best bed." He heard Gabriel's rebuke.

There was a thud as Stephan hit Gabriel on the arm. Alejandro opened his eyes and sat up. Aurielle was missing from the group and presumably, she had already got up. Taking in the surroundings a little more, Alejandro realised he had never really looked around Shumuti's room before. Maps and drawings covered the walls, from ceiling to floor. Alongside that were jumbled piles of teetering books resting everywhere, including dangerously close beside his head.

"I wonder if Elias and Evaine are still here?" Gabriel asked.

They got up quickly then and headed downstairs to discover there were still five others sitting around the table. Elias was speaking, and the one listening the most intently was Aurielle.

"...right up to the final battle."

"You two fought together?" Aurielle asked.

"We did," Evaine said, "the last time was on that day. We stormed the old ruins together with a large company from Attaching, including the old King."

"I don't remember you being there for that, Seaglen." Elias scratched his head.

"No," Seaglen said, "Astrid and I had business elsewhere."

"Doing what?" Elias asked.

"Clearing up the fight that had taken place to the east," Seaglen said, "far to the east."

"I did not know there had been one," Evaine said.

"It was very brief, of hardly any importance."

From the look in both Seaglen and Astrid's eyes, Alejandro doubted that entirely.

"But I am honoured that you have agreed to help again," Seaglen said.

"What do you mean?" Alejandro asked.

"We," Elias said, "that is, Evaine and myself, have offered to assist Seaglen in his new appointment. It is a demanding position, and we will gladly support him as best we can."

"Erdic has also agreed to help," Seaglen said.

"But how do we know they can be trusted?" Gabriel asked suddenly. The conversation broke off, and Seaglen eyed Gabriel curiously.

"I mean, not to offend, but all five of you were there yesterday to try and gain this position. You saw how insistent Drystan was to be the one chosen. By keeping quiet, you both now have gained yourselves a small section of power by pledging yourselves to support Seaglen."

"What are you suggesting, boy?" Elias asked.

"I'm just wondering what your intentions are," Gabriel answered.

"You know, in my village, speaking against your elder in that manner would not go unpunished," Evaine said.

"However, we are not in your village," Seaglen said, "you must forgive Gabriel his forwardness, but his words are not without sense. It is good to have a cautious voice on your side."

"Fortunately for you, we are of better character than you suggest." Elias looked slightly offended at Gabriel. "Our only wish is to support Seaglen."

"Forgive me," Gabriel said, "I come from the King's court in Lyria. I am used to those who say one thing and mean another."

"Believe me, Gabriel," Seaglen added, "I have considered this for a long while."

Elias waved a hand aside. "No matter. You are wise to apply caution. But we must stay unified if we are going to accomplish something, eh?"

"We must leave soon, Seaglen," Evaine said, "our villagers are restless to return to their homes and families, and it's our job to lead them back."

"Yes." Seaglen nodded. "I understand. If I have an urgent need of you, I shall send one of these three. They ride fast and will not be troubled on the road."

"If we do not see you before then, remember that we shall meet again at the end of this month to finalise plans and ready our forces," Elias said.

Seaglen nodded. All three stood and said their farewells before Elias and Evaine departed the house. Seaglen announced then that he would have to go down to the village and Stephan added that he had to leave too. Gabriel went over to the window to watch them go. With only four left inside, it felt unnaturally quiet.

"The house hasn't been this empty for months," Aurielle remarked.

"Imagine how strange it was when there were only Seaglen and myself," Astrid said.

Gabriel turned towards the table. "Are you sure this is a safe position for Seaglen to be taking?"

"Seaglen needs to unify Merrywater," Astrid said, "he is only making certain that as many people are behind him as possible. He knows what he is doing."

"I know, that's not what I'm worried about. What if people learn that a Magic wielder is leading them?"

"You heard the reaction to the Atabra at the council," Astrid said, "if they did not believe such a thing was real, they would not believe that Seaglen can use Magic."

"Until they see it with their own eyes," Aurielle said.

"I am not sure how a display of fire would have gone down," Astrid said, "to me, it dœs also feel like a precarious decision, but Seaglen is determined not to let Dagaz do harm and being able to command Merrywater puts him a good position to stop him quickly."

"Elias and Evaine have no idea what he can do then?" Alejandro asked.

"None at all," Astrid answered, "just as they had no idea last time."

Seaglen returned later than they expected that night, and seemingly later than he had planned for too.

"Yet more meetings and discussions!" he objected as soon as he came through the door. They looked up in surprise. "It is well that you are well on with your training and you all are skilled because I fear now that my days will be taken up by endless, useless talking."

"Useless?" Astrid asked.

"It is clear what must be done," Seaglen said, "we wait and practise and arm ourselves the best we can until the time comes that we are called out by the King. Now we shall have to endure meetings of countless variations and alternatives that people can think of, a waste of the time that we have left."

"Meetings? When is there another meeting?"

"In three days. In Thayll, a gathering of our village only at the Boar Inn."

"Well, that might prove to be some use."

"I agree, but I only hope that there are fewer after that."

"Yes," Astrid said, "because there's another problem. I've been looking around your wardrobe and that outfit that you wore yesterday is the only entire set of respectable clothes that you own."

Seaglen threw up his hands in mock despair.

"That, my dear sister, is the least of my worries."

Despite his evident frustration, Seaglen's beard twitched into the first smile Alejandro had noted since Shumuti's departure.

CHAPTER 19
THE SEA WIND

~SARA~

"Do you see that building?" Sara asked, squinting into the distance.

"What?" Shumuti asked, shielding her eyes from the sun, "are you sure?"

"No...but it dœs look like a building."

"Check again when we're closer."

They continued riding steadily onwards. Around them was nothing but desert rock and that had been their landscape for days. The heat of the sun here and the reflection from the ground into their eyes burned like blinding fire and the change in climate was a shock to both of them. Sara wondered if this was normal for early springtime in Boctor because compared to the temperature back in Thayll, it felt like the height of summer. She closed her eyes, preparing for the possibility that the grey shimmer on the horizon was sadly nothing more than that, an illusion.

"Sara, is it still there for you?"

She slowly opened one speculative eye and scanned the horizon again.

"I still see it," she said, cracking her lips open to speak.

Shumuti's face broke into a smile, and so did Sara's.

"I think we will reach the town by this time tomorrow."

The desert landscape around them had not altered in days now, so travelling had begun to merge into one continuous cycle of what felt like the same day again and again. A village on the route that they had been searching for, they had not found. It had either been obliterated since the map's creation or they had lost their way from it completely. Now, finally, the landscape had changed, and there was something in the distance that gave them hope.

That evening they heard the sound of something more welcoming than the sight of the building. Somewhere nearby, there was a faint trickle of water from a stream.

"Do you hear that?" Sara asked, no longer feeling as though she could trust her senses not to fool her out here in the desert.

"There, look!" Shumuti pointed. "You can just make it out in the light. It's almost shimmering."

They made camp beside the water about an hour later and drank plenty. That night, Shumuti and Sara lay down quietly under the sight of stars that they had not appreciated for days, grateful for a place to refill their supplies.

"It is a hard life out here," Shumuti said, "it makes you appreciate what you have."

"All my life I was warned to stay away from Boctor," Sara said, "but there is more beauty to the region than I first realised. The desert is so unique."

A movement across the plains caught Sara's eye as a pair of large ears perked up from behind a nearby rock. A small, sandy coloured fox noticed them and froze, before darting back the way it had come to hunt in the cool night air elsewhere. Every creature they had seen out here differed from home, and she assumed had been adapted to survive the desert sands. She wondered whether they ought to be copying the animal and travelling at night instead of during the draining heat of the day.

"You're right," Shumuti said, "beautiful, but also more dangerous. We mustn't let our guard down here. At least now we certainly look like everyone else who is travelling in Boctor. We have the story that should get us inside, and once we are there we can find food. After that, we'll gather information as best we can. All the while, I'll keep alert to see if I can sense any Magic."

"How has your practice been going?" Sara asked.

"Not well," Shumuti answered, "all of us can detect one another when we are nearby, but Seaglen has spent a couple of decades honing that talent. A week of properly trying hasn't really got me anywhere yet."

Sara blinked slowly, realising she was barely listening to what Shumuti was saying. She did not remember the exact moment that she slipped into an exhausted sleep, but she woke the next morning to find Shumuti sitting cross-legged in the sand, facing away from the camp. Her eyes were closed and her face set in concentration, much as she had done every morning since they had arrived in Boctor. Sara noted the darkened circles around her closed eyes. This trip through the desert had taken more of a toll on both of them than they had thought it would. Sara packed down the camp around her as silently as she could and just as they were ready to leave, Shumuti stood up with a sigh, sand falling from her clothes as she stood.

"Any sources of Magic nearby?" Sara asked.

"Nothing," Shumuti replied.

Instead of riding that day, they both walked beside the horses. The journey to the landmark on the horizon they had spotted the previous day took a couple of hours, and they arrived weary but energised by nerves. The grey building they had seen yesterday materialised itself as a tall gatehouse. The windows of the building were shattered and boarded up by wood, while the top was beginning to crumble. As they glanced further up, Sara noted with trepidation that the flag flying above it was not Boctor's, but Nimaz's.

"It dœsn't look particularly inviting," Sara said.

"Well, we can't turn back now."

"Then, after you," Sara said.

Shumuti turned Fynne and walked forward, pushing her scarf back from her head as she went. Sara tailed nervously behind, constantly scanning around for any signs of movement from the broken tower. They passed under its shadow and out the other side unchallenged, but as they crossed in front of the door, Sara saw that it was open and rested solely on one hinge.

"Shumuti, look," she uttered, hardly daring to raise her voice.

Silence drifted from the open door. Sara glanced uncertainly at Shumuti, feeling like they should move on. Gently, Shumuti handed her reins over to Sara and inched forward towards the shadowy entrance. There was a smear on the door frame, something dark in colour that ran down the length of the wooden board, staining the surface as it had dried. Shumuti drew her sword.

"Wait here."

"Are you sure we need to go in?"

"I'll be back soon."

Sara held her tongue as Shumuti vanished around the darkened door frame. As the glint from her sword blade faded, Sara cast another worried eye around her, but there was still no sign of life at all.

Five minutes passed in her routine of keeping watch in each direction until there was a flicker of movement by the doorway and Sara tensed. Shumuti reappeared, pale but otherwise unharmed. Sara breathed out in relief and waited for her to speak.

"Are you all right?" Sara had to ask eventually.

"Sorry." She shook herself. "Yes, I'm all right. But it is a real mess inside there."

"Were there bodies?"

"Not that I could recognise," she replied, "the damage inside has not happened recently. If there were people here, they have been taken away."

"We should move on," Sara said.

Shumuti nodded. "Let's go."

They set off again on the horses and soon left the destroyed gatehouse behind. For a short time, the natural desert landscape was all that rolled by under their horses' hooves. But that changed as they came to the edge of a dry, grass sprinkled embankment. Spread out below them was the first settlement that they had seen since leaving Cirrus. An indefinable smell drifted on the cool breeze, and Shumuti smiled as she caught it.

"What is that?" Sara asked.

"The scent of the sea," Shumuti answered.

"Really? I've never been to the sea."

"You haven't? Then we should go while we're here if we get the chance."

Sara nodded, finding herself feeling a little revitalised.

"Can you detect any Magic?"

"Nothing yet."

Late afternoon came when the pair rode steadily into the village near to the sea. A milestone marker by the road named the settlement as Newark, and Sara felt her heart quicken nervously as ten men blocked the way into the town. These were the first people they had seen in days, and each carried either axes or pikes slung over their shoulders. From the scratches and notches, the weapons appeared as though they were well-used.

"I'll speak," Shumuti whispered.

"Fine by me," Sara said.

"Your business in Newark?"

"We're travellers, come to find an old friend of ours who lives here. We are to bring him back to his family in the north."

"You do know we are at war, don't you? Your preparations to serve Boctor should be more important than family reunions."

"It is because of the war that we were urgently requested to find him."

"Where are you from?"

"Harland," Shumuti replied, quoting a name directly from their map. Sara prayed it was still a relevant one.

"Harland..."

"Will you let us pass?"

"Go on through. I hope to meet you again on the field of battle."

That was an odd thing to say, Sara thought, remarking at what she assumed was a custom and remembering the similar experience with the traveller in Cirrus.

"Er... as do I," Shumuti answered.

The man tilted his head in satisfaction. Quickly, they nodded and continued. Sara heard the voices of the men as they moved away.

"Don't look back," Shumuti whispered.

Once in the centre of Newark, they halted. Sara risked a scan around and found there was nobody in sight. Slightly disturbed, she pointed this out to Shumuti.

"I know," Shumuti murmured, "come on. Let's head further in."

It was a good while until they came across another human. A young woman of a similar age to them appeared out of a side street and Sara felt hopeful she might help, but when they moved forward to greet her, she shied away with large, white eyes and said nothing. Just before she turned to run, Shumuti desperately called after her if she knew of anywhere they could get food, and she waved an arm vaguely towards the north of town before disappearing.

They explored the silent alleyways until at last, they came across a sign of activity in the town. A cramped market had been set up in one of the wider streets that almost passed for a square. Shumuti and Sara guardedly approached one of the vendors who appeared to be selling seafood, but at this point, Sara was too hungry to care much about what he was offering. As the trader bent down, his coat swung back, revealing a nasty looking and rusted dagger at his waist, before he stood up again and spotted them. A wisp of grey hair escaped from underneath the hood he was wearing.

The man froze, just staring.

"Shumuti, I could wait to eat," Sara said, starting to back up.

"He might be able to offer us information as well as food," Shumuti said.

"I don't think we should trouble him. Really, I don't. Let's pick someone else."

"All we need is a little guidance."

"Agreed, but it doesn't have to be from him."

Then the man extended one arm and beckoned them towards him. Arrow shied from Sara's increasing nervousness.

"We can deal with an old man."

Sara made a non-committal squeak of uncertainty followed by a failed attempt at speech.

"You put your point across well, Sara. Come on, we have to start somewhere."

Grudgingly, she shadowed Shumuti as they moved towards the man. He lowered his arm as they drew close and Sara saw it drift over his cloak to hide his dagger before falling neatly to his side.

"Can we buy two fish, please?" Shumuti asked.

The vendor grunted and began wrapping up two of his cooked fish in what looked like the leaf of the same trees they had seen growing in Cirrus. He handed it over and Shumuti produced a tiny chunk of gold from her pocket in payment.

"Could you tell us where we could stay for a night? Is there an inn here in Newark?" Shumuti asked.

"No inns here in Newark anymore," the man said.

"Right." Shumuti paused. "Do you know anything about strange sights in the sky above Boctor in this area? We don't want to head that way by accident."

"Do not venture west of here if you wish to return. Ghosts haunt the skies above the coast there and the seas as well."

"What kind of ghosts?" Shumuti asked.

The man stared blankly.

"It dœsn't matter," Shumuti said, "well, thank you for your help."

"What you need is free shelter?"

"Oh no. No, we're fine, thank you."

"Not right for two ladies to spend the night on hard ground." He indicated towards Sara.

"No, I'm fine on hard ground," Sara said, "I actually prefer it."

"Why don't you come with me?"

"We'd hate to trouble you. We couldn't."

Sara gathered up Arrow's reins as a spur in preparation to move on. Another couple of customers appeared in front of the stall, and they stepped aside swiftly to let them through. Before the man could speak again, Shumuti and Sara moved away back into the streets and mounted up, not giving the man a second glance and decided to leave the area immediately. They nibbled on the fish as they went, which turned out to be surprisingly good and soon found themselves on the far side of Newark.

"I know we need to rest, but I don't want to stay here," Sara said.

"No."

"It sounds like we just keep heading west."

"He mentioned the coast. I think the location we're searching for must be as far west as we can travel. If we can keep going just a little longer, we might make it."

"We already smelt the sea earlier, so it can't be that far away."

"Then let's let our noses guide us."

Shumuti encouraged Fynne into a trot and soon they had left the town far behind. Sara found the evening desert almost welcoming and drew her hood and scarf around her face as the wind picked up and sand buffeted her cheeks. The winds began to worsen as they rode further on though and Sara began to question whether it had been wise to set out here in the dark. Their distrust of the town had forced them into a hasty decision and might have led to putting themselves into more danger.

Their vision soon concentrated into a five-foot sphere around them, making it hard to tell if they were still travelling in the right direction. The sandstorm continued to grow in size as they rode under the darkening skies and Sara had to focus to make sure she could still see her companion a few steps ahead of her. A short while later, Shumuti halted Sara in her tracks.

"What is it?"

"There is Magic in this wind."

"Are we in danger?"

"No, I think this storm is just meant to deter anybody from venturing closer. Follow me, and keep close."

Sara set off after Shumuti as she picked up the pace and soon noticed the terrain switch under their feet from softer sand to harder stone. Then, as if they had crossed a threshold, the winds suddenly dissipated entirely and the desert fell calm around them once more.

Now that their vision had cleared, the sky reappeared once more but it was a sky unlike anything either one of them had seen before. High above them in the moonlit night, it appeared as though a range of mountains hung in the air, suspended by nothing, with what could be a tower rising from the central peak, surrounded by a backdrop of stars. Sara had grown used to strange visions and illusions in the desert, but this was on a whole other level.

Brushing the sand from her shoulders and pulling down her hood, Sara saw for the first time that they were standing near the edge of a line of cliffs and before them stood the sea. Waves crashed onto a shore below them that was currently just out of sight. There were some similarities between the shape of the ridge formed by the cliffs and the one in the sky, almost as if the existing landscape had been duplicated somehow. Sara turned to Shumuti for an explanation.

"This is insane," Shumuti said.

"Is what we're searching for up there?" Sara took in the floating landscape in trepidation.

"No, the whole image is fake," Shumuti said, "just like the sandstorm, it's all a distraction to keep people away from this place. Somebody has worked hard to protect-"

Shumuti slumped forward in her saddle and sharply gasped as if all the air had been knocked out of her. Sara watched on in shock to see a long, feathered arrow shaft protruding from Shumuti's left shoulder. Shumuti growled in pain, trying to push herself back upright.

Behind them, came the sound of a high-pitched neigh and the echo of several horses' hooves. Turning, Sara recognised the faces of the guardsmen from Newark emerging out of the edges of the sandstorm and galloping in their direction.

"Hand me your reins," Sara cried quickly.

In a panic, she scrambled to gather control of Shumuti's horse as well as her own. Shumuti clutched the saddle to remain on horseback as Sara urged both horses into flight and down a narrow opening between the cliffs that she presumed led down to the beach. Their pursuers could still be heard clearly above them as the track steepened and Sara feared they would both be thrown off.

Shumuti twisted back angrily in her saddle towards the pass as the beach levelled out below them and a new sandstorm whipped up out of nowhere across the path between the cliffs to block their pursuers' passage. They carried on riding to put some distance between them and the marauders from Newark until the horses kicked up saltwater among the sand and stones. When they reached the water, they halted and Sara saw Shumuti slide from the saddle beside her onto the beach. In the distance, the sandstorm faded away into nothing.

"No!"

Sara slid off as well and their two horses bolted a short distance away as the sound of their hunters grew louder again.

"It's so painful to use Magic here," Shumuti said, her face pale.

"Don't use it if it hurts you," Sara said.

"Help me up," Shumuti said.

"You're in no state to fight," Sara said, bringing her friend onto her knees.

She heard the whistle of another volley of arrows shoot towards them in the darkness, but they fell short and protruded out of the sand a few feet away.

"We can't run any further," Sara said, the waves already lapping up against the heel of her boots.

Shumuti pulled her down to shield her as they heard bowstrings twang once more and Sara buried her head in the salty mud as a fierce wind whipped up above them and scattered the arrows left and right. Lifting her face, she saw that their attackers were nearly on them, but Shumuti was not rising beside her.

"Shumuti!"

There was no answer. Sara pushed herself back up onto her feet and drew her sword, the blade grinding free of a sheath that had been clogged up by silt and sand. Wearily, she dropped into a guard position to defend her friend, struggling to keep her footing on ground that was constantly shifting beneath her feet, and prepared for their approach.

Chapter 20
The Boar

~Gabriel~

"Alejandro?" Gabriel asked all of a sudden, "what happened to your parents?"

They were sat by the edge of the White Lake. Gabriel was with Aurielle and Alejandro, while Aztec patrolled up and down the shoreline, tracking the scents of various animals that had come down from the forest to drink. The wolf was also now sporting a piece of custom-made leather armour along his back and chest that Gabriel had lovingly crafted at the blacksmith's. Gabriel had wanted to make sure that every companion he had would be protected as well as he could manage from danger.

Alejandro did not answer for a while. "My parents?" he said eventually, watching Aztec leap full-bodied into the lake, "why?"

"I was just thinking," Gabriel replied, "Shumuti and Sara are off in search of what may be a relative of Aurielle's, and we all seem to descend from the other ones. I want to piece their story together in my mind."

Aurielle lifted her head from her arms that were curled around her hunched up knees.

"Seaglen, Astrid, Dagaz, Lyria, Annah, Jemina," she recited.

"My father was killed in the last war, I was told," Alejandro said, "that was not an uncommon situation in Lyria after the fighting ended and a large orphanage sprung up in the city. I was sent there when my mother, Jemina, fell ill soon after and died, until I left to live on my own. I have never really known what it's like to have a family. What about you, Gabriel?"

"My mother was Annah." Gabriel smiled. "My parents met each other on the battlefield. She saved Ewan, my father's life, and he immediately fell for her. Ewan was Captain of the King's guard then and after the war ended. From what I remember and heard, he was a talented fighter. That was why King Eric was so keen to train me up and for me to enter the guard at a young age, once he had learnt that Ewan had had a son. He had hopes that I would be of the same quality."

"What happened to them?" Aurielle asked him with interest.

"My father was sent to lead a scouting party into Nimaz over ten years ago. They had been checking the area for a while to make sure that all was still safe. But unusually, Annah accompanied him. Neither of them returned and nor did any in the company. It was not long after that event that King Pala took his father's place on the throne, and we began to fear the Nimaz border again."

"You never saw them again?" Aurielle asked.

"No, I think they thought they would return," Gabriel said, "but something prevented that, maybe Dagaz himself. I'll probably never know."

"Would you go to search for them?" Aurielle asked.

"I nearly did," Gabriel said, "that's what I was preparing to do before the three of you found me. When I fled to the volcano above Lyria, I was considering going into Nimaz myself to track down what happened to them.

I don't really know why, there's not much of me believes they're still alive out there."

"Do you think I should have gone into Boctor?" Aurielle asked him.

"No," Gabriel said, "not if it did not feel right to you, but I hope you don't regret the decision."

"You don't think there's a chance your family might still be alive?" Aurielle asked.

"After all this time?" Gabriel asked, "I doubt it, but I would still like to know how they met their end."

Aurielle fell silent.

"Do you remember Lyria at all?" Gabriel asked her tentatively.

"How could I?" Aurielle's tone sharpened. "I had only just been born when she left. My father has forgotten her. He couldn't even describe to me what she looked like. That, or he does not want to remember."

"Well, there's no relation between any of us," Gabriel said, "but you may have a new family in Boctor, Aurielle."

"If they exist, I shall have a lot of questions for them," she said.

At that moment, Aztec emerged from the water. He strode up to the three of them, before shaking wildly and spraying water droplets over their faces. They got up soon after and walked the long stretch back to Seaglen's house above the village. On the way back, Alejandro noticed a group of villagers training out on the fields. Sessions like these had been arranged soon after the council, and everybody who had signed up was now undergoing combat training. The sound of clashing metal had become commonplace in Thayll.

Once they got back, they found that Erdic had arrived at the house with a horse and cart, and was standing outside the door with Seaglen and Astrid. Erdic looked tired but pleased as he drew back the cloth that covered the items in the cart. They approached to see an assembled collection of glistening armour and weaponry. Most of it, Alejandro and Gabriel recognised as the gear they had helped to make at the forge.

"I see that hound of yours is still sporting my best leather," Erdic said, spotting Aztec lope through the door.

"He deserves the best," Gabriel said.

"He even included a pouch in the armour to store items," Aurielle said.

The blacksmith shook his head in disgust at what he believed to be a waste of good material.

"I've been training him," Gabriel said, "it's not a waste. I'm turning him into one of Merrywater's finest warriors."

Erdic ruffled the wolf's ears. "Ferocious. At the moment, he is the least threatening wolf I have ever met."

"Is this for the meeting?" Aurielle gestured to the cart.

Erdic nodded. "We are going to distribute it among the villagers."

"You have done a fine job," Seaglen said.

"We ought to head on down now," Astrid said.

Seaglen, Astrid and Erdic rode at the front of the cart on the way to the village, while Aurielle, Alejandro and Gabriel walked beside them. Getting down the tilting track proved to be a small obstacle for the cart, but it was delicately managed, and before long they had arrived at The Boar Inn.

Grim-faced villagers were beginning to cluster around the doors already. A few shifted to get a good view of the cart as it arrived and cast several furtive glances towards the concealed goods within. Seaglen, Astrid and Erdic climbed down from the front, and the innkeeper opened the doors of the tavern. Men and women turned and began to file inside, talking as they went. Erdic paused and turned to the three of them.

"Would you mind looking after the cart?" he asked, "I'd hate for anything to happen to what we have made."

Disappointed, they reluctantly agreed to keep watch. Seaglen, Astrid and Erdic vanished inside, and the door clicked shut. They watched a few stragglers hurry inside the tavern before settling down to wait.

Aurielle went over to the door and put her ear against it to listen.

"Do you hear anything?" Gabriel asked after a minute of watching her.

"Bits and pieces," she answered, "I think they're talking about the organisation of the troops during the fighting and battle strategies. I suppose Seaglen will pass on to us anything that we need to know once we get back."

Gabriel nodded. "Let us know if you pick up something interesting, though."

They sat by the cart for well over two hours and Aurielle had long since given up standing by the door. Alejandro went over after a while to take over the watch.

Aurielle came and settled in among the piles of swords and armour next to Gabriel at the back of the cart. He noticed a scar on her neck from the Lifthayll Bridge was healing nicely and Gabriel thought back to the last time they had been at this inn. He opened his mouth to say something to her, before stopping. They were about to go into a battle together. Aurielle stared up at the horizon and suddenly straightened. Alerted, Gabriel lifted his eyes over to where she had hers and scanned for what she had spotted.

"Can you see the rider?" she asked.

Gabriel had just noticed it that second, the movement of a blurred shape in the distance, of red against green.

"There are three," Alejandro said, coming to stand in line with them.

He was right. Two more shapes rolled into view, moving down through the plains towards the village.

"Do you suppose they have come from Attaching?" Gabriel asked.

"That route branches off from the Ember Way," Aurielle said, "so they've at least come from Elmdale."

They watched the riders until the trio descended below the level of the rooftops in Thayll. Gabriel, Aurielle and Alejandro were standing on the main road through the village. If the riders were coming here, they would be more than likely to use it. When nobody emerged, Gabriel left the other two and paced down the road a little. He had made it around the corner when he heard the jingle of bells and the tread of horses' hooves in warning before the three riders came into sight, making their way down the road. Gabriel recognised the lead soldier instantly as the Marshal from Attaching. The other two were yet more soldiers dressed in the livery of the King.

Aurielle and Alejandro came forward to where Gabriel stood.

"Ah good," the Marshal said, "I had hoped I would be able to find you this easily."

"We did not expect to see you back here," Gabriel said.

"I need to speak with the Commander for Merrywater. Where is he?"

"They are inside," Aurielle said, "Seaglen is busy with the others from the village at the moment."

"I see. I have been sent with messages from the King important enough to interrupt this meeting. You need to hear this as well."

The Marshal dismounted and left his horse with the other two guards. Apprehensively, Gabriel, Aurielle and Alejandro followed inside as the wooden door creaked open, and he strode into the inn.

Erdic cut short whatever he was saying as the four of them entered. What felt like the entire village fell silent and turned their attention in the Marshal's direction.

"It is too late to be still deciding things now," the Marshal said, "a large hoard has been spotted approaching the Nimaz bank of Winterburn River, level with northern Elmdale. More and more are joining their ranks each day. It appears that they intend to cross and declare war any day now."

It only took a moment for the Marshal's words to sink in before the inn erupted into a hive of activity.

Chapter 21
Alexia

~Shumuti~

Shumuti had feared the minute she had slipped onto the sand that she might never rise from it again, so the sense of pain that shot up her back came as quite a surprise as she came back into consciousness. With a set grimace, she pulled herself into a sitting position, leaning against the rock at her side, and looked around for clues as to where she was now and what had happened. She reached gingerly for the wound on her left shoulder to find that it had been bandaged up and now only felt slightly wet to the touch.

Once her surroundings came back into focus, the next thing Shumuti realised was that night had now become day. She could hear the sea still, but it was further away and now seemed to echo in the distance. She was still next to the sea but lying in a cave with sea-beaten walls and a curved entranceway, hollowed out by the power of the waves.

The entrance of the cave darkened as a figure stepped through to join her and Shumuti tensed, backing away even closer to the wall. A young woman entered, and she was watching Shumuti with concern. Her hair was half tied back behind her head and fell in waves that looked as though they had spent a lifetime buffeted by a sea breeze. She was dressed in mismatching pieces of armour and tattered fabric, covered at the neck by a wide and frayed scarf that could also serve as a hood. As Shumuti took in her appearance, she noticed that in addition to holding a bundle of cloth in her hand, she carried a longsword by her side and her boots were stained by both sand and blood.

"You're awake." The figure sounded relieved.

Shumuti realised then that Sara was not with her.

"What is your name?" the stranger asked her, coming forward slowly.

She sat down near to the bed, and Shumuti noticed an extended cut running down the outside of her right arm. Her shirt had torn at the same time it had been made.

"Who are you?" Shumuti asked.

"My name is Alexia."

"Alexia?"

"Do I get your name in return?"

Her heart skipped a beat. "My name is Shumuti."

"Ah," she nodded, "how are you feeling, Shumuti? You were badly hurt."

"What happened?" Shumuti asked.

"We saw you on the beach, fleeing, and looking like you needed help. I was glad to find you still alive after the battle. You were lucky, the tide had nearly swept you out."

"You saved my life?"

"I think I did, yes."

"Where is my companion?"

"She was determined to defend you and fought bravely until we arrived. In the process, she was hurt and is still sleeping, but we're looking after her and I believe that she will fully recover, given a little time."

"I didn't expect to find friends in Boctor," Shumuti said.

Alexia cast a glance at Shumuti under her eyebrows.

"I came to change your bandages," she said, "it has been a good few hours now since I last checked the injury."

Shumuti felt the dressing run from her shoulder under her arm and across her chest, under the shirt she was wearing. "You bandaged my wound?"

Alexia blushed slightly. "Yes. I'm sorry, there was little time and you were bleeding heavily. Don't worry, I took the arrow out cleanly. We are used to injuries like that around here. May I change the dressing now?"

"Fine." Shumuti shuffled around begrudgingly until she faced the wall and uncovered just enough of her shoulders to remove the bloodstained bandage. As Alexia carefully applied a balm to the injury, Shumuti felt an instant jolt at the touch and in her weakened state, she realised something she ought to have noticed from the moment Alexia had stepped into the cave. She had just felt a surge of Magic.

Alexia had frozen behind her and Shumuti glanced over her shoulder as a tingle of Magic pulsed back and forth between them. Typically, Shumuti would have shied away from a stranger, but this connection was giving her strength, so instead, she sat still as slowly the pain in her shoulder began to recede, thinking of what to say next.

With her head clearer, she focused her attention on Alexia. Now it was apparent, she could not believe she had not noticed it straight away. She sensed her Magic as clearly as she did with any of the others. It was like a comforting glow around her. Alexia finished tying off the bandage. From the look on her face, she had not come into contact with Magic for a long while. Shumuti pulled the shirt back over her shoulders once more and swivelled back around to face her.

"Do you know what I am?" Shumuti asked finally.

"You're a Guardian of Magic," she answered a second later.

"What? How do you know that?"

"My mother. She told me."

"Your mother? Wait...Lyria?"

"Yes." Now Alexia also seemed caught off guard. "You know her?"

"We thought we might find her here."

"My mother died some time ago."

"Oh." Shumuti frowned in confusion. Then there was still part of the story that she was missing. Her mind raced through what should be the next question, but in her weakened state, she was beginning to feel unwell again.

"I will have some food brought for you," Alexia said quickly, seeing her face drain of colour, "we can talk after. When did you last eat?"

"Yesterday, but only a fish."

"Then I had better hurry. There are some spare clothes there if you want to change."

Alexia left the cave, and Shumuti felt a wave of relief. For the first time since entering Newark, she felt reassured that their journey out had not been for nothing. Lyria was no longer here, but she had found her daughter and the source of Magic here in Boctor.

Motivated by her success, she stood up and slowly changed clothes. They were a little too big for her, but she fastened them tight with her belt and made her way out into the open air. Standing by the entrance, Shumuti leant against the rock and stared out. They had moved, as far as she could gather and remember, under the cliffs that she had stood on top of yesterday. Where the beach had been empty yesterday, men and women now littered the coastline. Some huddled over, lighting fires and others were rushing about, carrying items back and forth from caves next to the one she was standing in. If it wasn't for the constant movement, their clothes made them almost invisible against the sand.

Shumuti distinguished Alexia amongst a group of men and her heart leapt again with achievement. She wondered if this company knew who she was or what she could do. The Magic radiated powerfully off of her, like shimmering heat.

The group she was with stood by the water and it took a moment for Shumuti to realise they were fishing with spears in the water's shallows. Alexia took up a spear from the pile and strode forward, looking for a target. A moment later, she aimed, and as she threw the spear, Shumuti felt a rush of Magic as the weapon hit the water's surface and a celebration as apparently it struck a target.

Alexia turned.

Shumuti walked a step forward, waiting for the inevitable consequence of using Magic that she was used to in Merrywater. Nothing happened. She frowned and looked around at the landscape, slowly realising. The land here already appeared so lifeless that while using the same amount in Merrywater might have caused obvious damage to the immediate area around them, the effects here were unclear. Alexia had probably been using Magic here for years, unaware that there were usually consequences.

She passed her spear on to another and departed from the group, carrying a steaming bowl. Shumuti's stomach let out an audible grumble as she approached.

"Here." Alexia handed it over. "I had this prepared for you."

"Thank you."

They sat down on a large rock as she ate the stew out of a smooth bowl, carved from driftwood. Within minutes, her meal was gone, and she set the bowl down on the sand. Down by the shoreline, some of the group were cleaning and stockpiling a set of weapons and armour that she recognised had yesterday been on the backs of the marauders chasing them from Newark.

"You've built a lot of defences to keep anybody from reaching this place," Shumuti said.

"I have to protect my company from the rest of Boctor, whatever that takes."

"I'm sorry we led some to your door."

"It was nothing we couldn't handle."

"You are in hiding from the rest of Boctor?"

"Only the ones who have aligned themselves with Nimaz. Everybody you see before you fled from Newark with me when Nimaz arrived to take over the town. We have found a sanctuary here."

"You use Magic in front of them?"

"Of course," Alexia answered, "they all know what I can do, that's why they followed me here. I had hoped that one of them might have the same skills as me. It would have been useful. But I have had no luck, until now."

"Useful?" Shumuti asked.

"To fight back against the raiders from Nimaz that have overtaken the village. I couldn't protect them all on my own, so I led those who wanted to come here."

"And the illusion in the sky, that was you as well?"

"It was."

"How?"

"It was something I created myself, after seeing mirages in the desert all my life. I studied them and learnt that they are created from air currents of different temperatures. The desert creates the right conditions for a mirage where images are duplicated below. By switching the currents and manipulating their location, I created the image of the cliffs duplicated above instead. Then it was just a matter of exaggerating tales back to Newark of the dangers of exploring too far west."

"You control the air," Shumuti said.

"So do you," Alexia said, "I saw your display last night."

"Have you ever noticed anything happen as a result of using Magic?"

"Not so much with small things, but whenever I refresh the mirage, I fall ill for a couple of days after each time."

"It hurts you and you use it anyway?"

"Yes. I have to protect my company. Is that not a normal effect?"

"No, where I come from there is a much bigger abundance of Magic than here. But any we use causes damage to our surroundings. Whereas here, I suppose the largest source of Magic around would be...you."

Shumuti glanced at Alexia uneasily.

"Where do you come from?" Alexia asked.

Shumuti fell silent.

"I know it is hard to trust people from Boctor."

"Take me to my friend," Shumuti said, "once I know she's safe, then I will consider telling you more."

Alexia offered out a hand up and led her into an adjoining cave, where they found Sara laid out asleep and covered in a few small dressings of her own. Shumuti slowly knelt beside her. Sara looked peaceful enough, if a little exhausted, and her chest was rising and falling steadily. It seemed like Alexia was taking good care of both of them.

"I come from Merrywater," she said, without taking her attention from Sara.

"Merrywater?"

"Dœs that change your opinion about me?"

"There is so much I want to ask you." Alexia sat down hesitantly.

Shumuti smiled weakly. "Likewise. But you go first. I'll tell you what you want to know."

"Why did you come to Boctor?"

"To find you. I need your help."

"My help? I think you shall have to tell me the entirety of your story before I understand."

They talked well into the afternoon. Shumuti informed Alexia of what was happening on the other side of the Winterburn River and their fears about what might be about to occur from this side, including the invasion at the Lifthayll Bridge and the attacks from the Atabra. She finished up by explaining the reason behind her expedition into Boctor to try to find out why an old Guardian had decided to turn on the rest of them.

"We're fighting on the same side then it seems," Alexia said.

"My turn to ask you a question," Shumuti said, "can I ask you about Lyria?"

Alexia nodded slowly.

"Why did she come here?" Shumuti asked, "to Boctor?"

Alexia sat back, seeming suddenly reluctant to answer questions. "She came to look for her family."

"Here?" Shumuti paused. That didn't sound right.

"My mother had none of her own family left," Alexia said, "so she came to Boctor because that's where my father's had lived."

"But she did have family left," Shumuti said, "I have a friend in Merrywater. You share the same mother as her."

"That's not possible." Alexia waved her hand, discounting the information instantly. "I was born in Boctor, not Merrywater, in the town of Newark. My mother never had any other children than me."

Shumuti frowned.

"Are you sure?"

Alexia folded his arms. "Certain."

"Tell me about yourself," Shumuti said, "your life here, growing up. Talk to me."

She wanted as much information as she could gather, while she tried to make up her mind what to think. Alexia began to talk about her life. She had learnt all about Magic from Lyria, growing up. She had learnt quite a lot before her mother had died and Shumuti could already see that Alexia was adept and would not need the same level of training as Gabriel and Alejandro had. When Nimaz arrived to take over Newark, Lyria had been slain and Alexia and the others had been forced to flee to the coast.

"Do you know anything about why Nimaz is attacking the other regions?" Shumuti asked, "we need to know as much information as possible."

"No," Alexia said, "Nimaz has long been trying to overpower Boctor to add recruits to their ranks. But as to the reason why they are both now attacking across the Winterburn River and why now, I don't know. Perhaps both regions have finally grown too jealous of the fertile lands to the east and want to claim your woods, lakes and fields for their own."

Shumuti sat back against the wall of the cave, deep in thought.

"I want to help you." Alexia stood up and paced to the entrance of the cave. "My remaining family is out there on the beach. But my company and I can only hold out here for so long, I know that. The Nimaz garrison in Newark could order them, and me, to be killed at any moment. They've already done it once. I can do more by helping you to fight against Nimaz, but on the condition that you take us all back with you and give us refuge in Merrywater."

"If they fight with us, I am sure we can find a place for them," Shumuti said.

"Then I will talk with the company." Alexia stood up.

"Wait," Shumuti said, noticing her and Sara's saddle-bags were in the cave as well, "if you agree to join us, I have something to give you."

She unbuckled a long item from the bags, wrapped in cloth and offered it across to Alexia. Taking the gift, Alexia revealed the last of Seaglen's swords concealed underneath, drawing the blade carefully.

"This is the finest weapon I have ever seen," she said, examining the sword in awe, "we have never looted anything this good off of the raiders."

"Consider it a thank you in advance for getting us out of Boctor alive," Shumuti said.

"Thank you, Shumuti."

She exited the cave, leaving Shumuti alone with Sara. As soon as Alexia's footsteps faded from earshot, Sara's right eye flickered open.

"You were awake all this time?" Shumuti asked.

"Are we safe?" Sara asked.

"Somehow, I think so."

"Who was that who left?"

Shumuti caught Sara's full attention. "I have a lot to tell you."

Chapter 22
Departure

~Aurielle~

Astrid braided Aurielle's hair ready for war. Aurielle watched her reflection in the mirror as Astrid worked, not sure she liked who was staring back at her. Her hair was tied back from her face, and she could not deny the practical use that it would have while she was fighting. Astrid's shorter hair was plaited similar to her own, contrasting only where hers was dark and Aurielle's light.

"The last thing you want is to be unable to see," Astrid said to her.

"Shumuti and Sara haven't made it back in time," Aurielle said.

Astrid's fingers slipped slightly over one of the knots. "At least they will not be involved in this fight."

"Have you been in many battles?" Aurielle asked her.

"Not that many." She paused. "Not enough to be used to the experience. Do you think you are ready for this?"

"Well, I think we're all as ready as we're going to be."

Astrid waved a hand and met Aurielle's eyes in the reflection of the glass. "I am not talking about your training. I mean you. Do you think you're prepared?"

"I think so."

Astrid reached over and hugged Aurielle. After a second of surprise, she hugged her back in return.

"Well," Astrid said quietly, "I can only hope that I am too."

Seaglen dressed them ready for battle in the Guardians of Magic cave. Erdic had prepared a set of metal spaulders for Aurielle, to complement the leather armour that they already wore. He had offered to create a full metal set of armour for each of them, but Seaglen had refused the offer, and Aurielle knew why. Their Magic would protect them far better than heavy plate would.

The metal on her shoulder clinked as Aurielle settled her gear into place. It was a perfect fit, for which she was glad. Most of the armour was light, made of leather, interspersed with steel. It still granted her movement, and she was pleased that they were not burdened like the soldiers were by the heavy breastplates of the King's guard. In the style that Seaglen and Astrid had adopted before them, only their sword arm was armoured, leaving their second hand unencumbered to wield Magic swiftly.

She buckled her sword belt over the top of her gear, admiring how well Erdic had crafted the weapon to complement the armour. Finally, she added leather bracers to each arm. They had already packed what little they needed, and as she brought out her travelling coat to complete the ensemble, she knew she was ready.

"Now, I have one final trick to teach you," Seaglen said, "the runes in the swords you now hold are linked to Magic, as you know. You can store a portion of energy inside the rune here. Take some from the training room now, where it is abundant, and you will have some free power, if you like, out in the field. A boost can be useful in tricky situations. Additionally, you can use the Magic in your rune directly with your sword. For example, watch me. Gabriel, I feel you may especially appreciate this."

Seaglen drew his sword and Aurielle recognised the rune set there for the first time. She realised that she had never noticed it before because Seaglen's runestone was entirely blank, and Aurielle had always thought it was just an embellishment. She had only a second to make this connection before the stone glowed red and Seaglen swung his sword. A series of fiery patterns, of spirals and triangles and intertwining curves ran down the fuller of the blade. An eruption of red fire dripped from each of the edges and followed the swing of Seaglen's movement. A second later, the flames extinguished, and the sword dulled back to silver.

"You're right." Gabriel watched on ardently. "I do like that."

"Use the runes wisely," Seaglen said, "you may not always be in locations where Magic is so plentiful. I'm sure over time you will think of unique ways to make use of this."

Seaglen sheathed his sword once more.

"Then it looks like we're ready," Gabriel said.

Aurielle said nothing. Shumuti had not returned. King Pala had summoned them earlier than expected, and there was no time left to wait for her and Sara. She could not help but feel it had been a bad idea to separate at a time like this and without any knowledge from Boctor as to what Dagaz might be planning, they were going into this fight blind.

The three of them left Seaglen and Astrid to change and went to ready the horses. The entirety of Thayll's army was to meet in the village by mid-morning and the news had been spread all around Merrywater. Fighters from anywhere south of Thayll had arrived last night and were camped out on the fields in every space available.

Seaglen and Astrid came outside to join them at last. Seaglen was as settled and composed as he always was, but Astrid looked uncharacteristically uneasy. Aurielle watched her in concern as they prepared to leave.

"Thank you," Seaglen said as he took his horse.

Aurielle smiled. "I wish Shumuti and Sara were with us."

"As do I." Seaglen looked away regretfully. "Every day since they left, I have wondered if I made the right decision."

Aurielle stared at him, unsure what to say.

"Everything has happened too fast," he said.

"We have to go," Gabriel said urgently.

Aurielle turned down the hill to see a large gathering of armoured villagers assembled ready on the fields. Stephan and Ramin were riding up the hill to the house.

"Yes," Seaglen said, "past time that we were gone."

They quickly climbed up onto their horses and turned to go after the messenger and the soldier.

Filled with anticipation, Seaglen and the others met the army at the base of the hill. Aurielle scanned the line of soldiers from Thayll and felt a pang of slight worry, mingled with pride. Her father stood amongst the soldiers who had signed up in service to the King. She was proud, and a little surprised that he had chosen to defend Merrywater, but she was also troubled now that there was one extra person to worry about. Ever since the night she had accused him of lying to her, he had isolated himself even more. Whatever the heart of the problem was, he was not going to tell her, but Aurielle had resolved to get it out of him when they returned.

Seaglen looked around approvingly and steered his horse over to where Erdic was waiting at the head of the crowd. They followed dutifully, attracting inquisitive glances from those immediately nearby and rode proudly to the head of the column. Erdic nodded at Seaglen as they joined him. Ramin and Stephan rode up on either side, each now embellished with bright banners holding the standards of Attaching and Merrywater. Seaglen surveyed the scene. They were ordered and correct, and so he turned to face the north and waved to Ramin.

"Riders, ready!" Erdic called.

A bright note rang loudly on Ramin's horn. The assembled army shifted and gathered the reins of their horses. The families of the fighters cried out words of comfort and goodbye, before Seaglen, Garrin and Erdic began to move out. Astrid, Stephan and Ramin came next, with Aurielle, Gabriel and Alejandro in the next line. Finally, came the bulk of the Merrywater army, three abreast in each row as they moved out of the village.

Once out onto open land, the pace quickened. The force of so many hooves rocked the ground, creating a rumbling echo that made Aurielle shiver. Out towards the Ember Way they journeyed, the main road into Elmdale, aiming to make it near the Elmdale Forest before nightfall, and keeping up a regular rhythm all day saw that they reached their goal. Nothing eventful occurred that day, but the day of riding had taken its toll on those who had never journeyed very far beyond Thayll. More than a few were laid on their backs on the grass, resting while the food was prepared that night.

Any hope of lighting fires was dampened by the disheartening arrival of drizzle that descended on them out of the darkness soon after they had begun eating. Illuminated only by the light of the moon, Aurielle regretfully informed Gabriel that she had neither the energy nor the desire to stop rain falling from the clouds, and so they sat glumly in it with the rest of the army.

Sleep was a welcome prospect for all, save for the sentinels who had been duly appointed for that night. Continuous rainfall had become an accepted issue by the next morning, so it was almost ignored as they packed up and

Ramin sounded the signal to move on again. The fringes of the Elmdale Forest hung over them as they rode up to the edges and headed inside, riding between tall pines, in the direction of the Winterburn River. Birds took flight, and a pack of deer cantered away in alarm as the unit trotted the length of the tree line.

"We will cut through the break in the trees ahead," Seaglen called, from in front of them, "it leads through the shortest part of the forest and over the gorge into Elmdale. We shouldn't be far from the border now."

Tributaries of the Winterburn River naturally bordered Merrywater and Elmdale, much like in the other regions of Meteorath. Between Merrywater and Elmdale, the border river ran through a deep, forested gully for the most part, which had come to be known as the Elmwater Gorge. It took the best part of the day to reach the section of the trees that led to the canyon. The number on each row of the army diminished from three to one as the track narrowed. Their speed decreased as well and the tread of the horses became more cautious. The Merrywater army soon reached the bridge that spanned the gorge into Elmdale. It had been designed for horses to cross, but perhaps not for so many at once, so the border crossing took time and Aurielle, Gabriel and Alejandro remained at the far end of the bridge, overseeing the operation until everyone was across.

The camp that night was arranged on the hills that overlooked the starlit landscape of Elmdale. Aurielle, Gabriel and Alejandro got there late and eventually found Seaglen and Astrid amongst the mass of other allies.

"We have a few hours rest here, and then we must ride on to the King's camp by the river," Seaglen informed them, "I have sent scouts ahead, but the last we heard was that the Nimaz army had not yet reached the border on their side of the river. They have not attempted to cross yet, but it can only be a matter of time. It will still take us another few days to reach them at this pace."

"How will they manage it?" Aurielle asked, "the river is wider in Elmdale than at the Lifthayll Bridge, much wider."

"I do not think Dagaz intends to let the river prevent him from crossing," Seaglen said, "he will have a way."

"Do you think he will be there himself?"

"I would prepare for it."

Aurielle looked around at the army and wondered what they all were thinking right now. In the crowd, she picked out a familiar face and headed over towards where her father was sitting alone. She sat down silently next to him, not caring whether or not they spoke.

"I've asked Seaglen to place you in his flank of the army," she said after a while, "that way we'll be near each other in case one of us gets into trouble."

"I think the time has long past since I was able to protect you," Seamus said.

"Even so, I can still watch out for you," Aurielle said.

"You should not trouble yourself with me," Seamus said, "go back to the father you are worthy of having."

He looked back towards where Seaglen was in deep conversation with Astrid. Aurielle felt a rush of anger.

"You're my father," she said, "I want you."

Seamus did not answer, still staring transfixed towards Seaglen and after a minute, Aurielle reluctantly stood up to re-join the others.

The allotted two hours passed that Seaglen had given them and the army set off once more towards the King's encampment. It barely felt like they halted at all on the road up through Elmdale. Aurielle was conflicted by feelings of wanting to reach the King's army as soon as possible but also dreading the moment when they did. Sooner than she had bargained for though, the morning came when she crested the hill beside Alejandro and Gabriel that offered a close up sight of the Winterburn River and the transformation it had undergone.

On the far side, Aurielle could just about make out that a series of bridges had begun to span the gap between Nimaz and Elmdale, hopping between the islands that littered the distance in between. The Nimaz army had made considerable progress across the water but upon one glance, Aurielle could see why nobody on this side of the river had attempted to halt their progression. The islands would run out before the Nimaz forces could reach the Elmdale bank and Aurielle knew from sailing on it herself that the currents on the Elmdale side of the river ran fast and deep. She frowned, wondering how Dagaz was planning on traversing the final section to reach them.

Troops from Attaching and Elmdale had already gathered near to the banks of the river, and the number of soldiers was overwhelming. Their cohort arrived to join the others and was greeted by the other Captains of the King. Seaglen was summoned away, so Gabriel, Alejandro and Aurielle were left with Astrid, until a uniformed man approached Aurielle and asked her to follow him to join Seaglen in the meeting with King Pala.

Aurielle had forgotten that Shumuti had appointed her to speak on behalf of the new Guardians, so it took a moment to realise why she had been summoned. Escorted by a guard, Aurielle made her way to a large red and orange tent in the heart of the army. On top flew three flags of red, blue and green but inside, the colour of silver armour predominated the scene.

The King stood in the centre of the space, surrounded by his Marshals and Captains, and before him was Seaglen and a woman who Aurielle assumed to be the Commander for Elmdale. Trying to hide her nerves, Aurielle took a place next to Seaglen and made a bow to the King. He acknowledged her arrival with a frown.

"You are not Shumuti," he said.

"She's away, my King," Aurielle explained quickly, "on a task. She has not made it back in time."

"No. This cannot be. I need all of you here." The King's confident tone slipped ever so slightly. "Don't you realise how important that is, given what we face?"

"I sent her," Seaglen said.

"You, the Commander for Merrywater?"

"I am her father, and let me assure you that Shumuti means more to me than she ever could to you."

"Ah." King Pala eyed Seaglen contemplatively. "Then I will need to speak to both of you privately after this."

Aurielle and Seaglen nodded. She stepped back, listening to the King giving direct orders on their placement in the battle. Aurielle knew that Seaglen would ultimately be the one to direct them, but it was useful to know the overall battle plan. As soon as the King finished speaking, the tent cleared instantly and orders were relayed on back through the army. Within seconds, only the three of them remained around the table.

"I have not confided to my army the nature of who you are." The King glanced between the two of them. "From what your daughter has told me, Seaglen, am I right to think that you possess the same skills as her?"

"You are," Seaglen replied quietly.

"I was promised four of you. Since you have sent Shumuti away from the battle, you will assume her place here."

"I sent Shumuti on a task to find out more about why Dagaz is doing this. There is someone else who can use Magic in Boctor. Either she will return with one more to add to our ranks, or she will eliminate another potential threat to you. I believed we had more time when I sent her, or else I would not have gone ahead with the decision. But as it is, yes, I will take her place here. Along with my sister as well, there will, in fact, be five of us fighting on your side."

"Will it be enough?" the King asked.

"That depends on what we face," Seaglen said.

"So far we have seen nothing inhuman on the far banks of the Winterburn," King Pala said, "I received your report on who leads them. This Dagaz, has he betrayed you then?"

"You could say that," Seaglen said, "I believed him to be dead. He was a friend to me once, but now he is unrecognisable. I would know if he was over the other side of the river, and thankfully, I can detect no sign of him at the moment."

"That is good to hear." The King sighed. "All we can do now is wait for their attempt to cross. I have positioned scouts for miles either way down the riverbank. If this is a decoy of sorts, we will be informed quickly. There was a report not long ago of a large part of the Elmdale Forest near here being ripped apart, and now the reason becomes clear. But do you know any way they will be able to ford the final section of the Winterburn?"

"Dagaz controlled the air element," Seaglen said, "he should not have been able to take apart a forest as you've described. But whatever happened to him in Nimaz resulted in him gaining power, I would not be surprised if things that were once impossible for him now came easily. But at the moment, he is not out there with his army."

"On these bridges they have created we can pick them off before they even cross," the King said, "if the situation changes and Dagaz appears I need you to inform me immediately. Now Seaglen, you will still lead the Merrywater segment of the army, but Aurielle, I want your focus and that of your companions to be on anything Magic-related that enters the battlefield. Only the five of you will be able to deal with a threat like that, and you must understand that you are my only hope. I do not intend to allow our enemy to cross the Winterburn River, or set foot on our borders."

Aurielle nodded. "I understand."

"I don't know how long you will be able to keep your Magic secret from Meteorath after this," the King said to Seaglen.

"Dagaz has not helped to make Magic seem like a positive thing," Seaglen said, "this is not the way I wanted Meteorath to find out."

"Then fight by my side against him," King Pala said, "show the fighters from Attaching, Merrywater and Elmdale that you are prepared to bring down Nimaz with me. They will see that Magic is something to be celebrated."

Seaglen gave the smallest of bows, his expression troubled.

"Is that all, my Lord?"

"For now, yes."

Aurielle and Seaglen exited the King's tent and walked back through the swirl of soldiers to find Astrid and the others. As they climbed the hill towards the Merrywater encampment, Aurielle looked back over the assembled army to see the Winterburn River and beyond, the shadow of a dark mass gathered along the river as far as she could see.

Chapter 23
Events are Set in Motion

~Sara~

Sara's head was reeling from an overload of information about Alexia and her life in Boctor. With nothing else to do but recover, she had spent the past few days thinking over what Shumuti had said. Shumuti thought that Alexia could be trusted, but Sara had barely met her and was yet to decide that for herself.

Shumuti had spent her time learning the life of the company here, becoming involved with the everyday jobs of the group and getting to know most of them reasonably well. They numbered into the hundreds and all were all young and held Alexia in high regard. The company was cheerful and got on well together, but under it all, Sara could discern a steely determination that aged them more than they looked. This was a group who did not fear dying. She was also bothered by the story about Lyria. Either Alexia or Aurielle had their information wrong about her and Sara was not sure who else they could turn to in order to learn the truth.

Sara was dozing in the cave as night fell and Shumuti was somewhere in the fading light, sitting beside her. Alexia had left early that morning with a handful of others to learn if another party from Nimaz was likely to come investigating the fate of the first one and if the road out of Newark was a safe one to travel on.

"Sara." A hand shook her in the dark. "They've returned."

Sara jerked upright and squinted outside the cave. Shumuti rushed to her feet and ran out onto the beach. Hastily, Sara followed her out into the cold evening under a glittering starry sky. Alexia had returned and Sara got the sense that something else had happened while they had been away. The others that had clustered around had suddenly moved into action, gathering up everything on the sand.

"Shumuti," Alexia said, "I bring back some bad news with me."

"What has happened?"

"Newark lies abandoned. We found a command order in the old guardhouse. The town left days ago to join the rest of the Nimaz army assembling at the Winterburn River, and I can only assume they are preparing to cross over."

"What? No, this is too soon!"

"I'm sorry."

"We have to go," Shumuti said, "but I'll understand if you and your company choose not to come with us now. Sara and I will not be heading to Merrywater, but straight to Elmdale."

Alexia cast an eye around the faces of her group, considering. "No, we will fight with you."

"Are you sure?" Shumuti asked, "the town has been abandoned. This could be your chance to take it back."

"For a time, maybe," Alexia said, "but this may be our only opportunity to get out of Boctor. My fighters are loyal, and we will not let you down. But it will take you too long to travel back the way you came. There is a quicker route to Elmdale. It is the same one the army from

Newark will have taken, and it will lead us to the rear of the Nimaz army."

"You can guide us?"

"We will be ready to leave in minutes," Alexia said. She called a few men over and sent them running off in different directions along the beach.

"Then thank you," Shumuti said.

Alexia gave them a small smile and ran off to ready her horse.

"Are you sure we can trust her?" Sara asked.

"I've never been completely sure we can trust anyone we've met so far," Shumuti said, "but if she can get us to Elmdale quickly, I will let her help us. Will you be all right to travel?"

"I'll be fine, don't worry about me. All I want right now is to get back to the others."

"Me too."

The two of them hurried back into their cave and strapped on their swords, before gathering their horses and riding along the beach to where most of Alexia's company had gathered. More and more joined them every minute, materialising from more tunnel entrances than Sara knew had existed. One handed Alexia a flaming brand, before distributing more torches around the group.

It felt like they were only waiting there a moment before Alexia sounded the call to move out. Lighting up the darkened sky with a line of flickering fire, the company streaked down the beach, charging down the sand and shooting up spray from the sea. Alexia rode at the head, flanked either side by Shumuti and Sara and turned the column sharply left off of the beach. The horses slowed to manœuvre across the softer sand but soon regained their speed above the cliffs as they came closer to Newark.

Passing through the deserted, ghost-like settlement, they moved in the direction of the guardhouse on the outskirts. Alexia gripped her torch firmly as the building came into sight.

"Ready!" she shouted as they reached it, "not all the torches!"

With that, three men threw roaring torches through the window, shattering the glass. A fire sprang up, and the flames hissed menacingly under the window. Alexia gave it one satisfactory glance and turned away.

"Move on!"

They rode on. Behind them, now and then a rider flung their brand into the guardhouse, increasing the inferno within. They charged out of Newark and up onto the embankment. The company turned briefly at the top and wondered at the force of the fire that they had created. The guardhouse was now nothing more than a whirling tower of flames, and they could feel the heat from where they stood. Sara exchanged a nervous glance with Shumuti before they rode away after the group.

That night, Alexia did not stop. Sara and Shumuti's need to get to Elmdale as quickly as possible spurred the whole company onwards. The light from the fires that the group carried lit the way as they returned to the deserts of Boctor. Alexia's company found shelter when the sun was at its highest and alternated between running and riding for nights until they finally conceded that both riders and horses needed to rest. They directed themselves towards the north of Boctor, and as dusk fell on the third day, they finally reached their goal. Sara was glad that she had spent the last few months training because otherwise there was no way she would have been able to keep up with Alexia's company.

Camping out by the river's edge, the group took care of the horses and only after they had been attended to did they think about the welfare of themselves. Alexia brought food over for Shumuti and Sara before they joined the rest of the company, who were sat in a giant ring, eating and talking.

"We can cross here?" Sara asked.

"Yes," Alexia said, "the current of the river slows here and it's at one of its narrowest stretches. The horses can swim across here relatively easily."

"Yours might be able to," Sara said.

"We will get you across," Alexia said, "we have made good time already."

"How is everybody doing?" Shumuti asked, looking around.

"We've been through worse together," Alexia said, "but they keep asking about you two."

"Too right we do," one of the men said, "it's not much short of cruel dragging you up the length of the country, and to war at the end of it."

"But it's our fault you're even here at all," Shumuti said.

"We are used to this life." He shrugged.

"Is it true that the King of Attaching will accept help from us?" another asked, "from Boctor?"

"We will vouch for you," Shumuti said, "and we will help you take back Boctor from Nimaz after all this, if we can."

Sara saw Alexia smile at Shumuti appreciatively. Several of the others around them mumbled between themselves.

They attempted the crossing early next morning and Sara was relieved to find that Arrow only took a small amount of encouragement to follow the other horses into the water. She detached her feet from the stirrups just in case she needed to quickly dismount into the water but Alexia kept a close eye on them both until everybody had reached the other side. Sara crossed into the new region, immediately feeling that this was not somewhere she should be.

"Welcome to Nimaz," Alexia said.

As was always the case at borders, Sara knew they could not see a true representation of Nimaz before them. The initial surrounding area was not that different than the terrain they had travelled through on their way here. On the other side of the river from the desert, she found that they could see plains that more closely resembled Attaching, spread out in the distance to the north, as well as a large portion of moorland which had been scorched and burnt down until it was reduced to almost nothing.

"Where do we go from here?" Shumuti asked.

"We stick to the river," Alexia answered, "it is safer to venture into Nimaz as little as possible, although hopefully the region will be distracted at the moment and we'll not encounter anyone on the road. When we reach the eastern edge of Nimaz, we can cut up from there. I'm sorry there is no time to rest anywhere before the battle."

"I do not want to be caught anywhere in Nimaz," Shumuti said, "let's push on for as long as we can."

Alexia resumed the lead once more and thundered alongside the riverbank. Sara wheeled Arrow around and headed after the others, closer to Elmdale and heading towards war.

CHAPTER 24
THE EVE OF BATTLE

~ALEJANDRO~

"Alejandro!" Gabriel called over, "Aurielle and Seaglen are back."

Alejandro poked his head out of the tent that they had only just been given as their own and searched the crowd for the two figures he would recognise. The silhouettes of Aurielle and Seaglen stepped out from between the haze of a dozen smoky campfires and met them amongst the crowd of men and women gathered in the makeshift Merrywater camp.

"We have somewhere to stay this way," Gabriel said, leading the way back to the flap of the tent. Aztec rushed around beside them, still sporting his newly crafted set of armour. Their tent was a deep red colour, embroidered in blue thread and plenty large enough to hold the five of them. It was circular shaped, with a high conical awning and room spare for beds to be arranged around the sides. Their saddlebags had been stored around the edges by Gabriel and Alejandro, and the horses were picketed outside.

Astrid had arranged somewhere to sit in the centre out of rugs and cloaks, and that was where they gathered in a circle now. Seaglen and Aurielle recounted to them all that the King had said as they listened in silence.

"We must be prepared to answer the King's summons at any moment," Seaglen warned them all, "we don't know when and how Nimaz may launch their attack."

"We just have to wait?" Gabriel asked.

"Yes. The King has no intention of striking first and attempting to cross the Winterburn."

"What are they doing out there?" Alejandro asked.

"The report from the other side of the river is still the same. Ever since the Nimaz army had arrived, they have begun to construct short bridges to cross the river on their side. There are many islands in this section of the Winterburn but it is still a foolish endeavour. Even with a whole army toiling away, there is no way to cross the final open stretch of water into Elmdale."

"Do you think Nimaz's army is waiting for something?" Aurielle hesitated. "For Dagaz to come?"

"He's not out there with them?" Gabriel frowned.

"No," Seaglen answered, "he is not close, not yet."

"If he comes," Alejandro began tentatively, "do you think we can stop him?"

"As yet, I don't know the full potential of his power," Seaglen answered, "but there are five of us, and he is only one, that has to count for something. The King is right on this matter. We must not forget that our first priority is to deal with any Magic on the battlefield. No one else can face that except for us."

All five of them fell into an uneasy silence.

"I'm going out to see the river for myself," Astrid said after a little while, "to see if there is anything out there the King has overlooked."

She exited the tent.

"I'll be back in a minute as well," Aurielle said, "there's someone I want to see before the fighting starts."

She also left, and Alejandro drifted back to his anxious thoughts. Wanting to find anything that might preoccupy him, he suggested the idea of a spar to Gabriel. He eagerly agreed, and they set up a small area in the centre of the tent. They drew their swords and went through the most recent moves that Seaglen had taught them. Gradually, Alejandro began to feel less on edge. Seaglen remained in the corner, pouring over a copy of the battle plans and map he had received from the King.

Not wanting to wear themselves out before the real fight, they stopped after a while as Alejandro heard footsteps approaching from outside. Aurielle re-entered the tent with a distraught expression on her face.

"What's the matter?" Gabriel asked.

She looked at him and stumbled on the words she was trying to say. "My father. He's missing from the encampment. I was told he ran away."

"What?"

Seaglen stirred slightly in the corner but said nothing.

"Why?" Gabriel asked.

"I...don't know," Aurielle said.

Gabriel looked like he was about to draw Aurielle into a hug, but then she spoke again.

"I'm sorry. I want to be alone for a while, I think."

With a lost expression on her face, she turned back around before he could react and vanished out of the tent again. Gabriel stared after her with concern ingrained on his face.

"Let her be for now," Seaglen said, "I will return soon. I have to go meet the other Marshals."

A few minutes after he departed, Astrid appeared around the corner flap of the tent.

"Where is Aurielle?" she asked.

"She wanted to be alone." Gabriel looked up at her helplessly.

"I heard what happened," Astrid replied, "I will find her."

"I'll come," Gabriel offered immediately.

"No." Astrid held a hand up to him. "No, I'll go on my own."

Astrid whipped back around the flap of the tent and Gabriel slumped back down, burying his head in his hands.

"Don't worry," Alejandro said, "Astrid will bring her back."

"This waiting is awful," Gabriel said.

"It is." Alejandro agreed with that statement whole-heartedly.

Aztec rose from over in the corner and dropped his head into Gabriel's lap, staring up at him with mournful eyes. Gabriel scratched the wolf behind the ear and took a steadying breath.

They waited in the tent for what felt like an eternity before Alejandro heard what sounded almost like a tearing noise and Astrid ripped open the flap in her haste to get inside. Neither of them had managed to get any sleep. Outside, Alejandro listened to the distant ring of horns and got to his feet nervously. Behind Astrid, Aurielle lingered by the entrance with a numb expression on her face.

"It is time," was all Astrid said.

Already prepared, they grabbed their saddles and wordlessly followed Astrid out into the chaos beyond the tent.

"It appears," Astrid said as they half-ran to the horses, "that Nimaz has also been making boats from the wood taken from Elmdale's forests. A portion of the Nimaz army has crossed the river further upstream. The scouts managed to return in time to warn us, and the King has sent the Elmdale army to deal with them. He is sure this is just the beginning of their plan."

They reached the paddock, and Alejandro fumbled with the saddle as he tried to put it on his horse as quickly as possible. Gabriel stood ready next to him as Astrid came up and laid a hand on each of their shoulders. It was the most comfort Alejandro had felt for months and to his surprise, he felt slightly reassured. Last of all, Astrid hugged Aurielle tightly, before the four of them turned to where Seaglen was waiting.

CHAPTER 25
A BREACH IN THE WINTERBURN

~GABRIEL~

"We must hurry." Seaglen ushered them onwards.

Out on the horses, they joined with the line of allies who were heading to the river. Seaglen found Erdic, and together they marshalled the army into order, forming ranks with the soldiers from Elmdale and Attaching. It was just before dawn and the shock of the sudden rousing had left everybody dazed and confused. Gabriel was worried for them, and he sensed that Seaglen was too.

They rode at the head of the Merrywater line as the signal was sounded to move out and quickly joined with the main bulk of the King's forces. Gabriel tried to catch the attention of Aurielle on his right, but she stared out ahead of them in a daze.

"Be prepared for what you see at the river," Astrid said back to them.

"Why?" Alejandro asked, "what exactly is happening there?"

"Their numbers have grown overnight, and they have crossed as far as possible out into the river."

"Has Dagaz ridden out himself?" Alejandro asked quickly.

Astrid paused. "I guess we shall find out soon enough."

Their pace increased as they breached the last slope before the Winterburn, and Astrid had been right to forewarn them about what was happening. On the shores of Nimaz, countless numbers of armoured fighters stood below them. Overnight, they had progressed forward from the banks of Nimaz close enough to where Gabriel could pick out individuals now standing opposite them.

"Dagaz is still not here," Seaglen said.

"What is he doing?" Gabriel asked.

"His army has made a lot of progress overnight," Astrid said.

"It is still not enough though," Seaglen said.

For the moment, the deeper and faster currents in Elmdale waters still held a strong enough barrier to halt Nimaz's approach. As they halted, Gabriel saw a detachment of their army split off and ride north. Green banners fluttered in the wind as the Elmdale fighters rode to deal with the ones who had crossed the river by boat. Seaglen led them down the hill to where the King was waiting below. The Merrywater army neatly joined ranks with Attaching, facing the threat across the river. Gabriel and the others entered the front row as he picked out the face of the Marshal mounted close by the King's side.

Directly in front of them, the water ran fast and reliably between the two armies and Gabriel was comforted slightly that the river was still too wide for them to cross here without losing too many soldiers in the process. As if to reinforce that fact, the King had positioned three lines of the best archers from each region at the edge of the bank, should anyone from Nimaz dare to enter the water.

As they watched the scene, a rider urgently galloped up from the south and skidded his horse to a halt before the

King. He spoke the few words of his message before the King answered and sent him off once more. King Pala turned to Seaglen.

"More have rowed across from the south," Seaglen loudly relayed to his flank of the Merrywater army, "it is our job to deal with them."

He drew in closer to Gabriel and the others. "Astrid, Aurielle, Alejandro. The King has ordered that you remain here in case of a magical attack. Gabriel, you are with me in case the threat lies downstream. I get the sense there may be something approaching from the south."

Astrid began to open her mouth to protest but stopped as she saw the look in Seaglen's eyes.

"We will return soon," he promised her.

Astrid backed down, and Gabriel moved forward to Seaglen's side as Erdic approached his other. He caught Aurielle's eye and only for the second time ever, saw that she was afraid.

"Keep Aztec with you," he managed to say to her, "look after him."

He sent the wolf to her side, the last piece of protection he could offer her. Then Seaglen's horn sounded again, and with one last look back, Gabriel thundered away at Seaglen's heels alongside Erdic. He heard the rumble of the Merrywater fighters behind him as the scout who had relayed the news rode ahead of them.

It was not long before they came across their target. Invaders from Nimaz overran the banks, and a cluster of small rowing boats constructed out of timber that could only have come from Elmdale's forests were already heading back to the opposite bank to collect further reinforcements. Seaglen did not let up as they charged onward, drawing his sword and using the horn once more to signal the attack. Gabriel drew his blade as the Nimaz ranks frantically prepared themselves in defence.

"Let's see how you wield my steel, boy!" Erdic cried across as he, Gabriel and Seaglen hurtled into the front line of attackers.

Their horses cut through the crowd beneath their feet without Gabriel even needing his sword. He focused on remaining upright and not losing Seaglen as they carved a path through to the other side.

"Erdic, take the ones on the right," Seaglen ordered, turning back and examining the forces that were left, "Gabriel, the left."

"You'll want this." Erdic threw across a pole wrapped in cloth from his saddlebags.

Gabriel unfurled a banner of Merrywater and Erdic raised his own. Suddenly, back as a Captain in training at the Lyrian Citadel, Gabriel summoned the Merrywater soldiers who were close to him and led them towards a cluster of Nimaz fighters near the river. The fighting was short, and the company made quick work of the enemy. Gabriel looked over to check if Erdic needed help, but the blacksmith was almost single-handedly clearing up any stragglers that remained.

A roar of fire, accompanied by a rush of Magic caught Gabriel's attention, and he turned back towards the river. The rowboats that had been making their way towards the Elmdale bank simultaneously caught alight and those aboard scrambled to jump free from the flames that engulfed them. Seaglen watched the spectacle from the riverbank with a set expression, before turning his horse away from the sinking fleet.

Above the smoke on the water, Gabriel then noticed something else in the distance, drawing closer in the skies over in the direction of Boctor. Quickly, he spurred his horse into action.

"Seaglen! Behind you!"

Hearing Gabriel, he turned back and noticed the large shadow in the sky.

"Is it an Atabra?" Gabriel asked, reaching him.

Seaglen stared up at the sky, examining the shape silently. It was covering ground fast, and soon Gabriel began to realise that whatever he was watching was far larger than the vultures had been described to be. He also realised that it was carrying something. Two enormous wings cut through the smoke, clearing the air and the sight before Gabriel's eyes made him waver. Several behind them swore loudly and openly.

"What the devil is that?" Erdic asked from behind them.

A vast entity covered the skies, soaring ever closer from the direction of Boctor. Gabriel had never seen a creature like it. The beast was long in the body, like a snake, but a hundred times larger and thicker skinned. The underbelly of the animal was a pale blue, almost white and matched almost perfectly with the sky that was now beginning to lighten. The gigantic snake was suspended in the air by two immense, sinewy, green and purple wings, which whipped up a wind that Gabriel could feel even from the other side of the water.

Running down from steel collars at several points along the creature's body were thick, long chains that connected the beast to the cargo that swung below. It was only the winged snake's size that made what it was hauling appear deceptively small. It was chained to a rock formation, a weathered arch that looked as though it had been lifted straight from the deserts of Boctor.

"What is that?" Gabriel asked in awe.

"A final bridge," Seaglen answered.

The creature carried its burden using its immense strength, although Gabriel could tell the snake was using enormous effort to do so. As the rock arch swayed closer,

Gabriel realised the structure was coated in Magic. It flowed like a layer over the cargo, aiding in keeping the structure lighter and airborne.

Whatever kind of creature this was, it was clear which side it served. Gabriel's heart sank even further as he noticed the beast was not alone in the sky. There was a rider sitting high on top and fear stabbed at Gabriel as he began to panic that all their hope was gone. Dagaz was about to lead the charge into battle.

"It's him."

"Is it?" Seaglen asked, "check for yourself."

Gabriel did. He searched out for Magic in the air as tentatively as he could and then to his uttermost surprise, and immediate relief, Gabriel realised the figure emanated no Magic.

"But then..."

"It is the Atabra," Seaglen said.

"Seaglen!" Erdic cried, "that creature will be the death of our army!"

Seaglen sprung into action.

"Erdic." Seaglen wheeled his horse around. "I need you to take my place and lead the Merrywater army back to the King. He will need reinforcements. I have to deal with this threat."

"It's out of range," Gabriel said.

"Not from us." Seaglen turned to him. Gabriel began to piece together what he was thinking. He drove the stave of the Merrywater banner into the ground. There would be no more use for it now.

"It can't be taken down," Erdic argued.

"Do as I say!" Seaglen commanded, handing over the horn, "Gabriel, with me."

Erdic thundered away back down towards the main army, blowing the horn as he rode. Knowing the meaning behind it, the Merrywater forces streaked after the blacksmith and back to where the King was waiting.

"Further up the slope, come on," Seaglen ordered Gabriel.

Racing level with the creature, they galloped away from the battlefield and up to the summit of the grassy hills that overlooked it. The Merrywater army kept pace, galloping below them. Gabriel and Seaglen reached the crest above where the King was stationed just minutes before the creature arrived at the river.

"I am going to need from you the same level of power I first sensed when I detected you from halfway across Meteorath," Seaglen said.

"I don't know if I can summon that much at will."

"You have to. Too many people down there are relying on us."

Gabriel glanced down at where he detected Aurielle within the ranks of the army. The flying snake was aiming for the head of the Nimaz forces.

"Archers!" Gabriel dimly heard King Pala cry from below.

Down below them, riders streaked towards the cohort of archers and set down braziers in front of them and fresh quivers of arrows. A single rider with a torch passed in front of the line and lit each as he passed. The archers swiftly stepped forward and sent out volleys of flaming arrows upwards into the sky. A couple hit the underbelly of the snake and bounced off harmlessly, while the rest fell short.

Gabriel shook his head.

"Now it is our turn."

He felt the shift around him as Seaglen drew on his Magic. Gabriel copied suit and concentrated all his efforts on the creature before them. The air ignited around the animal, and the force knocked it off course slightly. The stone arch rattled loudly in its chains.

"Again!" Seaglen's voice was strained with effort.

Gabriel gritted his teeth and tried to call on the same amount of energy that he had unleashed on the top of the volcano. He remembered the look on Aurielle's face when he had lost control and knew if he didn't find that same strength again, this time he really might lose her.

A mournful cry suddenly emanated from the centre of the fiery inferno in the sky. The sound caught Gabriel off guard and raised the hairs on his neck. It was the sound of an animal in pain. Both of them lost concentration as a result of the haunting sound, and the flames died a little. On the back of the creature, Gabriel could now see a second Atabra had joined Chana. As the snake swung into position over the water and hovered, the two vultures sought to unlock the chain collars linking the creature to the bridge. The snake began to descend slowly. Their flames were not going to be enough to deter the beast from its task.

"I'm going to aim for the chains!" Gabriel shouted, "maybe we can make the bridge fall in the river, not on the bank!"

He directed his fire away from the creature and focused on melting the iron holding the bridge in the air. After a few seconds, he heard a satisfying snap as one link broke and the stone arch swung dangerously over the heads of the Nimaz army.

There was an audible scream of fury from the snake spiralled out of balance, but a second later, both collars dropped from its back. Gabriel watched in suspense as the arch fell through the air. The stone slammed into the riverbank with the force of an earthquake. The reverberation threw Gabriel and Seaglen from their horses, along with many down below them on the hill. Both of their mounts panicked and bolted.

Deafened and winded, Gabriel crawled forward to the edge of the hill to see what had happened. His heart sank as he saw the arch had landed diagonally across the Winterburn, just long enough to join the two regions for the first time. From below, three riders broke out from the ranks and approached the rock formation. Astrid, Aurielle and Alejandro attacked the bridge with their Magic, attempting to break apart the stone. Two fissures of earth hurtled towards the rock, as water from the Winterburn rose in a wave towards the thinnest part of the arch.

The water passed over the rock harmlessly on either side and two rifts of earth hit the arch and juddered to a halt as if the stone was crafted from impenetrable material. Gabriel realised then that the Magic coating on the rock was doing more than merely making the structure weigh less. From across the water, he heard a roar of triumph.

The Nimaz army wasted no time beginning to charge. Armed with shields, the first fighters dashed onto the bridge as the archers in Elmdale hurriedly got to their feet, under the Marshal's barked orders. Aurielle and the others become enveloped in the mass of bodies below as the two armies clashed.

He watched on, distraught, unable to shake the feeling that they had failed. Above it all, Gabriel heard another wail of pain. Chana was wrestling to get the creature under control. One of its wings was now severely blackened and weakened as it battled to remain airborne.

"That creature could take out half the army with one swipe of its tail," Gabriel said.

"We need to draw its attention," Seaglen said, from above him.

He offered Gabriel a hand and helped him up.

"I'm not sure how much more Magic I can use," Gabriel said.

Still, he turned to face the creature once more as Seaglen aimed a bolt of fire towards the snake's unharmed wing. It spiralled in the air and Gabriel heard another enraged cry from Chana.

Then, finding more strength from somewhere, the creature straightened out both wings and ascended, aiming directly for the hill on which they stood. Beside him, the rune on Seaglen's sword flared red again and taking inspiration, Gabriel drew his own blade fearfully and prepared to call on Magic once more.

CHAPTER 26
BATTLE ON THE HILL

~AURIELLE~

As the first attackers from Nimaz and Boctor touched Elmdale soil, the Attaching army galloped past where they stood. King Pala led the charge himself, and he tore through the front line with a whirl of steel.

As a unit, the three of them charged their horses forward after the King, swords blazing and attacked the right flank of the enemy. Suddenly finding themselves in the heart of the battle, Aurielle, Astrid and Alejandro fought their way to the King's side with the rest of the Attaching army.

Daylight had finally begun to break fully over the Winterburn and lightly glazed its surface. More red than usual tinged the earth as the horn of Attaching blasted out over the noise of clashing steel. Aurielle ducked down out of the path of an incoming arrow, and her heart leapt as it zoomed over her scalp. She grimaced as she looked behind and saw another Attaching soldier thrown from his horse.

"Keep together!" Astrid shouted to her and Alejandro.

Determined not to lose Astrid, Aurielle sent an immediate onslaught after a pair who were trying to bring her down off her horse. Choosing her next target, she saved another ally from an attack and then widened her field of vision to stay alert for whatever was coming next.

Alejandro was temporarily distracted as a company of determined challengers rushed up behind him, and he was forced to swivel Oz around to deal with them. Together, Astrid, Aurielle and Alejandro beat them off and also the next tide that came after that. Their horses fought as hard as them, kicking out with their hooves at any who dared to approach them too closely.

Then they heard the cry from above. As it had done before, the wail stopped Aurielle in her tracks, as she almost felt a trace of pity for the creature high above them. She saw a fireball streak out from the hilltop, and the snake turned its concentration away from the battle on the ground. Aurielle was forced to shield her face as the creature's wings pounded the air above them, her hair whipping in front of her eyes.

"It's going after Seaglen and Gabriel," she heard Astrid yell, "we have to get to them!"

The whole battleground stood between them and the hilltop. Aurielle eyed the hilt of her sword and the rune set there. At that moment, another group charged them from Nimaz. There were far more this time, and Aurielle was in danger of being pulled off her horse. She scrambled to regain balance, scared of being trampled, when suddenly a giant ball of fur, teeth and leather leapt into view, taking out one of the men with it. Aurielle stared down in astonishment. Aztec had followed them into battle, heeding Gabriel's orders. The fur on the wolf had risen, doubling his size. Blood dripped from his jaws, and Aurielle looked down shakily at the animal that had just saved her.

Close to them, the King was also in trouble. He had been separated from the main body of his army and was struggling not to be overwhelmed by forces from Nimaz.

"He needs help," Alejandro said.

Aurielle turned her attention to the sky and the flames that engulfed the hilltop.

"You two get to Seaglen," Alejandro called, "I'll reach the King."

"We shouldn't separate even further," Aurielle said.

"There's no time," Alejandro said, "both Seaglen and the King need reinforcements."

Aurielle knew Alejandro was right.

"Take Aztec with you!" she shouted.

He nodded. Vines sprung up from the blood-soaked grass between where they stood and the King. Dozens of Nimaz fighters fell, and Alejandro took the opportunity to ride through the opening, urging Aztec along beside him.

"Follow me!" Astrid cried in a hollow voice, before turning away. The ground split before them as Astrid carved a second path towards Seaglen and Gabriel. Aurielle risked a look back to see with relief that Alejandro had safely reached the King.

Out of nowhere, a tall Nimaz soldier lunged at Astrid's horse, attacking the legs. Aurielle cried out as she saw Astrid fall before her. Quickly, she rode up and fought the attackers away, giving Astrid time to climb up behind her. Aurielle sent out a powerful jet of water in all directions, casting their attackers to the ground. With Astrid behind her, Aurielle urged her horse forward, finally seeing the perimeter of the battle. Astrid dealt with any who dared to follow them and in a minute they were free, galloping over the open ground.

"Alejandro," Aurielle panted.

"He'll manage," Astrid assured her.

They had escaped from the clamour of the battle, and it took a moment before Aurielle realised she could speak at a reasonable volume again. She jumped as a large shape beat its wings overhead. They were almost directly underneath the snake now. Her horse reared in fear, throwing them both off, before bolting far from the battle. Aurielle coughed, lifting her face from the grass and checked to see if Astrid was all right. After falling for a second time, her left knee looked unnaturally bent. Astrid clutched her leg for a moment before Aurielle felt a tingle of Magic and realised she was healing herself.

"Seaglen," Astrid turned her attention to a nearby hill, her face still pale.

Gabriel, Aurielle thought at the same time.

"Come on."

They ran forward as quickly as they could, on towards the hill. It got harder to breathe as they climbed and Aurielle remembered it was a similar feeling to when Gabriel had lost control of his Magic. She felt sick as she realised how much had been used up here. Around them, deep cracks had started to form in the bare earth and the vegetation had already been stripped away.

Aurielle and Astrid picked up the pace, hearing a screech from above them. The creature opened its jaws and roared defiantly. As the hairs on Aurielle's neck rose, she was surprised to detect an enormous sadness again in the creature's voice, and unconsciously slowed her pace.

"Do you see?" Aurielle caught Chana shouting above the wind, "you may have taken my wings, but my master has furnished me with a much greater pair! You have no hope against me now."

"Gabriel!" They heard Seaglen's shout.

Simultaneously, two barrels of twisting fire engulfed the creature and its rider. The beast dived forward in an attempt to land, and something leapt from its back as it fell. The creature writhed in pain as it began to fall, its body smoking and singed like charcoal. As it twisted, its tail flicked out, and Aurielle heard a heart-stopping scream from above them. The snake slammed to the ground not far from where Aurielle and Astrid stood. Astrid turned away from the creature as it writhed in pain.

Aurielle still could not help but feel sympathy for the animal and directed some Magic towards the creature to ease the flames. It was then that she realised another shape was tumbling down the slope. Drizzle now obscuring her vision, Aurielle recognised the outline of a body sliding lifelessly towards her.

"Gabriel!" Aurielle cried and threw herself towards him.

She caught him and broke his fall, collapsing beside him on the ground.

"Astrid! Help!" Aurielle cried desperately, knowing she was no healer.

Aurielle flipped him over onto his back and winced at the large bloodstain spreading across his side. Gabriel's face contorted with pain as Aurielle unfastened his armour to allow him to breathe better. Without thinking, she ripped off his undershirt and took in the full extent of the damage. Aurielle and Gabriel had only a moment to glance down in horror at the wound before Astrid threw her to one side and set about casting her healing.

"Too much Magic has been used on this hill," Astrid said, infuriated. She reached for her sword and the blade glowed a deep jade for a second. Gabriel inhaled sharply and shuddered.

"I'm sorry," Astrid said, "this is the best I can do for now. You'll live, but you'll have to bear the pain."

Up above them, Aurielle heard a shriek from Chana. Astrid got to her feet.

"Seaglen needs my help," she said, "stay with him, Aurielle. Protect him and cover up that wound."

Astrid stood up and drew her sword. With one last look at Aurielle, she bounded her way up the slope. Aurielle watched her go and turned her attention back to Gabriel, washing his wound out with a little water and using the shirt to bandage it up tightly.

Below them, Aurielle and Gabriel watched two dozen fighters from Nimaz detach themselves from the back of the army below and start to make their way up the other side of the hill. Gabriel's bloodstained hand grasped for her own, as his face contorted in pain.

"Aurielle," Gabriel managed to say, "you have to go... Seaglen and Astrid are going to need your help."

"I can't leave you," Aurielle said, tears springing to her eyes, "not like this."

"I'll be fine for a minute or two," he said softly, "I'm not going anywhere."

Aurielle heard the clash of swords from above and felt torn.

"They need you," Gabriel whispered.

He released her hand and gave her the smallest of smiles. Aurielle got to her feet shakily and picked up her sword from the grass.

"I'll be back soon," she promised him.

"I know."

Sword ready, she began to scramble her way back up the scorched hillside. When she reached the top, she discovered the summit of the hill formed a long ridge. Seaglen and Astrid were pushing Chana back along the top. If they kept on, it would not be long before they forced her off the end. Aurielle hauled herself over the crest of the hill at the same time as the detachment from Nimaz appeared on the other side of the ridge.

Seaglen and Astrid had not even noticed them yet. Aurielle threw herself forward now, forcing her legs into a sprint.

"Behind you!" Aurielle screamed at them.

Losing her own element of surprise, Aurielle provided Seaglen the split second he needed to twist and parry the oncoming attack aimed at his head. Single-handedly he turned to fend off the attacking group, and Astrid was left to fight Chana alone.

Leaping forwards, Aurielle flung herself into the fight to try and reach Seaglen. She used the emergency cache of Magic in her runestone to let loose an angry whirlpool of water and knocked several off the hill. The extra boost allowed her to make her way to Seaglen and fought side by side with him, more ferociously than ever before in her life. Their attackers slowly fell around them, and they gained ground back. Exhausted, Aurielle was distracted by a cry behind her. She dispatched another opponent and flew around to see what had happened. Astrid's sword had gone from her hand and skidded across the grass.

Chana aimed an assault on Astrid, but Aurielle launched herself towards them with a shout and threw the vulture off balance. All of a sudden, she was facing Chana. Leering evilly, the Atabra charged Aurielle, and she desperately parried the attacks. Astrid was gone now, and so were Seaglen and the rest. All that was left in the world was Chana, and her face filled Aurielle's mind. The vulture's speed and accuracy astounded her. It had not been much of a fight with her before, and somehow her abilities had been enhanced since. She fought with a sword in one hand and with the claws of her hand her other. The unusual weapon threw Aurielle off guard.

With inhuman agility, the vulture forced Aurielle back the way she had come. Aurielle fought back with grit and determination, so much so that she held her ground for half a minute. Magic was not an option, the complexity of it had no room in Aurielle's brain, and she did not dare to let her concentration falter for a second to reach out for it. A part of her cursed using up the supply in her sword earlier. Chana's defence never faltered once and she left no openings. Aurielle was hit once, twice, across the hip and cheek.

Chana lunged forward with both sword and clawed hand again, and Aurielle twisted wildly to escape the blow, only physically able to block one of the attacks. She fell severely and felt her weakened ankle collapse under her, this time feeling like something had broken. She wiped the mud off her face and parried one final blow from Chana on one knee. As time seemed to freeze for one second, Aurielle took note of the world around her again. Seaglen and Astrid were still fighting. Their opposition was nearly all down, but neither of them had noticed that so was she.

Then the movement of time began again, and Chana took a few steps back from her. Aurielle looked into her eyes, and she saw a cold, emptiness there. The Atabra was not going to show her any mercy. She imagined then that she held the eyes of the soon-to-be murdered. Her sword was useless, and she could not defend herself from Chana on her knees.

Taking a deep breath, Aurielle focused what energy she had left and gathered all the Magic she could. But there was none left on the hill. As if Chana was sensing what she was doing, she screeched and flew forward with inhuman speed. Aurielle did not manage to form a defence in time and slammed back into the grass and mud that was riveted with blood and coughed. The vulture loomed above her with her long blade aiming for Aurielle's chest.

As she dimly registered the final attack, Aurielle was thrust aside, out of its path. She rolled several times as a sword whistled down, and a target was struck. Horror-stricken, Aurielle raised her head to see Seaglen swing the flat of his sword and slam Chana clean off the side of the hill, her back buckling as she fell. Seaglen let his blade fall angrily to his side as she disappeared.

His attention was caught elsewhere, at something behind Aurielle. He was staring at something with so much grief written on his face, that she almost did not look. When Aurielle did, she instantly wished that she had not. Chana's blade was also covered in blood and rose directly up from the earth, impaling a body belonging to the person that had thrown Aurielle out of the way.

"No. Astrid, no."

"Aurielle..."

Astrid had saved her. Now she was pierced to the earth by the same blade that had been meant for Aurielle.

She was still alive, but barely. Aurielle crept on her hands over to her side and felt for her weak pulse. Astrid smiled back at her and with one frail hand, took Aurielle's own.

"You were not supposed to die," Astrid whispered to her.

"Neither were you!" Aurielle's voice choked.

"Well, it is too late for that now."

"It's never too late, you can heal yourself."

"Aurielle, you know as well as I do that we have depleted this hilltop."

"Alejandro can heal you," Aurielle continued, barely listening, "he'll save you, I know it. If you just hold on..."

"No, Aurielle. I won't make it back down the hill."

"But we need you," Aurielle mouthed, "I need you."

"Aurielle, it's all right. Tell...tell Sara that I love her as well, won't you?"

"Astrid," Seaglen breathed, kneeling beside them.

"Goodbye, brother. I'll miss you."

Tears blinded Aurielle's eyes.

"Aurielle," her voice had suddenly become hoarse, "for Sara, there is a le..."

She fell silent. Aurielle's body froze up as the grip on her hand fell slack, and Astrid's wrist felt numb below her fingers. She gasped as her Magic connection to Astrid was snuffed out a second later. Seaglen closed his eyes. Aurielle's breath choked, and she bowed her head, letting herself shake with anguish.

What felt like an age later, Seaglen spoke again.

"Aurielle, you need to get up."

"I can't," she murmured, "my leg."

A cry rent through the air from below them.

"Gabriel." She remembered he was still below them.

Aurielle felt herself being lifted to her feet. Seaglen slowly gathered her up in his arms and began to carry her back down the hill. Unable to take her eyes away from the body, Aurielle suddenly had a bad feeling.

"We shouldn't leave her," she whispered, looking back along the ridge.

"The battle is not over yet," Seaglen answered, "and we need to find Gabriel."

They made their way slowly down the slope, back the way that Aurielle had come. When they reached the location on the hill where Gabriel had been, they paused. Blood still stained the ground around, but he was no longer nearby, and there was no sign of him in any direction. A moment later, Aurielle heard something whistle through the air and Seaglen twisted. She was thrown from his arms with a cry and tumbled down the slope out of view. Overhead came the whistle of another arrow, and she shied away as it missed, desperately looking around for her attacker. Aurielle reached for her sword and found the scabbard empty, realising that it must be still on top of the ridge.

With effort, she forced herself over onto her knees to crawl up the slope back to Seaglen. She only made a few paces before armed soldiers from Nimaz emerged up the slope beneath her. Rough hands grabbed her, and one of them pulled out a small dagger, coated in some strange, viscous oil, but Aurielle had little time to observe more than that as it was stabbed into her side. She cried out and tried to use what little strength she had left to lash out with Magic, but pain radiated from the dagger in her side and coupled with the damage in her leg, she almost blacked out. The world swam in hazy colours before her eyes.

Aurielle felt herself being bundled onto someone else's back. Beyond sense, the image of Astrid lying on the hill filled her mind, and she gave up struggling. She was thrown down onto something wooden a minute or two later. Weakly, she believed that she might be lying beside others. She knew not if the battle still raged around them or what had happened to Gabriel. She was lost.

CHAPTER 27
OVER THE RIDGE

~SHUMUTI~

Up through Nimaz, Shumuti, Sara and Alexia had ridden, keeping to the Winterburn River. Their horses were exhausted, and several of their number had already fallen behind a day or so due to fatigue. But they had begun to pick up the trail of the Nimaz army and the tracks were fresh, so they did not stop. Flying across the region, it did not take long to reach the eastern border of Elmdale. Once everybody had caught up again, they halted to consume what was left of the food and water and let the horses rest for as long as Sara and Shumuti could bear. As soon as Alexia was satisfied that the company could continue, they started again.

Re-energised, their horses thundered faster and faster until they knew they were getting close. Smoke rose in the air ahead of them and Shumuti began to fear that they were too late. The sound of clashing weapons could be heard as they got closer and Alexia spurred the company onward, knowing that the battle was not yet over.

They reached the river and began to traverse the series of boardwalks that the Nimaz army had used to cross into Elmdale. The company slowed to navigate between the islands on the Winterburn and Shumuti took the lead. Finally, they closed the distance on the Elmdale bank and took in the battle for the first time. The massacre still made Shumuti's stomach twist into an uncomfortable knot. The battle at the Lifthayll Bridge was nothing, nothing compared to this. The carnage of bodies was strewn everywhere, but still, the armies continued to fight on to the last.

Taking a moment to close her eyes, concentrate and expand her perception, Shumuti searched around in fear for any indication that Dagaz was present at the river. Aside from an inkling of Magic somewhere within the centre of the army, there were no other sources of it present on either riverbank. The only other source of intense Magic use was a hill on the perimeter of the battle, just on the limits of what she could detect.

"The two sides look pretty evenly matched," Alexia said.

"Not for long," Shumuti said, "a fresh battalion of fighters might be enough to tip the balance."

One large, out of place, sandstone bridge now spanned the gap between Nimaz and Elmdale in front of them. It was cracked and broken in places but not enough to prevent it from maintaining its purpose. Wasting no time, Shumuti led the charge of their reinforcements across the narrow gap and into battle.

Discarded and sticking out of the grass on the far side was a standard decorated with the colours of Merrywater, and Shumuti gathered it up to help reinforce the message to the King that allies had arrived and not more enemies to fight. The army from Nimaz did not expect anyone to come over the bridge after them and taking advantage of this brief moment of confusion, Shumuti and Alexia led the charge into the rear ranks of the army.

It was not long before Shumuti knew they were getting close to somebody with Magic on the battlefield. A heavily armoured clad figure fell from his horse in front of her, and she spotted Alejandro not too far away, fighting beside the King and a small group from Attaching. Urging Alexia in that direction, the company from Boctor bolstered the ranks of the King, and he noted their arrival with evident relief in his eyes.

Reinvigorated, the King sounded his horn and fought back with renewed vigour as Alexia's company fended off Nimaz fighters from all sides and created some breathing room around the King and Alejandro. Without even halting, Alexia continued to push forward further into Elmdale, allowing the disparate groups of the King's army to reform and strengthen once more.

"Alejandro! Where are the others?" Shumuti shouted across to him.

A bloodstained portion of his fringe stuck to his forehead as he whipped around at the sound of his name. "Shumuti! They went up the ridge, but that was a while ago."

Shumuti turned in the direction he was pointing and felt her chest tighten at the sight of the charred and smoking hilltop. Around them, the tide of the fight was turning and Shumuti wondered if perhaps she was needed more elsewhere.

"Alejandro, Alexia, stay here. Sara, come with me."

They abandoned the others and skirted the edge of the battle until they reached the bottom of the hill. Shumuti's eyes widened at the sight of a body of a gigantic winged beast that lay sprawled on the broken earth, near to where they stood. She turned to Sara, but her cousin's eyes were fixed firmly on the summit of the blackened ridge.

"Sara?"

"Why is it so quiet up there?"

Sara moved her horse forward and up the slope. Halfway up, the ground was trampled and had been the site of some fighting. Normally, she would have halted to investigate it but Sara was already nearly at the top and Shumuti did not want to leave her unprotected. Once they reached the summit, the crest of the slope was littered with bodies, but otherwise deserted. It was then that Shumuti saw the isolated body at the far end of the ridge.

"Sara, wait!"

Sara disregarded her cries and was almost at the figure. Shumuti spurred Fynne after her as Sara jumped down off her horse and ran full speed towards the body.

"No!" Sara cried in anguish. Shumuti skidded to a halt, and Fynne snorted in fear. Cold crept up her body as she saw Astrid spread out on the ground before them, embedded to the ground by a long thin blade, thick with drying blood. Astrid's eyes were closed, and her face set in an expression that resembled peace, but the marks of battle lay all around. Shumuti dismounted and knelt beside the shaking body of Sara, her mind racing as to what fate had befallen the others. After a minute Sara fell still.

"Sara," Shumuti said, "wait here. I'm going to see if any of the others are nearby."

Part of her knew that they weren't anywhere on the hilltop because the connection to Magic had run dry. Unless, Shumuti thought, fear rising in her again, they too had met the same end as Astrid.

"They did this." Sara's head rotated towards the soldiers from Nimaz still fighting down below.

"Sara." Shumuti's mouth could find no other words.

Her cousin pushed her aside and stood up, taking hold of Astrid's sword in one hand and her own in the other. Before Shumuti could make a move, she sprinted past and back up onto her horse.

"No!" Shumuti shouted after her, flying to her feet, "wait!"

Without a glance behind, Sara charged Arrow down the slope with an enraged cry. Shumuti jumped back onto her horse and raced after Sara, desperately trying to cover her before she reached the battle and became lost in it. Driven by her anger, Sara made a quicker time than Shumuti had thought possible and reached the first line of the Nimaz army before any of them had realised she was there. Sara will not die today as well, Shumuti promised to herself as she rode.

Sara fought with more strength and skill than Shumuti had seen before, but it was not long before she became unhorsed. The absence of height proved not to bother her as she flowed effortlessly through every technique that Seaglen had ever taught her, moving from one to the next with deadly accuracy. Had Shumuti not arrived then though, Sara would have soon been overwhelmed. Sooner than she had imagined, Alexia and her company appeared around them as well. Alexia and Shumuti cut down a swathe of soldiers and let Alexia's fighters attack the rest on either side.

No Magic was needed because that would have interrupted the flow of movement from her sword. Next to Alexia she fought, and the two of them cut through air and foe alike with their blades. Tears eventually began to shimmer in front of Shumuti's eyes, knowing that they had been too late. She felt anger that Astrid was dead and scared that she did know the fate of the others, fearful that perhaps she had failed everyone she had ever cared for.

Shumuti and Alexia guarded both Sara's right and left to stop the numbers around her from increasing in size by too much. Countless faces passed before her own and helmets masked almost all, their eyes hidden. But others were not. Then Shumuti felt the horror and pain of war so much that it nearly overcame her, and she almost failed to ward against a stroke aimed for the left side of her neck. Sara still had her grief to shield her, but Shumuti knew that the others felt what she did. Her legs grew solid, like boulders and her arms wanted nothing more than to throw her sword down for good.

Reinforced and motivated, the King's army was too much for their enemy to deal with, especially as soon, Shumuti, Sara and Alexia cut a path back through to re-unite with the King and Alejandro. Briefly, Shumuti shared an acknowledgement with him before another tide of fœs rose between them. Erdic and Stephan also came to fight beside her, until eventually, only allies surrounded them. The final victory took place there as the King slew the last of the resistance and wiped his sword clean on the grass. Shumuti dismounted from her horse and made sure that Sara was not injured.

A swell of cheering rose from the army and swords were rattled together. Horns were blown, and banners were raised as the King gave a smile at their achievement. Shumuti could not join in with the celebration. She felt sick with worry as she scanned the faces of the crowd in search of her father. Their victory felt stained with bitterness and lack of knowledge about the outcome of too many friends.

Sara slumped beside her. Seeing that she was about to collapse, Shumuti quickly called for Alexia. With her help and one of her men, they lifted Sara safely up onto Shumuti's horse.

"Well met, Shumuti." A familiar voice sounded in her ear.

"I've got Sara," Alexia assured her.

With Sara secure, she turned and gave a hurried bow to the King, unable to hide the fact that she was coated in blood and mud and that she barely had the strength to stand, let alone remember how to be courteous to him.

King Pala seemed to be thinking along the same lines though, as he sat down on a patch of unspoilt grass by the riverbank, resting his sword on his knees. Carefully and deliberately, Shumuti wiped every inch of blood from her sword and dipped it in the river. The King waited and watched as she finally sheathed her blade.

"Have you seen Seaglen?" Shumuti asked, unable to completely take in what was happening around her.

"I will send for him," the King replied, waving for a messenger.

"Thank you."

"I thought that you would not make it at all," the King said, "it would seem that your arrival turned our fortunes in this fight. I thank you, Shumuti."

"Don't thank me," she answered, "they are Alexia's fighters. Sara and I just found them."

King Pala looked in Alexia's direction, thoughtfully. "This is the one you brought back from Boctor? So there are still some in that region who do oppose the rule from Nimaz?"

"Quite a few, I should say," Shumuti said, "though most of them are too frightened or weakened to do something about it openly."

"I shall have to think on that."

"I'm truly sorry, my Lord," Shumuti said, barely listening, "but I need to find my father."

"He is a remarkable man. He was chosen to lead Merrywater, but I think he could easily have gained more support under him than I have managed to gain for myself during all the time that I have been King."

Shumuti looked up, startled. "My father would never want to be a king, I know that for sure."

"Just as well."

Shumuti said nothing, looking out across the field. Seaglen had still not appeared, and the King raised a concerned eyebrow in her direction.

"There are so many dead," she whispered, unable to control the worrying thoughts growing in her head. Once more, she urgently scanned the battleground in search of Magic, but there was nothing out there apart from Alejandro and Alexia. Shumuti swayed and thrust out a hand either side to prevent her from toppling.

"Forgive me," the King said, sounding almost parental for a moment, "you are hurt, in more ways than one I'll imagine. Now is the time for rest, not talk."

"No. I need to know what happened. I can't-"

"We will find them and bring them to your tent. The battlefield is large, it will take a while to locate everybody."

The ceaseless riding from Boctor had finally caught up with her, Shumuti realised. She felt the last reserves of her strength seeping away as she struggled to remain upright, and the next moment, she found herself being lifted by somebody into their arms. The King walked beside her as she was carried alongside the crimson Winterburn River.

"Take her to the healing tents that are being set up," Shumuti heard the King order, "and the others that she brought with her."

Dimly, she recognised Alexia had replaced King Pala as they continued on their journey.

"I need to find the others," she said.

"You're in no condition to go looking for anybody," the Attaching soldier carrying her said.

"Your father?" Alexia asked her.

Shumuti nodded once. "Something's wrong."

"I will find them."

She registered that Alexia had left her side. The image of Astrid on the hill flared into her mind and Shumuti let out a shuddering breath and felt for her Magic. It came and enveloped itself around her like a cloak, and she relaxed as it comforted her more than any medicines that the King's physicians could prescribe for her. She just hoped that when she awoke that Seaglen, Gabriel and Aurielle would once more be at her side.

Acknowledgements

Writing is something I've always done as a secret hobby, from discovering Lord of the Rings at probably too young an age, to forcing my friends to run around the garden in cloaks with wooden swords, fantasy has always stuck with me. I tried to hide it for a while, get a career and focus on that, but over the last few years I've discovered lots of people out there, not just writing but making videos, playing roleplaying games, drawing, making music, all storytelling in their own unique way, and I couldn't resist wanting to contribute a tiny part to that community. As I'm sitting here, writing this with a blanket wrapped around me like a cloak of cosiness, I'm pretty sure I can conclude I'm definitely still into fantasy.

There's a lot of other people I want to thank for helping me create this book. First, I thank all my friends and family for their encouragement, and for asking me when the next book will be out. I really hope you enjoy reading it. To everyone who preordered the first book in the first few months, a super thank you for your support right at the beginning.

Thank you to Liam for reading through chapters of the book with me in the run up to publishing and for listening while I explain the wilder plot ideas that I think up.

Thank you to my editor, Mark McFaddyn, and everyone at Sulis International for their work on Autumn and now the second book, Winter.

I also send a huge thank you to everyone who read my first book, and also now this second. It's a strange feeling to be sharing my stories with others and the fact that people seem to be enjoying them is still a little crazy to me. Reading a new review is a highlight of my day. I have plans for two more books in The Guardians of Magic Series, so if you're interested, keep an eye out for Spring and Summer.

About the Author

Melissa Nash was born in South Africa, grew up in Yorkshire and studied Geography at Aberystwyth University in Wales. She has spent the last few years travelling and working as a freelancer and musician, all the while gathering ideas to combine her interest in the natural environment and fantasy into her book series, The Guardians of Magic.

If you enjoyed this book, please consider leaving an online review. The author would appreciate reading your thoughts.

Follow the author on social media:
Instagram: *@_melnash_*
Twitter: *@_melnash_*

ABOUT THE PUBLISHER

Sulis International Press publishes select fiction and nonfiction in a variety of genres under four imprints: Riversong Books, Sulis Academic Press, Sulis Press, and Keledei Publications.

For more, visit the website at
https://sulisinternational.com

Subscribe to the newsletter at
https://sulisinternational.com/subscribe/

Follow us on social media
https://www.facebook.com/SulisInternational
https://twitter.com/Sulis_Intl
https://www.pinterest.com/Sulis_Intl/
https://www.instagram.com/sulis_international/